GAME FACE

The Waterfer Next Generation

by USA TODAY bestselling author
GINGER SCOTT

Game Face

The Waiting Series Next Generation
Book 2

Ginger Scott

For Isabella

Chapter One

Wyatt

I'm already mic'd and I've paced the green room about forty times—the approximate number of times Peyton has given me the "stay calm" speech. I don't know why she's lecturing me when she's the one with her hand in a fist and her molars crackling.

"Peyt, I'm fine. I swear. I've had an entire spring and summer to get used to the idea."

Bryce Hampton entered the transfer portal the second it opened after I broke my collarbone at the end of last season. This is his second transfer. He's on the hunt for playing time, sick of playing backup. And he smelled blood when I went down. I know I'll need to compete for my spot—half the reason I came to Arizona is because Coach Byers insists every spot is up for grabs. He believes in putting the best team on the field. So do I. And I'm the best guy to lead it.

"I just know how Bryce likes to get under your skin." Peyton pauses to straighten my shirt collar. I'm not great at shirts with ties. It feels like I'm being choked. Besides, if I adjust things now, I'll just screw up the mic.

"Hey." Her eyes stop on mine after she gives my tie a good

tug. I cover her hands with my palms. They're so soft and sweet, like her face. The golden flecks in her brown eyes sparkle sometimes, usually when she's stressed or excited. I prefer the latter. I squeeze her hand a little, then bring it to my mouth, kissing her knuckles.

"I promise I won't let him get to me."

She steps up on her toes and presses her lips to mine, her smile stretching as she falls back on her heels. She wants to watch, probably because she's as curious as I am about what Bryce is going to say in that media room. I should warn her that the minute she walks in there, the only thing people are going to see is her. Even in a white T-shirt tucked neatly into white slacks with what she called "a boring leather belt" this morning, she's drop-dead gorgeous. Peyton Johnson has this easy way about her but is always somehow completely put together, as if she simply walked off the page of a magazine.

"Good. Now go get 'em." She pats my chest before backing away and leaving me alone with my thoughts in the room just outside the stadium's media center.

I run through my talking points, muttering to myself. I didn't lie to Peyton. It doesn't matter what Bryce says in our joint interview sessions. There isn't a voice loud enough to drown out my own, which has not stopped cycling through negative thoughts since I felt the crack near my shoulder after Cal State's number seventy-four flattened me on my ass. I've fought hard to combat each negative thought with a positive one, the way my father taught me.

I'm never going to come back from this.

I can come back from anything.

Everyone will think I'm weak.

I'll show them I'm not.

Who am I if I'm not a quarterback?

I am a fucking quarterback.

It's that last question that attacks me most often. And my

fear is dismissing it will only last so long. Because I'm not sure who I am without a ball in my hand, without the grind, and without the weight of a team on my shoulders. I thrive under the pressure. Without it, I'm afraid I'll simply float away.

"Wyatt Stone."

My mouth sours at the sound of Bryce's voice. I may be able to handle this situation with grace, but underneath it all, I hate every second of it.

"Hey, Bryce. Been a while," I say, spinning around as he crosses the room toward me, his hand outstretched. We grasp palms, and I'm pretty sure he's trying to out-squeeze me. I know I'm testing his grip. Petty. I feel like I win, though.

"Crazy we end up in the same place after all this time, huh? Who would have thought?" He sniffs as he tilts his head up, a little act of fake bravado that's stuck around since he was in high school.

"I mean, not totally crazy. You did ask to come here in the portal, and it's not like me being here is a secret." Okay, maybe I'm not as ready for this as I let Peyton believe.

"Ha." Bryce snickers, his top lip sneering. He didn't *actually* find my observation funny. It wasn't meant to be.

"Right, well . . . maybe it was about time we teamed up. And with my extra year of eligibility, maybe we'll see this program winning back-to-back championships." His eyes lock on mine, and I bite my tongue behind my lips to keep my mouth in check.

"Yeah, maybe. We didn't really have anyone ready to step in when I leave, so . . ." I turn my back to him and head toward the craft services table, a little ashamed of my passive-aggressive taunt. He started it, though.

His shoulder knocks into mine a second later, and he reaches across me to take a handful of cheese and crackers. He proceeds to crunch in my ear.

"Well, I'm just here to win. Whatever it takes, right?" Pieces of cracker flake from his lips as he speaks. It's gross. I think he's trying to push all my buttons.

"For sure," I say, popping my fist gently-*ish* into his shoulder.

"All right, Bryce . . . Wyatt. We're ready for you." Sonia, the university athletics communication director, props the door open with her foot as she waves at us to hurry with the clipboard in her hand. She's wearing a headset and holds up a finger when I ask how feisty the media is this morning. I start to move through the door, but she presses her palm to my shoulder, urging me to pause for a second while she seems to be listening to someone on her intercom.

"Got it. I'll send him in first." She drops her headset around her neck and nudges her head toward Bryce.

"They want you first. Just to get through the transfer questions before they get into the team business. I'll send Wyatt in after about ten minutes, so you won't be hanging out there alone too long."

Bryce's lip edges up on one side as he nods to accept her instructions, and when his gaze passes mine before he heads into the media room, every bone in my body sears with a thousand volts, as if I were just struck by lightning.

I breathe in deeply, holding the oxygen in my lungs until it burns. My phone buzzes in my pocket, and I pull it out to find a message from Peyton.

PEYTON: *Just breathe.*

I shake my head and laugh quietly to myself. She's sitting in the media room, in the back. It took her about three seconds to see Bryce walk in alone and know just what to do to center me.

ME: *I am. Like I told you, I'll be fine.*

She sends back a laughing emoji followed by the words *bullshit.* I heart her response. As much as I say I'm the steady one, I still have my weaknesses and insecurities. And nobody sees me better than Peyton.

"You wanna listen in?" Sonia asks.

I nod and take up the other door jamb, leaning my shoulder into it in time to hear the roar of laughter among the media in the room. *Shit, he's going to be the funny one. That makes me the serious one.* Nobody likes the serious one.

"Jency, from *The Times*." Sonia's assistant is running the room. She's young, an intern. It's good she's getting her feet wet with pre-season media sessions. That room can get downright hostile after a game, especially if we lose a close one.

"Thank you. Bryce, it's good to see you. Weird to see you wearing blue and red." Jency covers all the Arizona college sports. He loved it my freshman year when Bryce and I were going to be rivals. That never manifested because Bryce red-shirted a year, which means Jency's probably foaming at the mouth to stir up something new, now that we're vying for the same starting spot.

"Yeah, I know. My path here was strange for sure, but I feel like I'm right where I am supposed to be. Sometimes you need to get the bumps and bruises to grow, you know?"

I spit out a quiet laugh at Bryce's response, and Sonia gives me side-eyes.

"Sorry," I whisper, but her scowl lingers for a few extra seconds. Her job is to keep the peace, at least according to anyone outside the locker room. She doesn't need me throwing out grenades.

I turn my attention back to the media room and she does the same. I can't see much other than Bryce's left shoulder and a few of the podcasters sitting up front with their phones held out to catch every word.

"That's a positive attitude, Bryce. I'm sure Coach Byers appreciates that. But I wonder, how do you keep that up when you're fighting for a starting spot against one of the best senior college quarterbacks out there? Why step into that situation?

You could have transferred into a situation that promised playing time, but you didn't. Why?"

I'll give it to Jency—he goes right to the heart of a sports story. That's the answer I want to know too. Why, of every school that was interested, did he decide to come here?

Bryce takes a few seconds to answer, shifting his weight and moving his left arm as he scoots closer to the table. I haven't paid much attention to his media hits over the last year, but fresh out of high school, he had quite a mouth on him. He was quick to the mic, a big fan of his own sound bites. Seems he has learned to think before speaking.

"I meant what I said about those bumps and bruises teaching me a thing or two. I've done a lot of self-exploration. Sitting on the bench gives you time to think."

The reporters in the room chuckle at his quip. *He's the funny one.*

"Anyhow," Bryce continues. "Not starting as a freshman bought me a little more time, and I really thought hard about what I wanted to do with that time. I could have stepped into a mediocre squad that was desperate for a quarterback, and maybe we would have won more than we lost. I probably would have gotten some attention for doing what I could with them. But that would have been the easy route. I looked at Arizona and saw an opportunity to learn, to get better. To be part of a team that fights for every inch. One that takes practices as seriously as games. And if that means I'm playing number two to one hell of a quarterback, then maybe that's what I need to do to step into the spotlight when it's my time."

The room is quiet for a few seconds after his response, until eventually, Jency utters, "Thank you," and passes the mic to someone else. Sonia elbows my side and drops her brow when our eyes meet.

"Those are some pretty complimentary words he had for

you out there." She purses her lips just to rub it in. I take my lumps and suck in a long breath as I nod.

He said the right things. I still don't trust him, though. Just because he spent a couple of years learning how to be polished at the mic doesn't mean he won't play dirty everywhere else. I'm down for a fair fight for the starting gig. It's the deceptive shit I'll be on the lookout for.

"When the school press is done with this question, we'll send you out to join him." Sonia holds the mic part of her headset close to her mouth as she mutters her plan to her assistant. I'm never nervous for the media room, but my pulse is racing now. My palms are a little sweaty too. I run them along my thighs and flex them to work out the nervous energy while Bryce rattles out a few softball answers about his idols growing up. At least he didn't say Reed Johnson. I'm already on edge about how everyone's going to piece our history together. Both of us having the same role model would make the puzzle way too easy to solve.

"Okay, go on out, Wyatt," Sonia urges.

I crack my knuckles and exhale like Peyton does when she's doing her weird yoga crap. She swears it works.

I walk into the room and take the open seat next to Bryce, and we exchange knuckles as if we've been besties since grade school. I can put on a show, too. The cameras catch our friendly interaction as we both set our expressions to jovial smiles, and I ready myself to be at my best for the next twenty minutes.

The first few questions are easy and obvious.

How's the collarbone?

What was my routine for physical therapy?

Do I feel ready for our first game against Northern Iowa?

And then they hit me with it. Well, Jency hits me with it.

"So, are we to presume Coach told you you'll be starting next Saturday?"

I take a beat, which I always do, but this time I give it an extra breath. I have to be careful here—show I'm ready but also respect the process. Never mind the raging voice inside, screaming at me to *fuck the process!*

"Jency, I think you know all too well that nobody speaks for Coach Byers but Coach Byers. What I can tell you is that I feel great. My reps are up to the same levels they were before the injury. I've somehow gotten a little faster, maybe from all the PT, who knows. And if he puts me in the game, I'm going to be ready to execute."

Phew.

"A follow up for you both—"

I exhale, and it irritates me that I don't hear Bryce do the same. Instead, he sits up tall, ready to take on more. I nod.

"It's been mentioned here and there that you two were rivals in high school. Is that correct?"

"Oh, I don't know that—" I stop short, my smile instantly tight, holding in the lie as I glance to my left, meeting Bryce's similar expression. He spits out a short laugh, and I exhale again, this time letting my lips flap. Fuck it. "Yeah, I mean, sure. We were rivals."

I hated this motherfucker.

"Do you think that rivalry will rekindle? And will it make you both better or worse?" The pregnant pause that fills the room sparks a few chuckles from the other reporters.

I glance back to Bryce and hike my shoulders along with my eyebrows.

"You want this one?" I prod. If he's going to be the funny one, might as well let him put out fires.

"Uh, sure. Well . . . I mean, there's only one quarterback in the game at a time. And do we both want to be in? Yeah, we wouldn't be here if that wasn't the case. But we're both grownups now, and it's probably fair for me to admit that Wyatt's always been a little more mature. Historically, our rivalry didn't paint me in a very good light. I mean, hell, Wyatt even got the girl."

Everything suddenly moves in slow motion, beginning with Bryce's hand as it gestures toward Peyton in the back of the room, and continuing all the way through every head swiveling to stare in her direction. Her eyes grow wide and remain that way, and the room is so quiet I swear I hear her hard swallow. A few cameras snap and Peyton's eyes flutter, snapping my world, and perhaps everyone else's, back to regular speed.

Somehow sensing the instant chokehold that revelation left in the room, Sonia steps in before Jency has a chance to monopolize the press room and ask yet another follow-up.

"All right, everyone. I need to get these guys to the film room. If you have additional questions, I'll be around for another hour to fill in any gaps you might have. In the meantime, please refer to the QR code on the screen for the materials we've posted." Sonia flips on the large presentation board, and Peyton ducks out during the distraction.

"Dude, I'm so sorry," Bryce says as I get up to leave. His hand grasps my shoulder, and it takes every ounce of restraint not to shirk him off.

"You put a huge target on her, Bryce. Not cool. And I'm not the one you should apologize to," I bark over my shoulder as he follows me down the steps and back into the green room.

"I know. I got carried away, and I didn't want people to think I was only in this to beat you."

"You're not?" My response surprises me, but the way saying it out loud soothes the raging fire in my stomach means it needed to be said.

I stop in front of my backpack and gear bag, dropping my hands into my pockets and turning around to face him. His mouth is slack, and he's chewing at the inside of his cheek with his brow drawn in tight.

"I meant what I said, Wyatt," he finally says. "I came here

because it's where I'll become the best quarterback before the draft. And if it means learning some shit from you before I get my shot, then I'm ready to do it."

We stare at one another for a few long seconds, sizing each other up, perhaps, and maybe feeling each other out. Eventually, we turn away from each other, grab our shit, and leave the media center. I let him get a head start to avoid more conversation.

It's hard to tell what's bullshit and what's real with him. It's not like I ever knew the guy well. I know what Peyton has told me about him, and I know what I saw of him in high school and after we parted ways for college. I know there was always something in him that Reed respected, and I have to accept that. But it doesn't mean I have to like sharing my space with him.

And I sure as shit don't have to like him talking about Peyton.

Chapter Two

Peyton

Tate's Steakhouse is my father's favorite place on earth. He says our home is his favorite, and then the high school field, but I'm pretty sure this old barn-looking joint complete with sawdust on the floors and never-ending hot rolls with butter has his heart. I'll admit the food is good. But for my dad, I think it's that literally every person who steps foot in or works here knows him. Intimately. As if he's a godfather—*that kind of godfather.*

"Babe, I'll be right back. Corbin just walked in, and it's been a minute since we caught up." This is the fifth time my dad has left our table to catch up with an old friend. I'm pretty sure he saw Corbin two weeks ago, the last time we were here with my grandparents and little sister.

"Okay, but hurry. Wyatt's on his way and we need to order, Reed." My mom shakes her head as my father flashes a thumbs up over his shoulder.

"You should have his funeral here," I say.

My mom chuckles and pulls another roll from the basket in the center of the table. She rips a piece off and stuffs it in her mouth.

"If he keeps ditching me for middle-aged men, that funeral might come sooner than later," she snarks mid-bite.

I smirk, then twist in the booth to track my dad. I spot him with his hand on his friend's back, laughing at the bar. Just then, Wyatt walks in, and for a moment, Reed Johnson isn't the most popular person in Tate's.

"That should get Dad back to his seat," I joke before scooting out of the booth to rush into my boyfriend's arms. He high fives a few Tate's regulars at the bar before patting my father on the shoulder, then immediately bracing himself for me. His arms wrap all the way around me, and a few patrons whistle when I nuzzle my face into the crook of his neck and wrap my legs around his waist.

"You saw me this morning," he chuckles, kissing the side of my head as I breathe him in. I love the way he smells after a shower. His hair is still wet, and it's soaked his T-shirt collar.

"You look good in jeans and a clean white tee, what can I say?" I slide down his body until my boots touch the floor again.

"Wait until you see me out of them," he whispers in my ear just before my dad sidles up next to him, slinging an arm over his shoulder and guiding him away from me and to more old friends he wants to introduce him to.

"You two have thirty seconds before Mom makes Joey pull the saddle seats out and forces you both to sit on them through dinner," I tease. Those chairs are usually reserved for birthday honorees, but my mom has the Tate's owner, Joey, wrapped around her finger. And he's planted my father's ass on that saddle more than once just to make her happy. Truthfully, though? I think my dad likes the attention.

"I saw the presser today," my mom says as I slip back into the booth and take my seat across from her.

My molars smash together as I wince. She and I have had a lot of therapeutic conversations about Bryce's transfer. It's easier to be honest with her about how uneasy it all makes me feel. My dad is too tangled in Bryce's playing history. But also, he's my dad, and any inkling of Bryce making me feel uncomfortable sends him into papa-bear mode.

"His answers were good," I say.

"Whose?"

I glance up to meet her expectant stare. My stomach tightens.

"Both of them."

My mom nods, I think a little bit in understanding my stress while also agreeing that yeah, Bryce didn't come off too bad. Before we can get into it more, Wyatt scooches into the booth next to me and my dad slips in next to my mom.

"You two done signing autographs?" Mom teases.

Wyatt chokes out a short laugh before taking a bite of a roll.

"It wasn't me they were interested in. This little shit is looking to take over my college records too." My dad nods toward Wyatt, a bit of pride flashing in his eyes.

"I don't know. I missed some games last year, so unless I play like I'm a Marvel Comics quarterback, I think your records will be just fine." Wyatt's being humble. He put up high enough numbers his freshman and sophomore seasons that even missing a few games late last season won't set him back far.

I'm about to say so when Bryce suddenly appears at our table's edge.

"Are you our server?" I blurt out. It comes out snarky, and my mother nudges my shin with the toe of her shoe.

Bryce chuckles awkwardly and I mutter a half-assed, "Sorry."

"Honestly, I'm willing to wait tables if that's what it takes for you to forgive me for my massive screw-up today."

"Oh," I utter, my gaze drifting to Wyatt, who's focus is on his menu.

"You know the press loves a good joke. I'm sure it will blow right over," my dad says, though he wasn't actually there for it, and nobody laughed.

"Still, I shouldn't have gone there. I'm sorry, to both of you," Bryce says, holding out his hand for Wyatt.

My boyfriend's eyes flit to his right and his jaw flexes before he eventually drops his menu and takes Bryce's hand with a firm grip.

"Sure. We're good." I can tell by his tone that he's far from good with any of this. Anyone in a five-foot radius can tell, and there are plenty of tables near us with eavesdroppers.

"Mrs. Johnson, it's good to see you," Bryce says, nodding toward my mom.

Ever the steady professional, her mouth curves into her famous smile, bright white teeth and dimples beside her glossed pink lips.

"Same, Bryce. I'm glad you're doing so well. And it's nice to have you home." I'm pretty sure my mom means it, too. Bryce's home life was always a little rough. Hs parents fought in public often and eventually divorced our junior year. My mom always had a soft spot for Bryce because of it. Family is pretty much a bedrock for my parents—it always comes first.

"Thank you, Mrs. Johnson. That means a lot." Bryce smiles at my mom, then turns his attention to me, the corners of his mouth dropping a hint.

"I really am sorry." His insistence makes me uneasy, even if it's an apology.

"It's fine, Bryce. Really—I'm fine." My eyes flutter above my forced smile, but thankfully, Bryce was never that great at reading my facial expressions.

He falls back a step and his shoulders drop. I'm pretty sure he just exhaled.

"Well, you all enjoy your night. Wyatt, I'll see you early for conditioning."

The two of them nod at one another, and from the outside

looking in, I'm sure it seems cordial. But most people can't see the way Wyatt's hand has gripped my thigh under the table—possessively. His palm rests on my leg for a few seconds before I clear my throat and he finally pulls it away.

For a few minutes, we all manage to fill the silence by chowing down the rest of the bread. Carbs can only tide us over for so long, though, and per usual, my dad is the one to break the tension in his super non-tactful way.

"So, seems his head games are doing the job, eh, Wyatt?" My dad takes a long sip from his beer as he settles into the leather seatback and stares at my boyfriend with a knowing smirk playing at his mouth.

Wyatt drops what's left of the bread he's basically been mashing back into dough and lets out a heavy sigh.

"Reed." My mom's tone carries the rest of the meaning. *Lay off him tonight. Can't we just enjoy dinner?*

"I'm just giving you shit. You know that, right?" My dad waits a beat for Wyatt to nod, but I can feel the tension rolling off him. I lean forward to catch his sightline, and when our eyes meet, his flutter shut for a few seconds as he exhales for a second time.

"It's just that I have to watch my back on the field, in the weight room, during freaking media day. I didn't think I'd be watching my back at Tate's is all. And you know full well, Peyt"—Wyatt leans in close to me, doing his best to keep his voice down—"He's not charming you because he wants to mess with me. He wants you to forgive him . . . for everything. And then he just wants *you*, period."

I drop my chin and draw my brows together a hint.

"At what point do you think I found any of that charming?" I hold Wyatt's gaze until his mouth finally twitches with the threat of a smile.

"My part was charming, though. Right?" He's fishing now, but also, he seems more relaxed.

I quirk a brow and turn my attention to the waiter who just stepped up to our tableside. After listening to him share tonight's specials, we all rattle off our orders, and by the time he finishes filling our glasses with water, it seems like the Bryce conversation is finally done.

Except my dad's had a few beers tonight. He's been here chatting up old friends for a while. He's feeling . . . punchy. And I maybe overshared some things last week when I went home to visit with Grampa.

"Bet you wish you went ahead and moved in with Peyton like she asked," he blurts out, throwing in, "Not that I like the idea myself, mind you."

My immediate instinct is to scout the space under our table to see if it can accommodate me. I give up on the idea when I see exactly how filthy the floor is, complete with peanut shells and straw bits. Next to me, Wyatt leans forward, dropping his face into his open palms and pressing his hands into his eyes.

"You're being a tad loud, Reed," my mom says, rubbing my father's arm and mouthing, "Sorry," to me.

I scan the restaurant, and the good news is fewer people seem to be staring at us now compared to when Bryce stopped by. The sound of a metal object clanking against the tabletop draws my focus to the space between Wyatt's and my plates. It takes my mind a second to catch up to the key now lying there, and when I pick it up and realize it's to Wyatt's apartment—the one he just moved into with Whiskey—I promptly set it back down and slide it in Wyatt's direction.

"Really? A pity key?" My pulse now thumps from irritability. But before I can push Wyatt out of my way so I can exit the booth, he takes my hand and unfurls my fingers, pressing the key in my palm, holding it in place with his thumb until I glance up and meet his gaze.

"Believe me, there is zero pity in this gesture. I planned on asking you to move in with me tonight, after a lovely dinner with your family. It's been in the works for a week; I just needed to make sure Whiskey was able to swing a one-bedroom on his own. He's moving to the unit downstairs next weekend. But since I seem to have veered onto the world's unluckiest timeline, I'm sure you've changed your mind, so—"

"Wyatt," I interrupt.

His lips fall shut, but the top one twitches a little as our eyes meet. It's a nervous tic I've learned he has, like it's hard for him to patiently hold in his thoughts.

"I'd love to live with you," I say, waiting for his nostrils to flex with his exhale. I know when he's holding his breath.

"Wait a second, shouldn't you have asked me?" I can tell from my father's tone that he's joking, but I'm pretty sure Wyatt's had enough of Reed Johnson's ribbing for one night.

"No, Dad. Because he's not asking *you* to move in. Just me." I wave my dad off, and he chuckles before immediately muttering something about needing to have a new "talk" with Wyatt.

"Yeah?" Wyatt says softly to me in the meantime, a crooked grin playing at his lips.

I nod as my eyes squint under the pressure of my growing smile.

"Yeah. I'll be your roomie." I close the tiny distance between us and push up enough to press a soft kiss to his lips. "On one condition," I add.

His eyes flicker for a beat and his head tilts with caution.

"*You* have to tell Tasha," I say.

My best friend. Who is tougher than most of the linemen gunning for Wyatt on the field. Who does *not* like the idea of living alone. And who is going to lose her ever-loving mind when she finds out she's going to have to find someone else to take over my half of our split floorplan.

Wyatt's eyes remain wide open, perhaps a little frozen in

fear. Without breaking our gaze, he feels for my hand and promptly pulls the key free of my grasp. Then, leaning to the side, he pushes it back into his pocket and utters, "Never mind."

Chapter Three

Wyatt

"Explain it to me again, dude. Why am I not going to move into the apartment downstairs?" Whiskey is going to take a little convincing, but not nearly as much as Tasha is, I'm sure. Peyton and I came up with the idea of encouraging Whiskey to move in with Tasha after the world's most uncomfortable dinner last night. So far, I think Whiskey is intrigued—but also skeptical. He and Tasha are what Peyton calls frenemies.

I line myself up on the bench press, hands wrapped around the bar as I stare up at my friend. Our eyes meet as I sigh before going through the plan yet again.

"Look, it's cheaper rent, and her building is way nicer. You'll have your own room, and you'll be doing me and Peyt a solid." I lift the bar from the support brackets and lower it to my chest, breathing out as I push it back up.

"Yeah, I hear you, but . . ." He waggles his head, and I bust out another four reps before sliding the bar back on the supports and sitting up.

"Is this about the kiss situation?" I snag my towel from my gym bag on the floor and wipe the sweat from my face while my big-hearted and big-boned right guard chuckles. Whiskey and Tasha spent an entire night making out over the summer during one of our lake trips. We never discussed it, or rather, I brought it up and Whiskey quickly told me to, "Fuck right off."

"There is no kiss situation. At least, not for me. I don't know what's going on in Tasha's head, but as far as I'm concerned, it was just another night at the lake with a few beers and a good time."

My friend is a shitty liar, but I don't push him on this. He's also sensitive, which is one of his best qualities.

"Okay, fine. There is no kiss situation," I say with my hands up. "Then, what's the big deal? Cheaper room, better building, closer to the stadium . . . and campus."

He shrugs, and his shoulders quickly sag with an invisible weight as his eyes dim. It hits me. The big lug is going to miss me.

"You know we'll still be hanging out all the time, right? And Peyt loves you like family, so you're welcome in our place anytime."

He breathes out a short laugh.

"Yeah, I'm sure she really wants my ass on the couch between you two while we watch the late-night rerun of *Sports Center*."

He has a good point.

"Well, no. I mean, she probably doesn't want us to have sleepovers and shit, but you know you'll still be a part of our Sunday night dinners. And me and you will still do our regular hangs, and—"

"Yeah, I know. It's not like I'm crying about it or anything, it's just . . . you two are really growing together. And it's beautiful. I don't want you thinking I'm not on board with what you two have built together, because I am. I guess I feel a little left behind is all. And I know that's all in my head, or my own fault, but I was sort of getting my head around the idea of living alone and finding out what I'm all about. I'm sure this all sounds stupid as hell."

I stand up and drop my hand on my friend's shoulder. Our eyes meet briefly before he clears his throat and masks his emotions, quickly busying himself by removing the clips on the bench press bar to load up another plate for his reps.

"It's not stupid, Whisk."

"Yeah, well, whatever," he mutters, sliding the second plate on and following it up with the safety clip. He straddles the bench and drops down with a heavy sigh before lowering onto his back.

"I don't know," he starts before I interrupt with, "I'll pay you."

He punches out a laugh so loud it echoes around the weight room and draws attention from the other dozen guys lifting with us. He powers through his set, lifting three hundred pounds like it's a bag of groceries. The bar lands back on the supports with a clang before he sits up and meets my gaze.

"Why is this so important to you?" His question is so direct, and so unlike him, it takes me a little off-guard.

"I mean, it's Peyton, Whisk. I want to marry this girl. Moving in together is a big deal for us, and—"

"No, no. I mean me living with Tasha. Why is that such a big deal? She could find someone else. I'm fine living alone. So, what's with the tag-teaming to force us together?"

He's smart enough to know that Peyton and I are working in tandem. I wonder how her side of the pressure campaign is going. I wonder if Tasha threw any punches.

I snag my water bottle from the spare bench and lean against one of the weight racks as I pull the cap and chug. It gives me a few extra seconds to choose my words.

"It's important to Peyton. That's why this is important to me."

"Yeah, I get that. But why? *Why* is it important to Peyton?"

My best friend and I lock eyes for a few quiet seconds before I respond.

"Because she knows Tasha will be safe with you," I finally admit.

This isn't anything Peyton's said out loud to me, but it's something I just know in my gut. Over the three years Peyton and I have been together in college, and even when we met in high school, I've gotten a pretty good look at how volatile Tasha can be. She's a great friend to Peyton. A ride-or-die. It's just that sometimes her inclination to live on the edge and toy with death is a bit strong. I was with Peyton the summer before college when she had to rush her friend to the ER after alcohol poisoning. And last year, we helped her out of a toxic relationship with a guy who put hands on her. Whiskey remembers that—he helped me send the guy a message at the bar on the outskirts of town. I'm pretty sure my friend's knuckle prints are permanently encased in that asshole's face.

"And you'll pay me?"

I shake my head, my pulse kicking with hope that my friend is on board.

"Absolutely," I say. "How much?"

My NIL deals are lucrative. My mom set up a few funds for me through the financial advisors the firefighters' association uses, but it still leaves me with plenty of "fun money." I know I make more on the side than Whiskey does. He's the face of Wildcat Pizza, but the deal comes mostly in the form of free slices any time he wants.

"Five hundred a month," he says. It's a little strange how fast he rattles off the number, but I push off from the weight rack and stretch out my hand to seal the deal.

"Done," I say, gripping his palm for a shake.

I dig out my wallet from my gym bag and fish out the five hundred bucks I have on hand, just to make sure he doesn't back out.

"Wow, you work fast." He chuckles, taking the money and slipping it into his wallet.

We both zip up our bags. I wipe down the bench with one of the cleansing towels, tossing it in the trash as we make our way to the exit. Just before I reach the door to push it open, it widens in a *whoosh* and I find myself face to face with Bryce. I probably should have timed my lifting session with him, played mentor and all that shit, but after yesterday, I simply needed a break from seeing his face.

Joke's on me, I suppose, because here's his face. *Right fucking here.*

"Hey, man! Good to see you," Bryce says, taking Whiskey's hand. They pull each other in for a half hug, years of history tethering them together, despite the way their high school careers ended in rivalry

"You look good," Bryce says, tapping the back of his hand against Whiskey's chest. My friend puffs up in response, as if he needs to make himself look any bigger.

"Thanks, man. I'm about two-eighty this year. Looking to make the senior bowl, get myself drafted."

Bryce and I exchange a quick glance, and I roll my eyes. As confident as Whiskey is on the field, the guy always sells himself short. He's been worried about being drafted since we stepped foot on the college field. I know for a fact he's going in the first three rounds. I guess it never hurts to put in the extra work, though.

"Well, I look forward to seeing you out there. Maybe if I get lucky, I can take a few snaps with you to my right this season," Bryce says.

"No doubt, for sure," Whiskey says, embracing Bryce one last time. An awkward silence quickly cuts in, and my friend clears his throat before excusing himself, claiming he's late for something.

Bryce and I are left alone in the doorway, the clanking of

weights behind me and the screech of basketball shoes echoing down the hallway behind him, where the women's team is getting in some off-season time in the fieldhouse.

"You think he just realized you and I are both quarterbacks and me playing means you're sitting?" Bryce squints at me as he points over his shoulder. He's not being a dick about it, and I get his tone.

I laugh softly and shake my head.

"He definitely put that together a little late, and I don't know what the hell he could possibly be late for besides a nap," I joke.

Bryce's chest shakes with silent laughter.

"Hey, naps are no joke," he says, making room for me to pass.

The tension between us is suffocating, and I know I won't be able to perform at my best if things keep up this way. But I still don't trust him. We aren't close. If I were in his position, I'd be looking for my in, even if it came at his expense. *Especially if it came at his expense.* Even more reason to step up and be a leader.

"Hey, about yesterday," I say, rubbing the back of my neck as I avert my eyes. I draw in a deep breath before meeting his gaze. He's chewing at the inside of his cheek. *Good. He's uncomfortable, too.*

"I want you to know I appreciate your apology to Peyton. I know she appreciated it, too. And I heard what you said, about learning and growing. I'll get over my petty bullshit soon, I promise. I'd like to be that guy for you, the one you think I am, I guess." I'm not sure how many of my own words I believe, but they seem to chip away at a little of the ice as Bryce's shoulders relax and his posture eases.

"Hey, I appreciate *you*. I know how hard it was to say what you just did. I have my own bullshit, so maybe we can get over it together. Or at least try. Yeah?" He holds out his hand, and for a second my mind drifts back to the night before. I smirk at his palm, then grip it.

"Here's to trying," I say.

Bryce breathes out a long laugh as we let go and trade places in the doorway.

"Oh, and tomorrow—let's hit the gym at six, get in some miles?" I'm asking him for two reasons. First, to make up for the shitty way I ditched him today, but second, I'd really like to see how he fares on the treadmill. I'm childish enough to race.

"Sounds great. It'll be good to get the legs loose before we take some snaps."

For a quick second, our gazes lock, and I swear I see the old Bryce somewhere behind his eyes, the one baiting me and ready for the challenge. It's our first full team practice on our home field tomorrow. And while he threw at camp last week, I still wasn't fully cleared. Tomorrow is a statement practice.

"Looking forward to it," I say, my brows lifting for a beat before I turn for the locker room to dress out and race to my place, where my girlfriend is waiting for me.

Not for Bryce.

For me.

Chapter Four

Peyton

Tasha is mad at me, even more than she normally is after we fight. Of course, we usually disagree about going out on a weeknight or letting her borrow my favorite leather boots.

This time is different.

She's more than mad. She's hurt. And it feels a million times worse. I'd rather worry about her slashing my tires than not answering my texts or phone calls.

I finish sending the tenth message, promising to buy all her rounds when we bar hop next weekend. I'm staring at my words to her and the delivered notice—not even read—when Wyatt toes open his front door. His arms are loaded down with three cases of water, so I pull myself out of the comfort of his oversized beanbag and rush to help. As if he needs my muscles.

"Thanks. I've been driving around with these for a week," he says, sliding two cases onto the counter then taking the third from me to stack on top.

I tug at the pocket of his hoodie and flatten my cheek against his chest as he turns into me. His arms wrap around me, and I take the first full breath I think I've had since Tasha stormed out of our apartment this morning and said, "Fine, I'll let Whiskey move in. Anyone else you'd like me to offer room and board?"

"She'll come around. She always does." He presses a soft kiss on top of my head, and I snuggle into him harder.

"I know, but also, what if she doesn't?" I tilt my head, pressing my chin into the center of his chest so I can look up at him. His eyes scan my face as he tucks the loose strands of hair behind my ear. My head hurts from the high ponytail I've been wearing since practice.

"At some point, Tasha is going to have to live with someone who isn't you. I'm not planning on an open marriage that involves multiple wives. Although . . ."

Wyatt twists his lips and glances to the side, as if he's intrigued. I wrap the strings of his hoodie around my fist and tug his attention back to my face, trying not to overreact to the fact that he just said the M word.

"I'm kidding," he laughs out softly. His gaze sticks to me as he cradles my cheek with his right hand and strokes my skin with his thumb. I could stand here like this forever.

"I know Tasha needs to work on her independence. She knows it, too. But she's never really had the support system that you and I have, and when she and I moved here together freshman year, it was like she finally had this solid family unit. Even when I'm gone with you, or traveling for a competition, she's never totally alone. Hell, how many times is she our third wheel?"

Wyatt chuckles at my observation.

Tasha's the daughter of a single mom who likes to work and live large, which usually meant she was jet-setting without her daughter. I've always thought that was at the root of most of my friend's envelope pushing.

"I love how you love your friends," Wyatt says, his touch slowly pulling the stress from my body.

My mouth slides into an easy smile as my cheeks warm

from the praise. He leans in, his forehead resting on mine as the tips of our noses touch. I hum as I close my eyes.

"I love how you pay your friends to deal with my friends," I jab. I gave Wyatt a little shit when he told me he offered to sweeten the roommate deal for Whiskey.

"Hey, I got him willing to box up a week early, which means you and I could have this place all to ourselves in a matter of days." His right brow lifts with his *very* obvious innuendo.

"We've got it to ourselves now," I say, my skin prickling with sudden interest in being touched on more than just my cheek.

"I might also love this new cheer uniform you're rocking," he says, his hand moving along my face to the back of my head, where he grips the base of my ponytail and gently tugs. I lift my chin until our lips touch, and his teeth nip at my bottom lip.

"We had the fitting today. I kept it on because I thought you might like it," I say.

Wyatt always comments when I wear red. It's the color of his favorite bikini that I wear, as well as his favorite sweater of mine, and dress. I should probably invest in red lingerie. I figured in the meantime, this tight red bodice with a short skirt that barely covers my ass would probably do the trick, and as my palm glides down the center of his chest to the waistband of his joggers, stopping at the tip of his swollen cock, my hunch is confirmed.

"Hi there," I say, smiling against his lips as I let my hand sink into his pants and over his hot shaft.

Wyatt groans, grinning right back into my smile as his hands drop to my waist. He swivels me back a few steps until my ass hits the counter and he grinds his hard-on into my pelvis. I swallow as my breath hitches. The things Wyatt Stone can do on the football field are nothing compared to what he can do to me.

"Whiskey won't be home for forty minutes," he says, his

hands gathering up the hem of my skirt as his short nails scratch against my bare hips.

"What if he's early?" I back up a hair and lift a brow, at this moment not caring what Whiskey walks in on. I know I'd care after, though. I lick my bottom lip, then hold it hostage between my teeth.

"What if . . ." A coy smirk colors Wyatt's expression as his eyes shift to the door, then back to me. "We both could keep watch."

I tilt my head, not sure what he means. He snickers deviously as his hands swivel my body until my stomach is pressed against the counter's edge and he pushes into me from behind.

"Oh," I gasp at the feel of his palms on my bare ass.

"I guess that could work," I say, though mentally, I'm kind of insisting on it. I stretch my palms forward and lower my chest to the counter, which pulls my skirt up high.

"Peyton, this definitely works," Wyatt says, running his palms over my smooth skin, then lightly smacking my right ass cheek. I yelp, then giggle.

"I fucking cannot wait to live with you," he says, shifting his body behind me until I feel the warm tip of his cock against my ass. I've been on birth control since the end of high school, which has made for many spontaneous moments. Surprisingly, we've never done this. My mind races to all the ways this counter is the perfect height.

My body warms as Wyatt leans over me, sliding my ponytail so he can kiss the back of my neck. He drags his mouth along the center seam of my uniform, between my shoulder blades, pulling the zipper down with it until the fabric parts. Fingertips trail down my spine until his palms move to the sides of my body and back to my hips as he lowers himself behind me. My ragged breath fogs the black granite countertop as I roll my head to the side, my eyes staring at the doorway that could open at any minute, though it probably won't.

It's the *could* that excites me.

"These are cute," Wyatt says as he hooks his fingers in the top of my bloomer shorts, rolling them down my hips and thighs until they fall down my legs to the floor. I kick them away as his hot breath warms the backs of my legs. I shiver at the feel of his cool lips against my bare skin.

"I'm glad you like the new uniform," I whisper as he kisses his way up my left leg, coaxing me to spread wider as his mouth travels higher.

"It's all right," he teases, amusing himself. His soft laugh tickles against my skin just before I feel the tip of his tongue taste me. I nearly sink to my knees.

"Maybe better than all right," he muses, again passing his tongue over my sensitive skin.

I whimper and bring my fist to my lips, biting my knuckle. I nearly come when his mouth covers me completely. He sucks hard, his tongue flicking my clit before he takes me right to the brink of orgasm and then pulls his mouth away. I lift my head from the counter in protest and glance over my shoulder, but before I utter a single word, he's standing behind me, stroking his cock with one hand and grasping my hip with the other.

I slip my arms from my open bodice and push it to the side before lowering myself back against the counter, the cold granite a sweet shock to my hard nipples. Wyatt's hand traces between my thighs, his fingers gliding along my wetness before he sinks two fingers inside. The welcome fullness makes me moan.

"Just wait until it's my cock, Cheer Captain," Wyatt says, pulling his hand away and leaving me exposed and desperate for him.

"Please," I hum, knowing how he loves it when I beg. He likes to call me little pet names, too. Last week, it was Madame President because my sorority had elections.

"Stand up," he commands, and my body quivers, knowing he's standing behind me, looking at me, waiting to take me.

My palms flatten on the counter as I push up and stand, my eyes zeroed in on the doorknob, ready for it to twist. My ears are tuned for any sound that isn't in this room.

"I'm going to fuck you like this every night when you live here," Wyatt says at my ear.

I draw in a quick breath as his cock slides deep inside me from behind. When I begin to fall forward, he grips my hip to steady me as his free hand flattens on my tummy. I ache for more, threading my hand through his and coaxing it lower until he's circling my clit with his fingers.

"Oh, that's my girl," he says, his teeth grazing the beaded skin at my neck. My tits shake as he pushes into me harder, his pace picking up as my cries grow louder.

Fuck, if Whiskey hears what's happening in here and still decides to open that door, then he's as big a pervert as I tease him for. But right now, I could not care less who hears or sees me being absolutely owned by Wyatt Stone.

I leave his hand on my pussy and grab both of my breasts, tugging at my own nipples to release the ache building in the hard pink skin.

"Fuck, that's hot," Wyatt says, the scruff of three days of not shaving scratching my bare shoulder as he peers over me.

My head falls back against him as his hips work faster, his cock pushing in deeper with every thrust until the pressure between my legs becomes unbearable and I fall over the edge. Wyatt holds me to him as he continues to drive into me, riding the wave of my orgasm and drawing it out until I nearly pass out.

When the burst of warmth fills me, I lean forward and brace myself on the counter once again so Wyatt can fully release inside of me. His body covers mine as his hips pump slowly, every thrust matched by the flex of his cock in my pussy. We lie like this, connected, half-clothed, and covered in our own sweat and cum, for several minutes. The door never opens. And I can't wait for this to be the thing we do every night.

Chapter Five

Wyatt

What Peyton said about leaving Tasha alone stuck with me, and I still can't shake the weight of it this morning.

She teased me about dragging ass on moving in together, saying I had cold feet or whatever, but it was never that. Hell, I'd drop down on one knee and marry that woman yesterday with zero fear in my heart. It's not me I worry about—it's her. And not that she'd say no, because we're rock solid on our feelings for one another. It's that I'm not sure how fair it is to leave her alone so much. Kind of the same way she worries about Tasha.

The next few years are going to be a bit wild, and while this season will pull me away for travel, our lives will still be pretty much in sync since she'll be cheering. That all changes when I enter the NFL. I don't want Peyton to feel isolated, as though I pulled her away from her support system just to abandon her.

But fuck was it nice waking up with her in my arms. And yeah, it's probably going to feel even better when Whiskey isn't sitting in the kitchen in his boxers when Peyton and I leave the bedroom.

"What took you so long?" Bryce's voice rattles me out of my thoughts as I enter the weight room, his shitty country music already queued up and blasting through the speakers. I'm regretting that olive branch, though now I'm feeling mighty motivated to kick his ass.

"I like my beauty sleep. What can I say," I respond, holding his gaze for an extra second, just long enough that it feels uncomfortable. I think he knows what I meant by *beauty*. I won't flaunt Peyton in front of him because I have too much respect for her, but I'll be damned if I don't drop a few damn good hints.

"Hope you're not too tired to hit the incline," he jokes back, a clear bite to his tone.

"Never too tired, brother." His eyes flicker to mine at my response, his expression temporarily devoid of the macho façade. I call most of my teammates brother, and I decided when I woke up this morning that I was going to set the kind of example this team deserves. Maybe Bryce will prove me wrong and turn out to deserve it too.

"Alright, let's get after it," I say, pulling my sweatshirt off and tossing it on top of my gym bag on the floor. I step up on the center treadmill and pull my right foot up from behind to stretch my quad, Bryce matching me stretch for stretch. We both start with an easy jog, and after a minute of running, I amp up my speed. Again, Bryce matches me, both of us cruising along at a solid eight miles per hour.

"You feel that burn?" I joke, mostly to show off the fact I have zero trouble talking while running at this speed. I've been doing nothing but cardio since my injury. My lungs are ready for the challenge.

Bryce is panting, though not hard. He glances my way with a smirk and shrugs his shoulder. "It's all right."

"Ha! Liar," I fire back. It feels good to give him shit the same way I would Whiskey. It feels almost natural. There's still this underlying tightness in my chest, though, and I'm not sure that will ever go away.

When his hand moves to raise his incline, I do the same, pressing the plus button every time he does. I usually stop at three, but Bryce pushes us to four, so I do the same. We run in unison, our heavy shoes slapping the rubber mat as it whirls beneath us in perfect sync. After a full two minutes, I notice that my mouth is hanging open, my bottom lip heavy with the rhythm of my pant. That extra percent on the angle might be kicking my ass a little bit.

"What do you think? One more?" Bryce's words come out choppy, and I'm glad to hear this isn't easy for him, but fucking hell!

No! I do not think one more anything.

"Sounds good," I say, because I'm a man, one step away from comparing dick sizes.

Bryce ratchets his speed up to nine, so I do the same, and it's not quite a sprint, but it's a quick stride. The soles of my shoes feel a little like they're igniting on fire, so instead of concentrating on how much it fucking hurts, I let my mind wander back to this morning and the feel of Peyton's bare back pressed against my chest. How smooth her shoulders were as I kissed them. The way her nipples hardened under the thin layer of sheets, and how she writhed next to me as my hand brushed over the cotton covering them. The way she tasted when I trailed my tongue down her stomach to her pussy, pushing my tongue inside her and making her come in my mouth—the perfect start to my day.

Ten minutes pass before I know it, my mental distraction pulling me out of my body while it works to prove that I'm the best athlete in the room. By the time I'm present again, I've crossed into my running high, and I could easily go another level, but I can tell Bryce is working hard to stay in his own zone to keep up. Four years ago, I would have pulled the dick move and demoralized him just to prove a petty point. But now? Now, we're teammates. He called me a mentor of sorts. And goddammit, I'm going to be one.

We finish out our four miles together, cooling down to a walking speed as our offensive line pours into the room to get in their morning lift. I reach across to my left, holding out a fist as I hit stop on my treadmill, and Bryce pounds his knuckles into mine as he slaps the stop button, too.

"You think maybe next time I can pick the music?" I joke through ragged breaths.

"Ha! Fuck, no. This stuff is good shit!" He hops off his tread-mill and snags a towel from his gym bag while I stare at him with an open mouth.

"What?" he says, finally noticing my reaction.

"Well, you got the shit part right," I fire back. I point up to the speaker, which is currently playing some forlorn song about a man's struggle to be sober and win back the love of his estranged family. "I think we need to reassess the qualities of a good hype tune, dude. Cuz this ain't it."

"A-men!" Whiskey says from my other side.

We both pound fists and Bryce waves us off. The tunes change after a few seconds when Deacon, our center, takes over the speakers with the pre-game playlist he made last season. The room thumps with heavy bass while laughter breaks out across the room, more guys piling in and getting amped to kick off the season.

I wipe my face off with my towel, then lean toward Bryce, forcing him to meet my gaze and admit I'm right.

"Okay, I see your point. But don't bag on country just cuz you don't understand it. Maybe you just need to join me on my next trip to Fort Worth to see my dad. Visit a real bar, listen to some real music." It's the first time he's ever mentioned his dad to me. First time he's ever brought up family, period. Rather than react with the surprise I feel, I give a nod in a show of consideration.

"Yeah, that might be cool."

Would it be cool? How well do I want to know this guy?

"I'm gonna take a two-minute cold one before we hit the field," Bryce says, gesturing his thumb over his shoulder toward the showers. I nod and wait for him to turn the corner out of view before I address Whiskey's hard stare that I swear is burning a hole in my temple.

Whiskey has been telling me for weeks to go at this thing with Bryce as if we're old friends, to just pretend the bad blood was never there. It's what he's done, though I could make the argument that he's simply practicing avoidance. But he may have something with the whole *more bees with honey* idea.

"I'm trying it your way, okay? I don't want to hear it, and no, I'm not going to say you were right. Just . . . let it be, and we'll see if this works out." I roll my eyes, but my gaze sticks to him. The fucker chuckles, and even though he doesn't say it out loud, he's sure as hell thinking it loud enough.

"I was right" is all over his face.

Maybe Whiskey's maturing, too, because he manages to keep it to a smug grin, not even adding commentary when we get out to the field and Bryce and I are tossing the ball for warm-ups.

After warmups and team stretching, we break off into our position groups. The two freshmen recruits—who will be redshirting this year—set up a few obstacles and targets for the rest of us. Shad Owens—the guy who was my number two last year as a sophomore—eyes Bryce just over his shoulder. As anxious as this situation makes me feel, it must be eating away at Shad. He was in line to take the reins from me next season, having gotten time on the field for some key running plays last year. But now, nothing is certain. Hell, *I'm* not certain at this point, and a year ago, I was part of the Heisman conversation.

"Owens, come here," I say, drawing him out of his mental spiral, at least I hope that's what I'm about to do.

Bryce follows my gaze and steps out to make room for Shad in our three-man circle. The dude is trying, and damn if it doesn't feel sincere.

"You wanna run the drills first, show Bryce how it's done?" I'm trying to set Shad up with some confidence, remind him that he's still got seniority on this squad even if Bryce is bigger, older . . . *better.*

"Sure," Shad says, his response clipped. He steps between us and takes a ball from one of the freshmen, tossing it in his hands a few times before dropping back and running through the various routes.

Bryce watches intently, though he and I both know he can do this drill in his sleep.

"He's on edge about you. You get it," I say as we both look on and avoid eye contact.

"That's the game. I've been on edge since my Pop Warner days ended." Bryce chuckles.

I join in, laughing at the way I used to run the football every damn play. Scoring a dozen touchdowns all on my own, I was forced to learn how to be a *real* quarterback.

"That was cool of you, by the way," Bryce says. I glance at him, and he nods toward Shad as our teammate talks with our quarterback coach.

"People need to feel important. They need to know they have value. And everyone out here does—in the game or not. Every single person has a role out here that impacts our result as a team." I sit with my own words, a little surprised at how much I believe them. Part of it is my dad's morals that I've carried with me, but also, I've learned a lot about leadership under Coach Byers. It's strange to see lessons stick.

Bryce's hand lands on my back for a second, and the weight of it knocks me forward a half step. He huffs out a short laugh, looking at me with a crooked grin and squinted eyes. It feels kind of rehearsed.

"See, I knew I'd get better just being around you," he says, patting his hand on my spine once more before jogging toward Shad and Coach to take the ball and run through the drills.

Shad nods and smiles at him, uttering, "Let's see what you can do, transfer," as he steps into place next to me. We both look on while Bryce talks through a few things with Coach.

"I get what you did there, Wyatt. I appreciate it, but you should keep your guard up. There's something about that guy. He feels off somehow. Too . . . nice. Nobody's that nice."

"Huh," I breathe out, pulling the corner of my mouth in tight, not sure whether I wish Shad got more out of my lesson or that I got more out of his.

My eyes snap back to the field at the sound of the whistle, so I bite my tongue and decide to let things be for now with Shad. At some point, I'll relay the same thoughts I did to Bryce a minute ago, to reassure him that no matter what, he has a place here—that he's vital.

Just then, Bryce drops back and spins as if he's broken a tackle, rushing to his right about ten yards before slinging the ball right on target. His moves are crisp, his feet sure. He seems taller now, and the power in his arm feels light years ahead of everyone else out here. The applause from a few of the receivers looking on, as well as from our quarterback coach, elevates what just happened a little more. And when I glance to my left, meeting Shad's *I told you so* face, I put my guard back up—just like he said.

Chapter Six

Peyton

"Are you sure you don't want me to tag along, do our famous third-wheel thing? I could turn around, be there in thirty."

Wyatt's pretty transparent sometimes, even over the phone. He saw me before Tasha and I left for our girls' night, and I think he's a little worried about my outfit, though he'd never say anything about it. I kind of like the way he bites his tongue when I dress sexy and he doesn't want to share. I wore my mom's white cotton eyelet sundress with her boots tonight, maybe wanting to channel a little of her strength as I reassure my best friend that everything will be okay.

"I'm sure you would cut through the desert to get here in fifteen, but we'll be fine. I promise. Besides, you know Whiskey will show up at Catwalk eventually. He always does."

I promised Tasha one last hurrah before I move to Wyatt's on Sunday, and since this is the last free Friday I'll have for a while, I gave it to her. I hate that I'm missing dinner with Wyatt and his mom for her birthday, but he assured me she'd understand. I think she's probably looking forward to spending a night out with her son, one-on-one. As much as they love

Wyatt, my parents secretly love when I show up back at home solo.

"Yeah, I've already sent Whiskey the rules," Wyatt says.

His voice is a little loud, and there's a lull in the music playing in the rideshare car Tasha and I are in. Her head snaps to me a second before she rips the phone from my hand.

"Wyatt James Stone, you do not get to give us rules. You're lucky I'm letting you live after stealing my best friend from me for our senior year of college. So help me, boy, if you tamper with our girls' night, I will—"

"Cut you," I say in sync with her, a grin on my face. It's her favorite threat, though it's all talk. At least, *I think it's all talk?*

She tosses my phone back in my lap, and I lift it to my ear, still laughing.

"I'm glad you find your psycho bestie amusing," Wyatt says, a hint of worry in his voice.

"You know she loves you," I reassure him, cupping the phone to try to block out the sound of Tasha saying, "Ehhh, do I?"

"Well, I love you, and that's really all I give a shit about. So, just be safe, okay?"

I glance out my window, leaning away from Tasha for a bit of semi-privacy. Catwalk is an enormous country bar outside Tucson, and it's basically where every frat boy and jock from the university goes to usher in the weekend. The bouncers do a good job of keeping the peace, mostly, but sometimes youth and alcohol mix for bad decisions. While Whiskey sometimes makes a few of his own, his are more of the fighting-for-some-one's-honor variety. Probably not a bad guy to have looking out for us.

"I promise. I love you, too."

I end the call and tuck my phone into my small leather crossbody bag before meeting Tasha's stare.

"Ugh, could you two be any cheesier?" she teases. I slip my

arm through hers and snuggle in close, hugging my tough-act bestie.

"You know you're happy for me, deep inside. You are. I can tell." I poke at her cheek with my fingertip. It dimples with the smile she can't hold back, and she lets out a soft laugh.

"Fine, yes. I'm happy for you. But I'm still sad for me. It's going to take a lot of drinks to get over being sad about you moving out. *Expensive* drinks."

"Ha, nothing but the best for you."

Our ride pulls up to the curb outside Catwalk, and the line has already started to form. Tasha dated one of the security guys last year, and he still has a thing for her, so she gets us to the front of the line easily, and we slip inside seconds after the ID checkers slap bright orange wristbands on us.

"One day, we'll be able to go to a bar that doesn't look like we paid for premium fair rides," I say to her, tugging on her orange band.

"Girl, that's because we'll be old and there to play bingo," she says. We both laugh and link our hands as we march our way to the bar for our first round, which I buy.

With drinks in our hands, we make our way to the edge of the dance floor, taking it easy until we finish our first drink and discard the glasses to really let loose. The music heats up, and so do our moves. I spin so my back is to Tasha as we both sway our hips and bend our knees. Tasha's hands find my hips, and it doesn't take long for our dancing to attract attention. When a tall blond guy wearing a black button down that's open halfway down his chest works his way to our sides, I jut my chin over my shoulder to Tasha.

"I'm taken, but she's single," I say, good at my wing-woman duties.

"Well, all right then," the guy says, holding out his hand for Tasha to dance with him. I nod when she looks at me for permission, and lean into her ear so she can hear me.

"I'll get us shots and wait over there." I nod toward the long table to our right.

I leave my friend with open-shirt guy. I sized him up as he was approaching. No ring, and expensive shoes. He might be one of the younger professors, or maybe just a young professional out with the boys after work. I spot his friends at the bar cheering him on. I'll keep an eye on her, especially if she doesn't join me when this song is done.

I buy us a round of shots and carry them to the side table, recognizing the wide shoulders and famous plaid shirt of my bodyguard for the night. I tap Whiskey's arm with my finger while I balance my drinks in my other palm. He jumps and spins like a kid startled at a haunted house.

"Wow, and you're here to protect me," I joke.

He leans back and lets out a bellowing laugh before taking my drinks and setting them on the table. He promptly sweeps me into his warm bear hug, spinning me around once, and marking me as taken for the night. I know his moves, and they're sweet.

"Tell me the truth, how much did my boyfriend pay you to be here tonight." I lift a brow.

He grabs the handle of his beer mug and hums with thought, taking a drink before answering.

"Let's just say I can drink here for free all weekend." He winks and takes one more chug before setting his mug back down.

His gaze quickly darts over my shoulder, and there's a little flicker to his eyes. I follow his stare to Tasha as she makes her way toward us through the throbbing crowd of twenty-somethings. I smirk to myself but keep my teasing in check. It's enough that I've gotten Tasha to sign off on Whiskey being her roommate. I don't need to push the matchmaking beyond that.

"She looks good, huh?" Maybe a little push.

"Always does," Whiskey says, filling his lungs and widening

his chest about a second before Tasha steps up to my other side.

"That guy was a tool," she says, picking up our shots and handing one to me. We clink glasses, then tip them back to drink.

"He seemed sweet." I know full well that's a bullshit statement. I let him cut in because he seemed safe.

"Here, you can call him to talk about your portfolio," she says, handing me a business card with his details. Whiskey snags the card from my hand.

"Joshua M. Turner, Jr. Accountant," he reads. He tosses the card onto the floor with a flick of his hand, then grabs his beer.

"Fucking junior. Not even a *full* accountant," he utters over the rim of his mug before gulping down the rest of his beer. Tasha snorts out a laugh, and once again, I smirk to myself.

I buy another round, and after a few minutes of rest, Tasha and I make our way back out to the floor. This time, we stick together, and I rebuff the two guys that try to edge their way into our space. After nearly a half-hour straight of dancing, my neck and chest are beaded with sweat. Tasha's pulled her hair up with a clip, but I don't have a tie with me, so I resort to twisting my hair in my right hand and holding it on top of my head while I close my eyes and rock to the music.

"Sweet ass."

I don't recognize the voice at my ear, and when I drop my hair and take a step forward, I'm held against a strange body.

"Hey!" I shout toward Tasha, who's moved a few bodies away from me with the crowd. My voice is instantly swallowed up by the music.

I push my hair from my face and twist to face the stranger pawing at me. I push my palm into a damp, muscular chest. All I'm able to see of the guy is his tight black T-shirt soaked with sweat from whatever high he must be on. Before my gaze makes it to his face, his arm is twisted behind his back, and a large man in a tight blue denim shirt is pushing him through the crowd and out the door.

"What the fuck happened?" Tasha says as she appears at my side and weaves her hand in mine.

My pulse is racing, and my eyes scan the room for Whiskey. That wasn't him who stepped in, but where the hell is he? And who *was* that? The answer comes about a second later when Whiskey heads toward us from the front entrance, Bryce trailing behind him—in a denim shirt.

"Oh, shit. This is gonna get messy," Tasha slurs. She's had a couple more drinks than I have. She always does. We're both tipsy. She's verging on sloppy.

"It's already messy," I mutter.

She laughs at what she thinks is a joke. I'm not being funny, though. And now I feel gross and uncomfortable.

"I think we should go home," I say, ignoring her when she whines at my side.

"Come on, babe. Bryce kicked that guy out. We can stay a little longer."

My eyes snap to her, and somehow the sharpness of my stare must break through her fog, because she swallows hard and nods.

"Hey, Peyt. I didn't see that guy. What a dick. I'm so sorry," Whiskey says as he meets Tasha and me at the long table where our next row of shots is already lined up. Tasha slams hers before I can push it away, but when she reaches for mine, I tip it over.

"Can you call us a ride?" I look Whiskey in the eyes, doing my best to avoid Bryce's stare.

"I'm sober. I don't really drink anymore." *Fuck. Of course he doesn't.*

My eyes flutter their way to Bryce, and I nod.

"Will you drop us off at Wyatt's?" Everything about this moment feels awkward, and I'm sure taking me to Wyatt's house is the last thing Bryce wants to do on a Friday night. But Wyatt will want to see me when he gets back from his mom's. And right now, I need to feel his arms around me to erase the feel of everything—and anyone—else.

Bryce's eyelids grow heavy, the reality of what his future has become maybe hitting him in the face. Here I am, his one who got away. It doesn't mean I don't hope the best for him, though. Or want to see him well. I just wish he wasn't here, directly in my inner circle. And Wyatt's.

"Yeah. Meet me out front. I'll pull my truck up." Bryce makes eye contact with Whiskey, then turns and strides back out of the bar.

"Did you guys beat that guy?" I ask Whiskey as he ushers me and Tasha out to the street.

"Don't ask questions you don't want answers to, Peyt. You know I don't lie to you."

"*Pffft*, you lie all the time," I say, my mouth ticking up with a welcome laugh. My pulse is still firing on all cylinders from the adrenaline rush.

"That's right, I do lie to you. In that case"—Whiskey pauses as he holds open the exit door—"We hailed him a cab and combed his hair, gave him a mint, and sent him on his way."

My mouth twists as I roll my eyes, patting Whiskey's chest as I walk by him through the doorway.

"Such a gentleman," I say, scanning the sidewalk to my right for any trace of what *really* happened.

Chapter Seven

Wyatt

I know something is off the second Whiskey texts and says he's bringing Tasha and Peyton to our place for the night. It's only ten or so, which means either Tasha went hard and got sick or something happened. The fact there's no way in hell Whiskey is in any condition to drive is also a red flag, but I figure they called a ride.

Then I see that fucker's truck in my parking spot.

It's ironic that I take the stairs to give my heart rate a chance to settle down. Not only do I stand by my reasoning that cardio pulse is different from rage pulse . . . I'm betting on it. Because when I open this door and see—fuck, I don't know what I'm going to see—I need to be in full control of my faculties.

The TV is on as I step up to my door, the familiar lull of late-night *College Football Central* running through predictions for next week. The door is unlocked when I open it, so I step inside to find Bryce sitting on the arm of our sectional sofa, Whiskey nursing a beer on the ottoman, and Peyton sitting on the chaise section with Tasha's head in her lap.

"We opted for a slumber party?" I had three or four lines

ready to go based on what the scene was when I entered. This one was the friendliest. It's a good start.

Bryce gets to his feet first, stuffing his hands in the back pockets of his jeans. His shirt is stretched across his pecs, the damn buttons stretching like some Marvel hero in a poor disguise. Jesus, how is he bigger than me?

"Hey, man. I was waiting around until you got here. I'll take off. See you at film review tomorrow?" He pulls his right hand from his pocket and holds it out. I eye it skeptically, briefly surveying the room, before shaking it.

"Yeah, at eleven . . . tomorrow. Uh . . . is everything okay here?" I glance around the room again as our hands part.

"Oh, yeah. Just your usual jackass thinking he can feel up Peyton on a dance floor—"

"I'm sorry, what?"

My whole heart rate plan just went to shit.

Peyton slides Tasha's head to a pillow and hops to her feet, stepping along the sectional cushions until she gets to the one closest to me. With her arms stretched out, she reaches for me, and I lift her up and over the back of the couch and rest her bare feet on top of my shoes. I'm instantly inspecting her for bruises or injury. She's no longer wearing that pretty—and short—white dress. Her skin smells like milk and honey, so she must have showered before crawling into my sweatpants and her favorite Coolidge High shirt that she stole from her dad.

"Wyatt," she says, clutching my face between her cool hands. I realize against her gentle touch just how clenched my jaw is. I meet her gaze.

"Caveman."

I wince. It's our term for when I get a bit overprotective.

She pulls her lips together into a tight smile.

"*Mmm hmm,*" she says as she nods.

Peyton runs her hand through my hair, stroking my cheek

with her thumb, and for a brief second, I almost forget other people are in the room.

"It was no big deal. Besides, when Bryce stepped in, the guy practically showed himself out of the club." Peyton's eyes scan my face, but when our gazes lock, her hand falls away.

My jaw flexes.

"Bryce." I repeat his name. Not loud. No anger, despite how much I feel. I had to say it, though, to make sure I heard her right. Not Whiskey, but Bryce.

The way her eyelashes flutter tells me she probably wishes she had left that part out. I wish she did too. But we don't leave things out between us. It's why I believe in us so hard. Still doesn't make petty jealousy any easier to wear.

"I should let you guys get some rest. I'm just glad I was there." Bryce's hand pats my shoulder on his way out, and he looks toward my face, but our eyes don't meet.

"Me, too," I croak.

"See ya, Whisk," Bryce says, pulling my friend out of his near nap across the room.

"Oh, yeah, man. Pleasure working security with you," Whiskey laughs out.

Peyton follows Bryce out, sending him away with a quiet, "Good night," before she shuts the door in his wake and twists the bolt. She turns to face me, leaving her back against the door, and everything in her eyes is telling me not to go there mentally. But I'm already there. In the jealous, *I-hate-that-she-ever-kissed-that-guy, why-is-he-in-my-universe* place.

"Welp. That's my cue," Whiskey says, grunting as he pulls himself up to stand. He flips open the top of the ottoman to pull out a blanket, then sets his beer on the side table before spreading it out over Tasha. I'd love to tease him about how he's already doting over her, but I'm too focused on the tightness in my stomach and the fact I can still smell Bryce's fucking cologne.

"Good night, you two." Whiskey lifts his brows as our eyes meet on his way to his bedroom for the last time.

Tomorrow, we haul his boxes to Tasha's and bring here the rest of Peyton's clothes and some of her appliances, along with her pots and pans. The purple velvet couch that Peyton bought last year is her parting gift to Tasha.

"So . . . do we want to talk about whatever this is?" Peyton taps the center of my chest and glances toward the door, where Bryce's ghost still lingers. At least, for me.

"Talk about it in your room, you assholes," Tasha groans from the couch, pulling one of the cushions down to cover her head.

Peyton tilts her head toward my room, and I follow behind her as she pads her bare feet along the wooden floors. She walks straight to my bed, plopping on the end and folding her legs up as she stares at me, eyes wide and blinking with certain hope that I'll say something smart. I shrug and lean against the door, dropping my hands into the front of my hoodie.

"You know I love you, and only you, right?" Her head falls to her right shoulder as she speaks, her mouth pulled into a pouty frown that I think is meant to show care and sympathy, but somehow only makes me feel like an idiot.

"You know it's not about that. And you know this is all me, in my head, and has nothing to do with you at all, right?" I step into the middle of the room, pull my sweatshirt off, and toss it toward my closet, dropping my hands in the front pockets of my jeans. I swear, Bryce made me feel underdressed.

"I do," she says, reaching out her hands. I kick my shoes off and move toward her, stopping when her palms slide into mine. I rub circles with my thumbs on the backs of her hands as I chew at the inside of my cheek and search for the words that can explain the noise in my head.

"I need you to know one thing, and that's it. If you hear me out on this and maybe understand it, I promise I'll try my best to keep this version of caveman in check." My eyes flit up to meet her soft, doe-like gaze. Her tongue peeks out from between her lips, and it clears all my thoughts away for a moment because she's so fucking cute. A part of me wants to abandon this effort to be the mature guy who can talk about his feelings and instead push her on her back and bite that tongue. I decide it's best I look down at the floor until I get this out of my system.

"Bryce being here, the whole competition for football thing, playing time, him being—" I waggle my head but keep my eyes down. "Good, I'll admit. He's more than good. And all of it has been harder than I thought it would be."

"I know—" she starts.

I lift my gaze and pull my lips in tight when our eyes meet. I shake my head slightly and she bites her bottom lip, letting me finish.

"I can handle the bruised ego when it comes to football. I'm strong enough for that. But when it's you—"

"Wyatt," she whispers my name. Her legs unfold as she tugs me close enough that she can press her chin into my belly and stare up at me.

Every day that passes, I swear she grows more beautiful. The girl I fell for in high school is becoming this force—this woman with an incredibly wide smile, with cheeks that wear the sun, and golden hair that frames her face like a queen. And she is a queen—*my* queen. I cup her face with my hands, weaving my fingertips into her hair line as she blinks up at me.

"It's not that I don't like that Bryce was the one to step in tonight and be your hero. It's more that I hate it wasn't me."

She blinks at me slowly, her mouth stretching into the barely-there grin of hers that I love so much.

"I understand," she says, her voice a little rough, but her eyes wide and locked on mine.

"Thank you," I say, drawing my hands along her jawline

until my right thumb reaches her mouth. I brush the pad along her bottom lip, and she parts her mouth open a hint as a tiny breath escapes.

I lift her chin more and run my thumb back across her skin, and this time her lips part fully, suckling my thumb and holding it briefly between her teeth.

"I get a little feral at the thought of some jerk touching you, you know," I say, and her lips smile around my thumb.

"You're mine," I add.

"I'm yours."

She brings her hands up over her head, and I take her hint, gathering up her T-shirt before lifting it over her head. My eyes drop to her perfect round tits. I love every curve of her body, but the way her breasts alone make me hard is some kind of sorcery. As her hands fall to the button of my jeans, I move mine to her hard nipples, rubbing a thumb over each as she works to unbutton then unzip the front of my jeans.

"What do you want?" I love asking her this. I love that she tells me.

"This," she says, tugging my jeans down my hips enough to free my cock from my boxer briefs.

She smiles up at me as her hand wraps around the base, then she leans forward and takes me deep in her mouth. The sudden shock of it nearly knocks me off balance. As it is, my head falls back and my eyes roll.

"Fuck me," I groan.

"You will," she says, sucking me as her hand slowly strokes my length.

I open my eyes to the ceiling and focus on the feel of her soft lips as they close around me and slide toward my body, her tongue swirling around my tip.

"Yeah, that fucking part is going to have to happen now," I say, ready to come already.

I drop my chin and take a step back so my dick falls from

her mouth. The way her lips glisten, the bottom one swollen—plump—*yeah, this isn't going to last long.*

I nod toward the bed, and a devilish smile pulls up the corners of her mouth as she leans onto her elbows and backs away from me.

I step out of my jeans and boxers before crawling on the bed, caging her hips between my arms. I kiss her tummy, tonguing the diamond stud she wore tonight in her belly button.

"This one's my favorite," I say, looking up at her with hazed eyes.

"I know," she smirks. "I was hoping you'd see it, along with those."

I drop my gaze back to her pelvis as I slide the sweatpants down her hips. There isn't much to the delicate panties other than some intricate deep red lace, but against her milky skin, it's like a Christmas bow wrapped around snow.

"These are new," I comment.

"*Mmm*, yeah." She writhes under my weight. I tug her pants lower, pressing my mouth over the silk strip that covers the thin line of hair above her pussy. I nip at the fabric with my teeth, pulling it away slightly before growling and looking up at her.

Her head falls back with laughter.

"You're like a bull, Wyatt Stone. So predictable. All it takes to get you to do what I want is wear some red."

She's not wrong

"And what do you want?" I ask once again.

She lifts her head just enough that her eyes meet mine, and her expression grows serious.

"I want you to fuck me."

My cock flexes at her demand. I roll the panties over her hips, and she works them down her body, parting her legs as I sit on my knees between them. I guide my cock into her fast, driving deep inside as I brace myself above her. The gold chain she bought for my last birthday dangles against my chin, and I take it in my mouth, giving me something to focus on other than coming. I need this to last. She feels too good.

Peyton grasps at the blanket beneath her, her fingers clutching it in her fists and pulling it close as I'm relentless with my hips. She lifts to meet every thrust, our bodies slamming into one another with a sense of urgency until her mouth falls open and she begins to whimper.

I move my right hand to her ass, pulling her up and into me every time I rock into her. She wraps her legs around my waist, urging me deeper, so I lift up on my knees and hold her hips as we fuck. We're so loud there's zero chance that Tasha and Whiskey aren't hearing this. Hell, Bryce might be hearing us from his truck miles away. Good, I hope he does.

"Yes, baby. Please, baby. Wyatt . . . oh, my God, Wyatt . . ." Peyton's body quivers as her orgasm takes over. I hold on long enough for her to fall limp from overstimulation, then I pull out and my cum covers her belly. I empty myself on her skin, painting her with proof that she is mine and only mine. Like a fucking animal. And when I fall onto the bed next to her, our arms and legs tangled, her hair stuck to the side of my chest, she rolls her head to meet my drunken stare.

"There's my caveman," she coos.

I pound my fists to my chest and smile on the side closest to her. She giggles, and it's the greatest sound in the world.

Chapter Eight

Peyton

I don't feel bad at all for leaving the boys to do the heavy lifting. And I don't feel bad for not feeling bad. I tried to tell them that we should get up early enough to beat the morning heat and so I could help before practice, but Wyatt wanted to sleep in. And Whiskey was snoring so loudly, it woke Tasha through the walls, and she went home to sleep off the rest of her hangover.

For having had a few drinks for the first time in weeks, I feel surprisingly wired. And I think it's because I know when I get done with practice today, I'm going to walk into Wyatt's place and call it ours.

My phone buzzes in the Jeep's cupholder as I pull into a spot just south of the track, near the gym. I pull it from the charging cord and wake up my screen to a message from Tasha.

TASHA: What am I supposed to do with these two?

My palm buzzes with the incoming picture. It's Wyatt and Whiskey standing shoulder to shoulder in her doorway as if they're stuck. Their hair is tussled like third grade boys who've just woken up from a sleepover, and Whiskey is already holding a beer.

I cackle, then thank myself for not feeling guilty about missing this.

ME: You put boxes in their hands and wave them on their way.

TASHA: This.

I chuckle at the mental picture, which I'm sure is exactly how Tasha executes my suggestion. And I bet Whiskey and Wyatt obey her every order, because my best friend has a way of being heard and minded.

I'm early to practice, the only car in the small lot next to the gym besides a familiar truck parked on the opposite corner. Bryce isn't inside it, so I don't think he's stalking me. But it's weird that he's here, and at eight in the morning. They don't have practice until four.

Pulling the straps of my bag up over my shoulder, I hop out of the Jeep and lock it behind me before heading toward the track. It's already nearing a hundred degrees out, the Arizona fall behaving a lot more like summer. It's what makes our desert football teams so formidable. People come play us here early in the season and simply can't hang in our heat.

I lean into the fence, spotting Bryce running on the opposite side of the track. His pace is steady, and his shirt is off. He may be my ex but I'm human, and the man has kept up with his fitness. I'd still take the feel of Wyatt's abs under my hand any day, but Bryce, he makes a good case for calling attention.

His run slows to a jog when he spots me. He peels off the track after a few more steps and walks across the field where our soccer team practices. His hands are linked over his head, his elbows out, and I can see how hard his chest is working to catch his breath as he nears.

"You know it's better to show off where people will see you," I tease.

I back up a step as he meets the fence, hooking his fingers through the links and resting a foot near the bottom as he lunges into a stretch. He lifts his head and squints from the sun as he looks at me.

"You saw me."

His mouth curves in that half grin he still wears well. It's a glimmer of the cocky fifteen-year-old I fell for as a kid. Man, was I an easy target.

"Yeah, but I have zero say over the starting quarterback slot." I shrug, and he laughs out hard, letting go of the fence and backing away a few steps to stretch his quads one at a time.

"You know, I still have shit balance," he proclaims as he holds his right foot behind him while he wiggles on his left.

"You've gotten better, though. A few years ago, you'd be on your ass by now."

He chuckles and lets his foot fall to the ground.

"That's fair."

He stretches the other leg, glancing up at me with his lips parted as if he has something to say. It makes my chest tighten.

"I know why I'm here early. We hit the mat today, first time with the new routine. Unless you're switching it up and coming to be a base, why are you putting in overtime?" I nod out toward the track, which is devoid of anyone else and looks fucking hot. The red all-weather rubber appears on the verge of melting, and I swear I see heat radiating from the concrete lip around the edge.

Bryce drops his other leg and licks his lips, shifting his weight, then running a hand through his sweat-soaked hair. He's been at this a while.

"Honestly? Wyatt kicked my ass on the treadmills the other day, and it made me realize my cardio is shit."

Huh. Wyatt seemed to think Bryce was on par with him. I won't tell Bryce that Wyatt was worried about the same thing, but he was. And he's been running a lot more on his own too. Granted, Wyatt likes the trails. He gets up at dawn and scales the mountain and back.

Bryce's head tilts to the side as his hands land on his hips, his breathing back to normal.

"Hey, you got a minute?"

I glance behind me, the lot still empty. I like to be early, but I guess I can handle not being the one to flip the lights on.

"Yeah, shoot."

He flashes a tight-lipped smile and holds up a finger, jogging to the edge of the track where his gym bag sits. He pulls out a towel and a white T-shirt that he slips over his head before jogging back toward me. I follow along as he makes his way to the gate between the track and the lot, near his truck.

He opens the front passenger door and tosses his bag inside, then props a foot on the running board while he leans against the side of the seat. He picks at a hangnail on his thumb, a nervous fidget it seems because he quickly stuffs his hands in his pockets after not getting anywhere with the random grooming. His gaze remains focused on the asphalt between us.

"I came here for you," he says, words spilling out all at once, landing at my feet like a pile of hot vomit.

What the fuck!

"Bryce—"

"At first," he cuts in, finally lifting his head to meet our eyes.

The churn in my stomach pauses, but the bubbling is still there. *At first* might make it better, but this still feels bad. On instinct, I scan the parking lot and nearby street for Wyatt.

"I know, I probably should have kept that to myself."

"You *definitely* should have kept that to yourself," I pile on, hugging myself with my arms and nervous energy.

Bryce lets out a nervous laugh.

"Yeah, I'm really bad at timing. I know. But I just have all this . . . *stuff* . . . on my chest." He runs his fingertips around the center of his body in circles, his mouth twisted like he's going to be sick.

"Did Bryce Hampton grow a conscience?"

He grimaces.

"Sorry, continue." I clear my throat and grab the sides of my T-shirt tighter. I need to hold on to something.

"It wasn't only about you. I wasn't getting time on the field, and nothing was going right for me with football. I felt like I kept making bad decision after bad decision. And Wyatt had this great year, and then he got hurt. And I'll admit, at first, I thought about the opportunity. Stepping in and filling his shoes. And yeah, you were here. And the idea of you seeing me at my best, maybe feeling . . . *something* . . . for me—I entertained that fantasy for a little bit."

"Key word—fantasy." I need to make sure he knows where the line is between us.

He nods and shoots me a quick, crooked smile as he holds a palm up.

"Okay, yeah. I got it, Peyton. No need to totally demolish my ego."

My nerves settle, and I warm with a touch of guilt for making him feel bad. I don't apologize, though.

"I'm not sure what Wyatt told you about camp workouts or the first week of practice, but Peyt . . . he's good for me." There's a tiny quiver to Bryce's bottom lip, almost like he's scared. I think maybe he's embarrassed to admit this. I won't poke fun because I get just how big this is. But I'm blown away hearing it.

I take in a long breath and hold it in my lungs, my gaze flitting down before rising back up to meet Bryce's.

"Wow, that's . . . kind of you to say. Have you told Wyatt?"

"Ha! I mean . . . in little ways. Mostly when he looks like he wants to punch me. I try to let him know that I'm grateful to him. That I'm learning a lot."

I nod, honestly flabbergasted at how different this Bryce is from the one I used to know.

"He's not going to let you have the starting job. If you want it, you'll have to take it." This is the part I've been dreading since word of the transfer hit—the battle to be on the field. I have all the faith in the world that Wyatt is the best man for the job, and that he'll keep his position. But there's that lingering sting in the back of my mind that whispers, "What if?"

What if Bryce knocks him out of starting QB?

"I know I need to earn it. And I'm not going to just let him have it. I'm going to work my ass off and fight for it. But if it shakes out that I'm his number two, I just want you to know I'm good with it. Better than good. And maybe you can let him know, if that time comes."

"*When* that time comes," I say, making sure Bryce gets where my loyalties lie on the field.

His mouth quirks up with a quiet laugh.

"Yeah, we'll see."

He pushes off the truck and steps toward me, chewing at the inside of his mouth for a few seconds before looking at me through his lashes.

"I'm sorry."

I blink a few times, taking in the non-verbal cues from his tight-lipped expression, the heaviness in his eyes, the sincerity of his stare. He means about me—about us, and how he was back then.

"I know." I won't say it's okay. He should know that about me.

He nods and steps closer, stretching his arms out with his head tilted a hair.

"Friends?"

I draw in a sharp breath, and without thinking too hard, I give in and hug him back. It's a quick embrace, but the way his hand drags against my back when we part, as if he's clinging to some kind of hope, sticks with me. I get this strange sense that a part of him wanted to kiss me just then.

"Friends," I echo.

The childlike smile makes its way back to his mouth. He looks lighter, too.

"Go kill it in there. Hope they're letting you fly," he says, remembering how much I love the gymnastics of what I do.

I start to walk backward, wanting to end on a high note with him.

"I fly a little. But mostly, I'm there to throw other people in the air. It's the damn Johnson muscles. My parents made me strong," I say, flexing a bicep.

"Apples and trees and all that," he says through a chuckle.

"Something like that," I say, spinning as I continue to walk away. I hold up a hand to wave bye. I don't hear anything more from him in return, but I can feel it without looking—he watches me all the way to the gym.

Chapter Nine

Wyatt

I should have listened to Peyt when she said to start early. My fault for assuming there wasn't much left to move.

It felt like we already had so much of her stuff at my place. Her clothes have filled half my closet for a year. My bathroom is basically hers. We make coffee with *her* Keurig and dinner in *her* insta pot. I figured since we were leaving the couch behind, we could get it all in one haul. And we're turning Whiskey's old room into a workout room for stretching and yoga. Hence, no bed to move. Whiskey never bothered with a frame so his was just a mattress, and we took that to Tasha's on our first trip.

Somewhere along the way, though, I miscalculated Peyton's affinity for shoes. And sweaters. And headwear, including four cowgirl hats. One is my fault since I bought it for her at the spring rodeo. After six hours of carrying Peyton's boxes into my place—*our* place—I'm wiped. And now I have to run through the entire playbook with our offense while Bryce watches, learns, and repeats. I only hope he doesn't do it better.

"Let's start with the wide receiver slants."

Coach is wearing his game-day sunglasses. They block his

eyes completely and obscure most of his expression so there will be no reading into his mood. At least not on his face. The man is always direct and to the point, so everyone's first assumption is that he's pissed off. I remind myself not to make that mistake and get caught up in my worries.

"Yes, Coach!"

I pop my mouth guard in and chew at the hard plastic while working the ball in my fingers. Keaton, our number one receiver this year, steps up to the line and I give him a nod.

"Blue, forty-two! Blue, forty-two!" I shout, then fall back a few steps, faking a handoff before spinning out and hitting Keaton mid-stride just beyond the first down.

"Good. Run it again," Coach says.

I flip my mouth guard around in my mouth, gnawing at it to keep myself from grinning like a child because he praised me. I shouldn't need so much reassurance, but damn if I don't. I glance at Bryce, his face stoic, eyes studying my every move. That fucker's part robot now, I swear. He's probably calculating every step I take and training his body how to shave off seconds, add in yards, double his speed.

"Blue, forty-two! Blue, forty-two!" I pivot again, letting my body do its thing. Keaton runs the route, and I hit him right at the line, a step before he goes out of bounds.

"Clean it up." Coach's criticism is warranted. It's a good pass if we're trying to save clock, run a two-minute drill down the field. But this season is all about scoring big. Coach made it clear that he wants us demolishing our opponents. It's a tough schedule.

"Yes, sir," I say, chomping on my guard again, this time to hold in the self-admonishing swear words.

I count it off again, dropping back and letting my mind go blank. It's all rote. Every cell in my body is trained for this. Keaton barely glances over his shoulder before the ball is there for him, and he tucks it in his arm and sprints ahead another fifteen yards.

"There it is. Yes!" Coach claps, then steps forward and points at Bryce.

I jog over to Coach's left side and give the field to Bryce. Coach pairs him with Nick, our number two. He's not as fast as Keaton, and a small part of me hopes Bryce overestimates his speed and biffs the pass. It's not what's best for the program, but it would sure as hell be good for me.

Bryce counts off and Nick takes off for his route, turning to find the pass right at his chest. The catch isn't as smooth, but that's more on Nick than it is Bryce, whose timing was actually right on target. *Shit.*

"I like it! Run it again." Coach shifts his weight, folding his arms over his chest as he chews at the toothpick in his mouth. The man has an endless supply of those things. It's more superstition than dental needs for him. He goes through at least a dozen every practice.

For the next hour, Bryce and I trade off running every single play, even the ones Coach only breaks out when he's feeling lucky. I feel good on my feet, and I'm smoother in the pocket, but I can't shake this nagging feeling that Bryce simply isn't going away.

Coach calls us to the sideline after he sends the rest of the guys off to the showers, and the fact the only guys out here are me, my former nemesis (easy on the former), our quarterback coach, and the man who holds my playing fate in his hands has my heart pounding.

"I couldn't be a happier man right now, gentlemen." He pulls his glasses from his face, a rarity out here, and his eyes crinkle on the sides from both the sun and his obvious glee. I, however, feel as though I'm slowly sinking into the turf.

"I agree," Coach Skye, our QB coach, adds with a nod.

I sink deeper.

I'm noting every detail of everything—the way Coach Skye's teeth are holding on to his thumbnail, his eyes set on Coach to take the lead, Bryce's slow rock from side to side, his hands knotted behind his back. I feel small, though I'm the tallest dude out here. And I'm getting smaller by the second.

"Wyatt, your recovery is incredible. I can tell you've worked your ass off to get back out here at one-hundred percent. You think you can handle the rush? Take the hit if our pocket turns to shit?"

I nod.

"Yes, sir. I'm stronger. I really worked to shore up my core and legs." I mean, I've been working on it, but I feel the same— no better, no worse. That's not what he wants to hear, though, and now, I'm selling myself like one of those dudes on Wall Street.

"Good. Good." He's nodding as his gaze wanders to the empty space between Bryce and me, as if he's still trying to decide what he's going to do. When his gaze snaps to Coach Skye, my heart stops.

Shit. Shit. Shit.

"I'd like to try something," he says.

Shit. Shit. Shit. Shit.

I nod and wish I had a mute button for the voice in my head. I glance to my right where Bryce has quit rocking, and his chin lifts a tick.

"Yes, sir." His Adam's apple bobs with a hard swallow. I'd feel a little bad for the stress he's feeling if I weren't in this fucking whirlpool with him.

"I want to run two quarterbacks."

My instant deep breath is audible, and my chest fills as I lean back. I'm no longer looking directly at Bryce, but I see his posture do the same in my periphery.

"It's not something we've done in a while, and with this

season's schedule, and the different approaches, we're going to have to tool to every defense. I'd like to give this a try."

"I'm all in, Coach. Absolutely." Bryce is practically bouncing on his feet.

I run my fist over my cheek, my mouth open with a million questions at the ready, but when Coach's gaze hits mine, I shut it. His mind is made up. And he's about to answer anything he cares to for now. I sink deeper.

"Wyatt, you're the starter. There's no doubt that your arm strikes fear in our opponents. We need that. And with our one-two punch in Keaton and Nick, I see big scoring games in our future. Lots of forty-burgers."

My lungs relax.

"For sure, Coach. It felt good with Keaton today. I think I could hit that dude with my eyes closed, and his speed is up, for sure."

Sell it, Wyatt!

"Good. I agree. And Bryce—"

My lungs cinch right up. My stomach hurts.

"I think we need your bulk for those running plays. Maybe we'll have you in for a pass or two, just to keep people guessing. I want that arm ready, and I want you learning from Wyatt. But when we need to move that ball a yard—punch it in the end zone—I'd like to see what you can do."

Bouncing. Fucking. Toddler.

"Absolutely." Bryce glances to Coach Skye, and the two share a nod, as if they've cooked this whole thing up together. Now I'm a paranoid lunatic. I need to stop my mind before it runs me out of a job.

"Fantastic. Thanks for today, guys. You were great."

"Thank you," Bryce and I say in unison. I feel his eyes flash to me, and I can sense his grin. I'm sure my mouth looks as if it's about to vomit, so I do my best to force my lips together tight. I can't muster a smile.

"Hit the showers. We run the full game plan against Tech starting tomorrow. We go hard all week. And Saturday we make a statement."

Coach says those last few words as he's walking away. Coach Skye shakes both of our hands, then jogs to catch up to his boss. Bryce is lingering, so I stay back with him, knowing he wants to talk this shit out. I'm not sure I'm ready to be the bigger man, though.

I walk over to the water station, the ground littered with paper cups, and I stoop to clean up.

"The student field crew will get that," Bryce says.

"Yeah, I know. But we're fucking pigs, and I don't mind." And I need to do something to feel useful. *Plus, this keeps my eyes off you, asshole.*

Naturally, Bryce picks up the dozens of cups near him on the ground. This new leaf he's apparently turned over is annoying as hell. I miss selfish Bryce, who would have walked into the locker room with Coach and left me out here to stew on my own.

"Hey, I wanted to run something by you. Uh, it's . . . awkward, I guess? But I thought it was better coming from me. If you heard it from me, I mean. And it's meaningless. But you know how people are. Anyway . . ."

I stand with my back to him, my fists full of trash. I walk to the metal bin by our bench and toss the paper cups inside before wiping the sticky Gatorade from my hands onto my pads. With my mouth sealed shut and molars glued together, I turn to face him.

"It's really nothing," he says, but the way he's tethered his hands behind his neck, elbows out as he tips his head back and looks at the blazing sunny sky, has me thinking it's far-ass-far from nothing.

I literally bite the tip of my tongue as I inch closer to him.

"Just spill it, Bryce. I'm kind of done with you today, and I'd like to get my shit and go home."

His head falls forward, and when our eyes meet, I get a glimpse of his old competitive flair. His lips part with a hint of a smile, and his head tilts slightly.

"You're pissed about what Coach said."

Fuck him, he knows I am.

"I'm fine, Bryce. What is it?"

I'm not fine. And I'm pulling further away from fine by the millisecond. When Bryce chuckles, I decide I've endured enough of everything for the day. I shake my head and walk past him, toward the stadium locker rooms. He follows, but gives me a welcome lead. Finally, fucking alone. I get about halfway there before he stops me cold with his words.

"You're so pissed off now, but wait until you see the picture someone got of Peyton and me at the club."

"That's it." I spin and close the distance between us with a few long strides, flying into him with both hands wrapped around his shoulder pads so I can force the top-heavy motherfucker onto the ground.

He topples quickly and I pin him down, straddling his flailing body while I push his shoulders harder toward the earth.

"Get the fuck off!" He shoves at my chest, but between my leverage and my rage, he doesn't stand a chance. I won't punch him because that would leave a mark. Last thing I need is Coach seeing my co-quarterback showing up with a black eye.

"Isn't it enough yet? Don't you have enough? Or do you want it all? My whole life?" I shake him, my weight landing on his upper body over and over. His eyes narrow as I continue to pummel his chest. Slowly, his body goes slack and I finally crawl off him and sit on the ground at his side, sinking my hands into my hair as I grumble.

Bryce sits up, brushing the bits of grass from his hair before leveling me with a hard stare that I deserve. My eyes flit up to catch it briefly.

"Fuck, man. I'm stealing your life? Are you that fucking clueless?" His words spill out in an exasperated, breathy laugh.

I wave my hand at him and shake my head as I drop my gaze back to the ground. He didn't even throw any punches. I'm not sure if we've grown or are just chicken shits now.

"I will never, in my lifetime, find a woman—let alone a whole damn family—like Peyton and hers. If I had one super-power, it would be to trade places with you in a heartbeat. So pardon me if I can't wrap my fuckin' mind around you feeling threatened."

My chest puffs with a short laugh, and I lean forward to spit out the pieces of grass that found their way into my mouth. Rolling my head to the side, I meet his stare, and that flash of arrogance I saw before is gone. Now he just looks sad.

"I'm not here to make some big play to get her back. I swear. But I am here to play football. I won't apologize for that."

I catch my bottom lip under my teeth as I take in his words. I start to nod, and the reality washes over me. Nothing is guar-anteed—Peyton, this game—but I can't lose sight of who I am as a man, the person I want to be. Todd Stone—my dad—he wouldn't let anything pull him away from walking his line. That's how I win.

My nostrils flare as I slowly let out the hot breath from my lungs. I lean to my right and hold out my hand, and Bryce grasps it firmly. We clutch each other, a little bit of a promise, and for me at least, a show of strength. Not who has the firmer grip, but who can rise above. We pull in unison until we're on our feet, then dust the scraps of grass and dirt from our white practice pads.

"Dude, you fucking stink. You should really shower," I say.

Bryce breathes out a quivering laugh that grows into a loud cackle.

"Says the man who smells like shit on roses." He nods at me.

I flash him my middle finger, then step in line with him as we head the rest of the way to the locker room. I muster the emotional strength to briefly place my hand on his upper back, and he does the same. I think, for us, that's as good of an apology as either will ever get.

Chapter Ten

Peyton

I think I got used to the clutter.

Now that my boxes are unpacked and I'm looking at the stacks of clothes lying on our bed, at the plastic tumblers for margarita night in the kitchen—all eleven of them—and my *perhaps* excessive collection of yoga mats, maybe I should have donated a lot of this stuff before Wyatt and Whiskey spent the morning moving it.

I finish tying up an extra-large plastic bag stuffed with a couple dozen competition sweatshirts from when I was fifteen as I hear Wyatt come through the front door. Not wanting to spoil the excitement of our first night in *our* apartment by asking for help hauling down to my Jeep three full bags of clothing and random fitness doodads I just had Wyatt move into this place, I push this bag to the far corner of the closet, along with the other two, and promptly close the door. I spin with my back to the door a second before Wyatt enters our bedroom.

It takes me about a half second to read the despair on his face.

"What happened?"

I move to him as he drops his gear bag at his feet and moves to swallow me up in his arms. His body is still damp from his post-practice shower, his T-shirt sticking to his stomach and chest, his hair damp and smelling of his cedar shampoo. He exhales a heavy breath into the crook of my neck, and then his body shakes.

"Baby," I hum at his ear.

Wyatt doesn't cry. Even when they had to cut his pads from his body when he broke his collarbone last season, he didn't shed a single tear. His face went stoic. His jaw locked. He ate the pain, and he processed the setback almost immediately. This man in my arms right now is hurting in a different way, and I think I know why.

"Saturday's game?" I swallow as I wait for his response.

His head nods against me, the cold tip of his nose burying deeper into my hair. I walk backward a few steps toward our bed. Wyatt loosens his hold on me, turning to sit on the mattress and scooting to the middle, pulling me to his chest and holding me between his legs. I lock his hands in mine against my chest, and together we breathe. Long inhale, then slow exhale. I wait patiently for him to feel ready, and eventually his chin lands on my shoulder, then his lips on my neck for a soft kiss.

"Coach is running two quarterbacks."

His revelation isn't as bad as I thought, but I'm sure it's bad enough to him. I was prepared for the worst—for Bryce to fully get the start. After seeing him putting in the work this morning, I realize he's here to fight for his legacy. Bryce's dad never made it in anything, peaking on his high school football team. For Bryce, being a college quarterback is a major fuck you to the man who abandoned him. Getting drafted has always been his dream. Somewhere along the way, he realized he didn't simply deserve it but would have to earn it.

"You're still the best," I say, wincing at my own words. His chest quivers against my back as a soft, breathy laugh tickles my neck.

"That was cheesy," he says.

"I know. I'm not sure what to say. I mean it, though. You are the best quarterback my dad's ever seen. This school has the program it does because you came here. Everything Coach is building is on your back. Bryce only came here because he knows where the competition is, and where he'll get the looks. Those eyes are on Arizona because of you, Wy. Nobody else. And if he's lucky enough to share a few snaps with you, he better not waste the chance to show off, because he won't get many. We can't afford for you to not be out there."

Wyatt's hands pull mine in tighter, his hold on me intense, almost desperate. I bend forward and press my lips on his knuckles.

"If it wasn't Bryce, it would be someone else. You made this the place to come—to *be*. The best want to follow the best—"

"But it was Bryce. It *is* Bryce," he interjects.

I suck in my bottom lip, thinking about my interaction with him today. Before I can mention it, though, Wyatt shifts slightly to his right, reaches into his pocket, and hands me his phone.

"One of those stupid campus gossip socials got a pic of you two at Catwalk."

I twist my head enough that my nose touches his, and I blink a few times.

"You know it was nothing—"

"I know. They made it look like something, but I know." He clicks his screen and pulls up the app, opening the search box where I see he's searched for my and Bryce's names a few times already. My stomach churns.

"Why were you looking for us?" I ask as I stare at the first photo that comes up. It's blurry, as if it's one of those sketchy *TMZ* shots. Worse, it was taken by some drunk student who wanted to perpetuate whatever rumors were fueled from the football press conference days ago. The angle makes it look like Whiskey and Tasha aren't in the picture, though they were mere feet behind us on our way out of the club. Bryce's hand is on my back, and I admit it gives off flirty couple vibes, but he was simply getting me out of the crowded bar without causing a bigger scene.

"Bryce told me about it. Of course, I had to see it for myself. Stupid, I know. But—"

"And why did Bryce tell you about it?" My eyes squint at the image for another second before I click the screen off and toss Wyatt's phone to the side of the bed. I shift in his arms, moving so my legs wrap around his waist and my hands hook behind his neck. He looks exhausted—his cheeks and the tip of his nose red from the sun.

He grimaces at me, and the longer he stares at me without speaking, the tighter my chest gets.

"Did he say it to be mean? To flaunt it?" Fucking Bryce, after that grand speech he gave me today.

Wyatt's shoulders rise, and the corners of his mouth pinch tighter.

"Wyatt?" I tilt my head. "Did you guys get into a fight?"

His eyes squint. I shift my hands around to his cheeks and bring his forehead to mine.

"I maybe didn't react so great to the splitting time at QB talk with Coach," he admits.

"Oh," I murmur. I close my eyes and roll my head against his.

"Was it in front of Coach?" *Please say it wasn't.*

"No, I'm smarter than that."

"Are you?" I tease.

He breathes out a soft laugh.

"Periodically."

I lean back, my hands still caressing the sides of his head as I stare into his dark blue eyes. God, the way this man can look like a storm all on his own. Dark hair, heavy brows, stubbled beard, and the ocean in his eyes.

"We kind of worked it out. Well, I mean as much as you can work out shitty things like competing for something you love." His eyes flicker, then settle on mine. I bite my bottom lip, and he does the same.

"I hope you don't mean me. Because there's no competition there. Ever." I run my hand through the side of his hair, and he leans into my palm, turning to press his mouth on my wrist.

"I let it all boil over inside. I feel like I'm being replaced out there," he confesses. "And it's turning me into something I don't want to be.

I nod and utter, "I know."

"I don't want to be a man like that. Someone you wouldn't want because he's jealous and angry all the time."

"And you won't be. Ever." I believe every word to my soul. Wyatt is built differently. I wish I knew his dad because from all I've learned about him, he's so much like his father.

"Do you want to own me, Wyatt Stone?" I bring his forehead back to mine, his bottom lip out enough for me to nip at with my teeth. He nods against me and lets out a ragged breath.

"Then do it. Right now." I pull back and hold my arms up over my head. He pulls his Arizona sweatshirt from my body; the only other thing I'm wearing is a tiny pair of white sleep shorts. In one smooth movement, he sweeps his right arm behind me and pulls my body to him, his mouth covering one of my breasts, sucking my nipple into a hard, raw peak that he catches between his teeth.

"More of that," I rasp, and he moves both hands to my back, pulling me into him harder, his mouth moving to the other breast and torturing it just the same.

"I fucking love you. You're everything to me. You, it's just you, Peyton," he says, scooting back and sitting up on his knees, lifting me with him, his mouth never leaving my breast.

Wyatt lays me on my back and continues to drop kisses down the center of my body, pausing at my belly button as he works my shorts over my hips. I kick them away, lying beneath him completely naked, my skin shivering from the apartment air and the ceiling fan above. Every part of me that chills, Wyatt quickly warms with his mouth, tasting my ribs and then my breasts again as he slips his hand between my legs.

I reach to touch him, the tip of his cock peeking out of his sweatpants, but he moves my hand away, holding it to the bed as he moves above me and shakes his head.

"Tonight, it's nothing but me serving you. I want you to come so many times that you fall asleep dreaming about it and wake up to me making you come again." He drops his mouth to my pussy and suckles my clit.

"Oh!" I barely get the tiny word out of my mouth before the first wave hits.

"All. Night. Long," he says, flicking his tongue against me and sending me over the edge. I lift my hips out of need, but he presses them down, forcing me to take every tease and lick at his pace. It's no sacrifice, and I feel spoiled that I'm the one getting this attention after the day he had.

But when he utters, "I love you so fucking much," against my sensitive skin, waking every nerve to life once again, I realize this is what makes him strong. Pleasing me. No matter what form of happiness I want or need. And right now, I need this. I need this so fucking badly.

Chapter Eleven

Wyatt

I can't imagine ever getting tired of watching Peyton get ready in the morning. I don't even care that it's five o'clock. Okay, I care a *little* bit. But not enough to pull the blanket back over my head and shut out the last few glimpses I will get of her for the day.

"Why do you all practice so early?" I rub a fist in my right eye so I can keep the left one open as she zips up her sports bra and slinks into her off-the-shoulder T-shirt.

"Uh, probably because all of the facilities are in use by various men's teams during normal hours," she says over her shoulder.

I give her a tight-lipped nod.

"Fair point." She's right. It's not even basketball season, but they get to dominate the gym facilities during the day. Even wrestling gets the space before women's basketball. Then it's cheer.

"Maybe if you had men on the stunt team," I joke.

She shoots me a hard look, and I retreat fast.

"Right. Not funny, and just . . . you're right." She is. It was a *little* funny though.

She flips her head forward to braid her hair from the base of her neck. I don't even understand how a person learns to do some of the things she does to her hair. She puts a band around the end of the braid and twists it into this intricate-looking bun that she locks in place with a hairpin.

"What?" She giggles when she catches me staring at her.

"You woke up seven minutes ago, and I swear you already look ready for the Oscars."

She laughs and moves toward the bed, kissing the top of my head as I wrap my arm around the back of her legs.

"What if you call in sick? Just once." I make pouty lips at her and tease her skin along the hem of her panties. She's wearing the plain cotton bikini kind, in red. My favorite.

"*Mmm*, tempting. But—it's the last full practice before the rally. Don't forget," she says, peeling my fingers away one by one. She brings my hand to her mouth and presses her lips to my fingertips before backing out of reach.

"Rally, right. I'm there," I say, not doing a very good job at masking the fact I forgot.

Peyton eyes me in the bathroom mirror across the room, her mouth open as she dabs pink gloss on her lips.

"It's for the alumni party, and your coach should really encourage you all to go anyway."

She's right again. He doesn't, though. Coach, in fact, has great contempt for all things tailgate, donor-appreciation, fundraisery. He would rather just win games to get butts in seats. I see both sides of the coin, probably because I'm beholden to people on both sides.

"I'll be there. I might be sweaty and gross, but I'll be there."

I cross my chest, drawing an X with my finger as she steps into her black leggings, then stuffs her sock-covered feet into her sneakers without bothering to untie them. It bends the heels of her shoes when she does that, and I've been preaching to her about ruining her shoes for as long as we've been dating.

At this point, I think she does it to spite me. What she doesn't know, though, is I secretly think her small acts of defiance are adorable. She scrunches her nose even, as if she's quashing my advice with her foot as she works on her shoe.

Fucking adorable.

"Four o'clock. Arena." She snags her bag from the chair and tucks her laptop and a binder from her animal therapy class inside.

"No break between practice and class?" I quirk a brow.

"We don't all get the football player accommodation schedules, you know. Some of us have to take the classes we need to graduate when they're offered. All of mine happen to be ass-crack of the morning."

I kick off the blankets and swing my feet to the floor, stretching my arms over my head as I let out a big yawn. Before Peyton looks away, I pound my chest with my right fist and grunt out, "Caveman like his online classes with no real due dates. Make him real good at business one day."

She rolls her eyes, but we both laugh. It's an ongoing joke we have with her family about the total scam the business education track is for football players. It's the one degree that can be "massaged," according to the booster members who demanded it when Reed was a student here. Most of the guys on the team who go this route figure they'll either land in the NFL or end up in sales and make big bank on their winning personalities. Personally? I actually want to learn valuable business skills so maybe one day I can build something like Peyton's parents have—a business that honors my father's name.

I guess quarterback fame and my winning personality will have to do.

"Don't forget!" Peyton hollers before rushing out of our apartment.

I grab my phone to set a reminder, then jump in the shower before logging in to my online portal to catch up on homework for my finance class. I spend an hour balancing a few sample spreadsheets, then buzz through an online quiz after a video that I don't watch but simply read the closed captioning for. I leave our apartment feeling absolutely zero-percent smarter than I did when I came home last night. But at least I'll make it to weights with Bryce and Shad on time, then a catered lunch paid for by the booster club, followed by hours of Tech football video from last year.

Bryce is already warming up on the treadmill when I arrive. I let myself feel the pangs that come with my insecurities for exactly four seconds, then tuck them away. The last few days of practice have all been mental works in progress for me, but I'm getting there. And I'm embracing sharing the field with him, despite the piece of me that still wants it all to myself.

"Slackers. Still stuck at eight?" I hop onto my treadmill between Bryce and Shad and warm my way up to nine miles per hour, but I back it down to eight after a minute.

"You know, not all of us are here for our arms, Wyatt." Bryce is doing a little shit-talking with me this morning because I started calling him Legs after Coach yelled the word at him at least fifty times at practice yesterday.

"Use your legs!"

"Why get legs that big if you can't use them to get your ass over that line?"

"More legs!"

"Legs! Legs! Fucking legs, goddammit!"

Whiskey caught on first, so full credit for the nickname goes to him. He was coined Bubble Ass our freshman year, which is fitting because his glutes are rock solid but enormous. He wanted the center job, but he's too fast to waste his speed. I think he's come to love playing right guard. I sure as hell love having him there. My collarbone breaker didn't get through him—he got through the left.

"You gonna start waxing those things, pretty them up?" I tease, pointing to Bryce's right thigh as we slow to a walk.

"I hear pale and hairy is in now," he cracks.

Shad spits out laughter on the other side, and for perfect comedic timing, the three of us turn just in time to catch Whiskey stepping into the weight room with his shirt off and his full chest of hair dyed half red and half blue for game day.

"What the ever-loving fuck is that, man?" Shad walks up to him and pokes a finger into the tuft on Whiskey's right pec.

"My new roommate thought it would be fun." He levels me with a quick grimace but cracks a smirk when he looks down at himself. He runs his hand through the center of his chest like he's trying to fluff it up.

"What have I done?" I say to him, putting a hand on his shoulder as I make my way toward the free weights.

It's a light lifting day, today's quarterback work out is more about arm care than strength. We're through our reps in less than an hour and upstairs for lunch before most of the team. I finish my first plate by the time everyone makes their way through the line of food, so I dash up to the serving station to grab one more cornbread muffin before Coach begins his talk.

"Too many of those and you'll start to look like me." I halt my hand under the heat lamp, the muffin pinched in my tongs as my grin slowly spreads at the familiar voice.

"Let me guess, they signed you to split time with me too?" I say to Peyton's dad.

"Shiiiiit, my knees can't handle that anymore," Reed says, slinging an arm around me and pulling me into one of those hugs that instantly reminds me he will always be in charge of whether I live or die because I'm with his daughter.

"Besides, if I *were* to join the team, all your asses would be benched," he chokes out in a half-cough-half-laugh.

"Reed, good to see you. Come on up," Coach says, pulling him away from me.

I take my muffin back to the table and sit a little taller. Something about having Reed in my corner gives me strength. Maybe it's his legacy. It's sticky. Whoever touches him gets a bit of the magic. At least, that's the lie I tell myself. So far, it's working.

Bryce leans toward me across the table.

"You know what this is about?" He nudges his head in Reed's direction, and I shake my head.

Reed takes a seat at the long table set up at the front of our dining hall. The windows overlook the stadium, and even though the sun is up, the lights are on as workers prep the seats and concourses for tomorrow's game. There's nothing quite as grand as running through that tunnel. One more year of it. Then, if I'm lucky, a whole new tunnel.

A few more men around Reed's age make their way into the dining hall, each of them embraced by a different player. And when Whiskey's Uncle Luke taps my friend on his shoulder for a surprise, it dawns on me. Whiskey's dad passed away last year, so his uncle stepped in for family day. Reed . . . he's here as my family.

"Oh," I murmur when the full picture hits me.

I glance across the table to meet Bryce's wide eyes. In a blink, his focus shifts over my shoulder. I follow his line of sight until I see the man I only saw once before. We were in high school, getting our asses handed to us by our high school coaches and a cop after a bunch of the players from both towns schools decided to drag race in the desert. Bryce's dad came to pick him up—or bail him out if things went that way. He stuck around while we all ran bleachers until the sun came up. He didn't seem angry or disappointed in his son. He didn't seem interested at all, now that I recall that night. He sure seems interested now, though.

"Fuck me." Bryce's voice is low, but it's easy to read his lips. I'm sure his father did.

Unlike everyone else with a special guest here today, Bryce remains in his seat. He clears his throat and holds up a hand to wave hello as his father walks along the outskirts of the room to take a seat near Reed. The two of them shake hands, but when Reed sits down, he holds up his phone to signal for me to check mine.

> REED: Bryce okay with this?

> ME: Define okay.

I look up to meet the straight line on Reed's mouth just before he slowly shakes his head. My gaze moves to Bryce, who is suddenly very interested in cleaning his plate.

> ME: He's gonna need some help.

I watch for Reed to get my new message, then catch the tiny nod he gives me before putting his phone back in his pocket. Coach starts to speak, and everyone in the room adjusts their seats to look at him head on. Bryce must turn his completely around, which means I won't be able to monitor his expressions, but I can keep an eye on his dad.

He's surprisingly older than I remember him, especially for only four years having passed. His hair is still the same buzz cut, and his build is a cookie cutter of his son, maybe slightly smaller. He's a lot grayer than I remember, though. And his face looks stretched, almost like he had plastic surgery or something. *Shit, did he?*

"I know you all are sick and tired of hearing me preach about our tough schedule—"

The room fills with our collective groans as Coach waves a hand and laughs it off.

"You'll see. We'll be six games in, and you all will be saying,

'Damn, if only Coach warned us about this tough schedule.'"
His joke garners a good laugh.

"I thought it might be nice for us to try a little something different, maybe a new tradition. I don't know. We'll see if we win or not."

A light chuckle filters through the room.

"I'm a big believer in family. When you all filled out your profiles for Media Day, you might remember a question or two about the people who inspired you to play the game. Well, we had help from the booster club to make it happen, and a lot of those people are here today. I'd like to give them all a chance to send you out there with some wise words. So if you don't mind getting things started for us, Reed?"

There's a wave of applause and a few whistles while Reed takes the mic. He stands at his seat and looks around the room before landing on me. My cheeks burn from the attention, but I like it. It means something. More than anything, this moment is one I will never forget, even if he doesn't say a word.

"I don't know how many of you know this, but your QB1 over there is dating my daughter." Shad punches me in the arm as Whiskey pounds the table, and the room fills with guffaws as hands slap over mouths. Even Bryce turns to face me and laughs, mouthing, "I'm so glad this is you."

I shrink down a few inches in my chair, my palms sweating on my thighs. Nevertheless, I can't get the grin off my face.

"You should also know that this little shit broke not one, not two, but *all* of my state high school records."

Our table shakes from pounding all around this time. Whiskey stands up and slaps his chest, shouting, "What *what*?"

"He's still short of the ones I hold here, though." Reed points at me and winks as the crowd eats him up.

"I got a year left, old man!" I shout back, this time the room roaring in my favor. Even Coach is laughing so hard that he has to wipe away a tear.

"We'll see, Wyatt. We'll wait and see. I hear your schedule is pretty tough." He points to Coach with that joke and gets our skipper to roll his eyes as he chuckles.

"Kidding aside, what I wanted to say to you today isn't about how great I think you are, and what I know you're going to do this season. I wanted to tell you how proud I know your dad would be if he were the one standing in this room right now."

Damn.

My eyes glisten without warning, the tears welling up fast. I run my arm along them only to face them getting full again.

"I mean it, kid. You're special, and I know he had to be one hell of a special guy to make someone like you. And he's still watching; I think you know that. He's got the best seat in the house, and he wouldn't miss a game. Love you, son."

I shake a little, spitting out my cry as I bury my face in my hands and draw in a sharp breath to try to make it stop. I can't shut it off so easily, though, and really . . . I shouldn't. I get up from my seat and Reed hands the mic off to the guy next to him. We meet at the end of the long banquet table, and I hug him as if he's channeling my father through his embrace. His hand pats my back, and I adjust my grip on his. I needed those words more than he could possibly realize.

"Thank you," I say over his shoulder.

"I mean it. I love you, son. You've got this. All of it."

I step back and our arms fall to our sides. A little nervous laughter gets me through the remaining tears, and I notice a few guys near me are tearing up, too. I'm not the only one in here with a dead dad. Hell, Whiskey is going to choke up like a baby too. It's a shared pain and a shared joy. I wouldn't wish it on anyone.

By the time I make it back to our table, Bryce's father has gotten the mic. I'm tempted to move my chair so I can sit next to him, maybe stand on his foot to keep him from leaping up from the table and picking a fight. But that's the old Bryce. I must start having some faith in him at some point, until he gives me a reason not to.

"Hey, son."

Bryce lifts his head to meet his dad's gaze, and he lifts a hand as he forces a smile on his face.

Bryce's father draws in a long breath.

"Yeah, that's the welcome I figured I'd get. It's all right, though. I love you anyway. And I know when you get your shot, you'll be a star. You were always so talented. Man, in high school . . . am I right, Reed?"

"You were never there," Bryce mutters. My muscles tense and I flash a look at Whiskey. He leans forward, cupping his mouth to whisper something to Bryce.

"I'm fine, it's fine," Bryce whispers back over his shoulder. His eyes meet mine for a blip, long enough for me to shake my head and silently beg him not to go down that tempting road.

"Anyway, good luck tomorrow, kid. We'll all be rooting for you." His dad takes his seat and hands the mic to his right. Bryce turns around and finishes his plate. And when lunch is done, he leaves the room before his father has a chance to cross it and shake his hand for real.

Chapter Twelve

Peyton

ME: Do you see Wyatt?

TASHA: Not yet. I'm here, though. You know, the superior roommate.

I purse my lips and blink at her text, deciding not to brand it with a laughing emoji because I'm anxious, and her jokes aren't helping. This is the first routine I've been a mid-base for since I started college cheer. It's not quite flying, but it's close—close enough. My friend Alicia is our main flyer, and I'm not sure I'm down for how high she gets thrown. I'm good to catch her on her way down, though.

The band is running through this week's show for the two hundred and fifty big donors who are sort of watching the stage. This whole event is set up for one reason and one reason only—NIL money for programs like ours. The ones who *support* the football game. What we do here today won't matter as much for me, but it will make a difference for the under-classmen supporting their education while pursuing their passions. I gave my NIL offers away. The one commercial I ran for a local coffee spot earned enough for one of my teammates to cover half of her tuition. It didn't seem right that I took money I didn't need. The commercial, though? That was kind of fun.

"We're on the mat in ten, ladies. Get ready." Coach Kane has a special way of clapping her hands—it produces a near-deafening boom that startles everyone in a twenty-foot radius to attention.

I check my phone for one last text from Wyatt or Tasha. Nothing new from anyone, so I put it away in my bag backstage and scurry my way to the other side of the stage for my opening tumbling pass.

My wrists feel good, but I add one more layer of tape, probably more to settle my nerves than anything, and chalk my hands as the band finishes their last song.

Horns blare at the audience while the drumline pounds out a rhythm so heavy I feel it in my ribcage. Half the reason the band is playing so loudly is to make sure everyone is paying attention. It seems to work as most people find their way to seats by the time the musicians form a long row across the stage and a second in front of it. As they blast out the final note, half the room is on their feet clapping and whistling.

Just wait until they hear our obnoxious music break through the speakers in this place. The mixtapes are everyone's least favorite part of competitive cheer. My dad could write a book of bad jokes he's told about the songs over the years, but he shows up anyway. He'd be here today, but he's busy wining and dining a few of the big donors to the football program.

When he told me he'd be on campus for that already, I had to ask him to step in for Wyatt at his luncheon. My mom mentioned that Whiskey's uncle had gotten a call from the boosters to show up for a family day, and I didn't want Wyatt to be left out, or for his mom to have to call off work when she's already coming out this weekend for the opening game.

Besides, as sexist as it is, it's very much a boy's club in that room. I couldn't think of a better man to stand in for Wyatt, besides maybe my grandfather. But Grandpa Buck isn't doing much out of the house these days. He still watches all the games, though, every single one of them—Wyatt, all the local universities, Coolidge and Vista High. The rivalry continues to be his favorite.

The lights in the arena dim, so I mind my pulse and take a few deep breaths before glancing one last time around the seats. When a door across the arena on the concourse level opens, everything in my chest settles. Of course it's him. And, of course, he's coming in the wrong way. And naturally, Whiskey is with him. And everyone is looking in *their* direction instead of at the stage where we're about to perform. Always stealing my spotlight, that boy.

I don't mind a bit. He's here.

Wyatt waves at me like a fool before he and Whiskey charm the security guard into letting them sit in the top row across the arena. It's not only the best view, but it will also be the least abusive assault on the ears when our music starts.

The arena manager turns on the spots, and at the first beat, I take a deep breath and haul ass across the stage for my first tumbling pass. I stick the round-off landing, then move into formation for our short dance routine before centering myself to help launch Alicia up her first fly. The roar in the room after we catch her sends a jolt of electricity through my body. This is always my favorite part of cheer competitions. The way an audience reacts feeds into our routine and makes it stronger, makes me tumble higher and move crisper.

The stunt we've been rehearsing all week is coming up, but I try not to focus on it so much that I lose my way through the middle of the routine. I think we could win nationals this year with this performance, especially if we stick everything. I've noticed a few mistakes so far today, but nothing anyone out there would recognize. I look at everything with a critical eye, just like Coach Kane.

I ready myself for the stunt, clapping out my count as I march backward into a back handspring and the grasp of two of my teammates. They catapult me onto a set of shoulders, and my feet feel solid. With a slight bend to my knees, I'm ready to absorb the shock for Alicia as my team sends her to the top. The hours of practice take over as she launches herself upward. I brace her right leg, holding her high in the air, smiling through the harsh stab of her heel against my bicep. The toughest part of stunt cheer is wearing a smile the entire time, especially when elbows and heels are digging into soft parts of my skin. But it feels easier today. Maybe this was the perfect audience to debut this routine in front of. They're natural fans, and the fact half of the room is businessmen with a thing for cheerleaders—*typical*—doesn't hurt either.

Alicia dismounts, and I fall forward into a basket catch seconds before we lead the room through the fight song. The band joins us, and for the next minute and twenty seconds, this arena bleeds red and blue.

It would be hard to miss the whistles coming from across the arena, especially because Whiskey can be so damn loud. But the fact our starting quarterback dropped in seems to really be the cherry on top for the alumni. While I busy myself taking photos with people, Wyatt does the same as he makes his way down the steps and across the arena to me.

"You made it," I say when he pulls me from my last photo op and into his arms.

"I told you I'd be running in right from the field." He lifts his sweatshirt to show his practice jersey underneath. I'm not sure what's underneath his sweatpants, but my guess is nothing. That's not for this room to see.

Two men in sharp gray suits step up to us, not seeming to care that Wyatt's hands are on my hips and my hands are linked behind his neck. I've watched my parents navigate this exact situation so many times, and I'm instantly struck with how similarly Wyatt handles it.

"You want a photo with the star? I could never do the crazy shit she does," he says, holding me close.

The men chuckle but quickly realize that if they want a photo with Wyatt, they're gonna have to have me in it too because there's no way he's letting go.

"Good luck tomorrow," one of them says after the selfie, shaking Wyatt's hand.

"Thanks, man. We hope to put up some big numbers this year."

He wears confidence well. It's nice to see him standing tall, both physically and emotionally. He's been doubting himself lately because of his injury and the pressure of splitting time with Bryce. He won't believe me because it goes against his humble demeanor, but Bryce could end up running every single touchdown this season, and Wyatt would still be the one everyone loves. They'll wear his number and name on their backs, and they'll pray he stays local when he goes pro. And not just because we'd never even get near the end zone without his arm. It's because Wyatt Stone is incredibly easy to love.

After an hour of forcing my smile into my cheeks and shaking hands with donors while they regale Wyatt with tales of my father, and even recite Wyatt's own great plays to him, the arena finally quiets. Whiskey bailed right after our show, but not Wyatt. He stayed for every moment, even when the praise was for our stunt team and had zero to do with football.

"Your cheeks are pink," I say to him as he hoists my gym bag over his right shoulder, threading his left hand in mine.

"I've had a lot of sun lately," he says. I chuckle and turn into him, lifting on my toes to rub my thumb along his upper lip and cheek.

"I don't think it's from the sun. I'm pretty sure you're

wearing more of my lipstick than I am." There's a fairly bright smudge on the corner of his mouth, and I decide to leave that one there. I like people knowing he's taken.

Wyatt backs into the exit door, holding it open for me as I walk through before he twirls me as if we're dancing. He rolls me into his body, then kisses me hard enough that I think he's trying to take the rest of my candy red lip color from my face.

He holds me close, locked in his arms as our noses touch. I close my eyes when his mouth moves to kiss my forehead. It's the little gestures like this, his quiet declarations, his soft adoration, that make my heart feel so certain.

"Thank you," he croaks.

My eyes flutter open, but I don't glance up, instead pulling my hands in to grab two fistfuls of his sweatshirt and rests them against his heart.

"My dad didn't embarrass you, then?" I smirk to myself, sure Reed Johnson got off a joke or two in the mix. My dad loves a captive audience. Especially a tipsy one.

Wyatt's chest shakes with his silent laugh and his lips land on the top of my head again.

"I love when your dad embarrasses me. Live for it," he muses.

"*Mmm*, he has you whipped," I tease.

"Ha, sure does. Nothing like his daughter, though. I mean, that music must be made in a torture factory. Why is it so loud again?"

I peel back and squint an eye, my mouth twisted.

"Cheer culture." It's the same answer I give for all the weird stuff that goes into my passion—the giant bows, the glitter, the uniforms that always seem to choke me a little but tout being "breathable" and offering "the ultimate flexibility." Liars.

"Ah, yes. Cheer culture." He takes a step back as his perfect damn smile fills my view. Dimples and sapphire blue eyes, wavy hair that looks sexy from the moment he wakes up. How did I ever resist him to begin with? It's as though he was cut from a mold I made with wishes and desires.

His smile settles into a softer one, and his tongue peeks out as he traps it between his front teeth like he's nervous.

"What is it, Wyatt Stone? You want to take me to prom?"

He shakes his head and pulls his lips into a tight smile.

It's quiet for several long seconds, and for the first time, I feel as though he may ask me to marry him for real right now. My heart thunders, and it gets difficult to hold his gaze. It feels hotter under his stare, as if I haven't stared into those eyes for nearly the last four years. It's like I'm looking into them for the first time, and the butterflies are so present my knees feel weak.

Wyatt chuckles and looks up at the sky, spinning on his heels and urging me to walk alongside him again. Our hands thread naturally, and we walk with a slight swing to them. And all the way home, those butterflies . . . they remain.

Chapter Thirteen

Wyatt

"Twenty-nine days, gentleman."

The locker room is hot as we all stand shoulder pads to pads, hands grasping helmets, eyes forward as Coach walks in the middle of our man-made circle. My feet are teeming with so much electricity I rock back and forth to tame my energy. Half the room does the same. We're primed, like race cars edging up to the line, the smell of gasoline in the air.

Game day.

Whiskey's face is painted for war, dark lines dripping from his eyes down his jawlines. His face matches the hurt he's ready to give anyone who gets near me or Bryce tonight. Nobody's getting through him.

"You've sweat on that field, put in the work, grinded your asses off for this moment. Right now!"

Whiskey starts to clap, and a few of the O-linemen nod their heads and shout, "Yes!"

"I tell you, in all my years, I've never had a team more ready than you are right now. Hungrier. More deserving. I feel it in the air. Can you?"

"Yes, Coach!" The room thunders with our united voice.

"Remember this feeling, gentlemen. Remember how your hearts feel. That burn in your legs. The taste you have for blood. Smell it. Can you smell it?"

"Yes, Coach!"

"Oh, I know you do! It's all right there for you. This game wants you to take it. It's yours to win. Those guys over there?" He points to the north end of the room, where the visitor's locker room rests beyond layers of brick and turf and glass and noise.

"Those guys think they can steal it from you!"

"No, Coach!"

"Yeah, that's what I think too. They're weak. They ain't ready for this!"

Coach begins to clap, and Whiskey steps into the center of the room to join him. I move in next, along with Keaton, our top receiver, and Deacon, our center. Captains—seniors. Our year. The last first game of my college career. It hits me in the chest all at once, but the feeling isn't like yesterday—it's not sentimental. It's war. Testosterone-fueled war. And there will be no prisoners.

Coach nods to me to take over, and my chest swells.

"Who are we?" My voice booms, the gravely howl coming from somewhere deep inside me.

"Wildcats!"

"I said, who are we?"

"Wildcats!"

I lean forward and pound on the wooden bench this program keeps around for this very reason. Hands join in, the storm growing in strength as we pound the wood, the room vibrating with our aggression—with our heart for this game. With our need to win.

"One—two—three!" I count off, ready for it.

"Bear down!"

We rush from the locker room down the concrete corridor,

the tight space echoing the thunder of our feet and the yowls from our mouths. The acrid smell of burnt gunpowder and chemicals from the fireworks leaks into the hallway and I breathe it in, letting it mentally transport me to every time before.

Twenty-nine days.

Three years of this tunnel.

My last year on this field.

My final first game here, in this uniform, wearing the same number as the man I grew up admiring—the same 13 that Reed is wearing out on the sidelines as he rallies our student section before we take the field.

One moment. This is it, and I'm going to be present for every single breath of it.

The team rushes out in front of us as I walk to the edge of the tunnel with my three co-captains, our hands linked, the feel of magic in our veins.

"Take it in, boys," I shout.

And we all do. Looking around as the crowd roars, the red and blue pompoms flickering against the stadium lights on either side of us as we step onto the field.

"Welcome to Wildcat Country!" The announcer's words are the signal, and the four of us drop hands and begin our slow run through the two lines of boosters, alumni, former players, redshirted freshmen, and cheerleaders.

My eyes find her instantly, on the end, as she promised. And after three years of holding myself back from kissing my girl in front of a stadium full of fans, I give in and kiss her hard, bending her back with my helmet held high in my other hand.

"I love you, Peyton Johnson. All for you, baby! This is all for you!" I jog backward and put my helmet on as she cups her mouth and screams, "Let's go!"

Reed's words yesterday at the luncheon resonated with me. He reminded me who I am. I'm Todd Stone's son, the man who pulled a woman out of her burning apartment building seconds before it collapsed; the guy who never missed a Christmas or a birthday, even if it meant we celebrated with him at the station. His roots are my roots, and I found the Johnsons because of the man he made me. And the man he wanted me to be would step up in front of Bryce just as I am now, helmet to helmet, my hands on his shoulders and his on mine.

"We got this!"

Our eyes lock and for the first time, I don't see an adversary. I see a brother. Past is past. This is now.

"You got this! My ass isn't even getting in this game today, you hear me? You're going to march down that field and score. They never saw you coming, Wy! Never saw you coming!"

Bryce builds me up as we push our heads together, helmet grinding against helmet, gritted teeth mirrored with my own.

"I got this!"

"You got this!"

We're in sync. Teammates. However we got here, it's happened. And Todd Stone's son is embracing it.

I sidestep my way down the line, bumping chests with teammates, shouting in faces, lifting everyone up until I make it to Reed. We leap and bump shoulders, which gets the student section on their feet as I turn and jog to the fifty-yard line to meet my co-captains for the coin toss. We lose, and Tech elects to kick off first, which plays right into our hands because of me —I've never been more ready.

Tech's kick puts us at the twenty-five-yard line, and Coach sends me out on the field with three words, "Give them Tombstone." I take my orders to my brothers, repeating it just as he said, and everyone nods, knowing exactly what to do. My eyes meet Keaton's for a blip, and I get everything I need to know out of the fire I see brewing behind them. The man is ready to run.

Run and gun. That's his call. It's a statement play, and we were working on it at the end of last season—before I got hurt.

I like it. I like it when we're bold. Tech won't see it coming.

I count us off at the line, then take the shotgun snap, rolling the ball in my hands as I bound on my feet. Our pocket holds, but Keaton needs more time, so I run to the right, opposite of him. Blocks are breaking down, but I've bought myself just enough time, and when Keaton passes our forty, I let the ball sail from my hand. I avoid the late hit and fold my hands on top of my helmet as I utter, "Come on baby. Come on baby."

The ball lands in Keaton's hands over his shoulder, his stride not missing a beat, and he leaves the Tech corner in the dust.

"That's a Wildcat touchdown!" The announcer bellows the words, letting them take up space and hover in the air, along with the roar from our home crowd. I rush to Keaton and meet him midfield for a celebratory chest bump, then run to the sidelines where I get another from Shad and Bryce. Coach pats my back as our field goal unit heads out to make the score seven.

My eyes snap to the scoreboard for a mental picture, then I jog down the sideline to Reed and leap into him one more time.

"That's how it's done, son!"

My face hurts from my wild, out-of-control smile. *Son.* That's my dad talking through him. With him.

I find Peyton's waiting gaze a second later, as she kicks and smashes her red and blue poms together. Her bright red lips—candy red, so I've learned—blow me a kiss, and I catch it and flatten it against my chest before returning to my brothers to do it all again.

Despite Bryce's prediction, he does get in the game for the final play before the half. I manage to get us to the one-yard line, and Coach sends him in to punch it in for the score. His body cuts through the Tech line with ease, and when he rushes to me, I give him the same dues he gave me.

"Nobody better, Legs! Nobody better!"

He laughs hard, but embraces his nickname, jumping up and pumping a fist in the air.

We head into the locker room up fourteen to zero, having held off two good drives for the lead. My lungs feel fresh, my muscles primed, as if I haven't touched the field at all, let alone played an entire half. I'm sure it will hit me tomorrow, or tonight when I finally collapse in bed. But right now? I'm high on the game.

"What did I tell you? That's how it's done! Welcome to Wildcat football, gentlemen. Glad you showed up!" Coach claps us into order, and we all take seats and hydrate while the staff goes through the few things they saw us miss on defense. Bryce, Shad, and I move off to the side to get some looks at weaknesses Coach Skye picked up in the booth. Tech is slow on the right, which means the third quarter might be a good time to get our running game going. They'll be guarding Keaton hard, might even double team him after the yards we've put up today. So we'll see what our running back Dickerson can do. He was born to run, and I think Whiskey can find him a hole to burst through and score. Coach leaves us to break it down, and I count us off to, "Bear down!" one more time.

The jog out to the field at half always has less energy, but for some reason, this time the tunnel feels thick with silence. I slap the side of my helmet, wondering if it's me, and push my helmet up, resting it on my forehead as I enter the field.

The band isn't playing, but that could be because they're still climbing into their section after the half-time show. They always play, though. Always. They'd play us on from the line to the bathrooms if they had to.

Something's wrong.

My head pivots to my right, to the Tech sideline, and I barely register the flash of red and blue before my focus zooms to Reed, pacing with his hands folded over his head.

Peyton.

I push my helmet from my head and race across the field, my cleats digging up turf as I lunge forward, angry that my feet aren't fast enough. I pass Reed and move right up to the stretcher that my whole world is strapped to, her neck locked in place, her eyes wildly searching the sky as tears pour down her temples.

"Peyton!" Her name comes out as a scream, and her eyes dash to me in a breath.

"I'm okay, Wy. It's okay. I'm okay! Win for me. Please. I'm okay!"

Nothing about her looks okay. And the tear stains would say otherwise. The candy red is smeared across her mouth and onto her chin, from who knows what or why. Her eyes blink uncontrollably, as the rest of her lies still, every bit of her strapped to a gray, aluminum gurney. I push through the emergency workers enough to grip her hand, but she slips away before squeezing me back and I'm left with nothing but the faint feel of her fingertips on mine as they hoist her into the back of the ambulance and shut the doors.

I turn into her father's chest, and he hugs me to him.

"She's going to be okay. It was a fall, but she's okay. It's going to be okay," he repeats, and I'm not sure who he's trying to convince more—him, or me.

Chapter Fourteen

Peyton

There are so many people in this room. My parents, I get why they're here. I want them here. I think. Why my Aunt Sarah is here, I don't know. Or maybe I do. It's a helpless feeling driving everyone. Helpless all around. Afraid. Frustrated. My Uncle Jason is out of town on business, but I've seen his face on my aunt's phone screen about a dozen times in the last ten minutes. He's FaceTiming into the room. I wish I was lucid enough to take notes and keep track of every little positive quip he's said to me.

I'd laugh if no one were here.

I'd cry.

I'm scared.

This room full of people isn't helping. It's loud. Crowded with questions and zero answers. There's not a doctor in this room right now.

My dad moves to my one side of my bed. My mom hasn't left the other. I'm bound to the bed with this cage-like structure of pins and slings. I've gone through so many scans. It feels like a hundred, but I'm sure it's more like four or five. Everything feels multiplied. My pain ranks at the top of all. I hurt.

"Wyatt's on his way," my dad says.

I breathe in deep. It hurts.

"Did they win?"

Nobody's told me about the game yet. I haven't asked because it probably makes me sound crazy. Wildcat football is very much not the priority in this room, but it's a priority in my head. It's my distraction.

My dad's mouth shifts into a soft smile as he nods.

"Twenty-four to seven. Wyatt threw an interception." He shrugs, but my mouth fills with a sour taste.

It's my fault he threw that. That's a stupid thought but I can't help having it.

"Did they pull him?" I ask quietly, not wanting the rest of the room involved in my conversation. My dad is literally the only one in this room who understands why this is important to me. I need to know.

A faint laugh parts my father's lips, and he shakes his head.

"No. He finished the game. And QB2 only went in twice." My dad's eyes linger on mine for a beat, and I blink because I can't nod.

My father's hand covers mine, and he moves his massive fingers between mine, squeezing. I feel him on the left. It's the right side that has everyone on alert. My mom is holding my right. Apparently, she hasn't let go since they moved me back in from the MRI and set up all of the braces. I only know because I see her holding it. I can't feel a thing.

It wasn't my fall that did it. It wasn't even my grip. I can recall everything in flashes, as if my eyes took snapshots as the world crumbled and set them aside for me to sort out later, to pull out as proof that this was not something I made happen. It happened *to* me.

Alicia wavered, her left foot slipped, and her body lurched forward. I did as I trained and worked to ease her fall, guiding her into a safe landing. But I was going down, too. And when I hit the ground, Alicia's knee hammered into my head and then everything went blank. My memory gets a little spotty after that too. Eyes blinking rapidly. Coach Kane holding my shoulders still. Our team trainer with a flashlight. The words, "Just a concussion."

Then the EMT. So many questions. Can I feel this? Can I move my right foot? Will I squeeze my right hand? Am I trying to? How about now? How about now?

What about now?

"Mr. and Mrs. Johnson? Can I have a minute with you and Peyton?"

My dad gets up from the bed, but my mom stays at my side. My gaze flickers between them as best I can without moving my head. I'm locked down.

"Guys, I'll update you out there. Sarah, if you can wait for Wyatt to show up and tell him I'll come get him in a few?"

My aunt nods at my father's request, then tells my uncle to hold on as she mutes the phone and steps over to me to give me another awkward hug where she basically just hovers over my body.

"You got this, honey." She's using her tough voice, probably to make sure I believe her. But do I? Do I got this? What the hell even is *this*?

In my mind, I nod. I think I smile, maybe.

"Jason's on his way, too," she adds as she leaves the room.

"Great," I utter when she's out of earshot. My mom chuckles. I definitely said that out loud.

"Hi, Peyton. I'm Dr. Klazmeric. We met earlier but you weren't really down for remembering names and stuff, so I figured we'd do this part again." He's young, maybe in his thirties. Young for a man in charge of making my limbs feel stuff again. Or maybe he's not. What do I know?

"Thanks for setting me up with this cool choker," I joke, doing my best to glance down at the surgical collar around my neck. His face tightens into a quick smile, and he nods with a short laugh.

"What can I say? I have the best jewelry," he jokes back.

I like him.

"All right, so . . . what we're looking at here, it's not impossible. It's tricky. And I don't want to make any false promises or distort the truth with any of you, especially you, Peyton." He makes eye contact with me, and I catch a glimpse of myself in the reflection of his dark-rimmed glasses.

My God.

I swallow at the sight but force another smile.

"I appreciate the straight shooting, doc."

"We all do," my mom adds. She shifts next to me, the bed moving a little with her weight, and I take a sharp breath.

"You should maybe use a chair for now," the doctor suggests, moving to the corner of the room and dragging an armchair to the bedside for my mom. She moves into it quickly then whispers to me, "I'm sorry."

It didn't really hurt, but it did make me nervous. And maybe I simply wanted some space.

"I'd like to get her in for surgery as soon as possible. She won't be under long for the diagnostic. Maybe two hours. But it's best for spinal cord injuries if we go in with a solid plan. We want to get a good look at what we're dealing with. We have some of the best spine and brain surgeons in the country here, and she'll have a team of us looking after her."

My mom looks to me and I give her a nervous, close-lipped smile.

"Okay," my mom lets out with a sigh. "How soon?"

"A few hours at the most," he says, and both of my parents stifle their gasps at his response.

So soon.

Not soon enough.

"So, we're sure it's her spinal cord?" My dad's voice wavers, and it's unlike him to show nerves. It makes my belly tighten, and I hear from the machine incessantly clocking my pulse to my right that it's amped up my heart rate.

"The scans all point to her fifth vertebrae. We're just not sure how bad the fracture is. And she has some severe swelling. That's likely why you're having a hard time feeling things on your right side. But we'll know more after we take a look."

"Am I . . ." I stop, swallowing the sandpaper that's instantly coated my throat. My eyes are burning with impending tears, so I breathe in slowly through my nose to hold them at bay. "Am I going to be able to walk?"

Dr. Klazmeric is quick to smile, and it honestly might be the first taste of hope I've had since I hit the turf hours ago.

"I don't want make guesses, but from everything I've seen on the scans, and the resources available, I have every reason to believe in two or three years you'll be walking again."

My lips quiver, and I can't hold them up to fake it. Neither can my dad, who looks as if he was just sucker punched. Probably because he was.

Two to three years.

"I know that seems like a long time, but when you think of it in terms of milestones and months, well . . . I don't want to get ahead. Right now, let's focus on getting all of the information in front of us, and then we can build our plan of attack. And you get to drive that, Peyton. That timeline will be completely up to you."

I swallow down the massive ball of doubt and croak, "Okay."

"I'll be back in about an hour with news on surgery. We'll get her prepped," Dr. Klazmeric says to my father, shaking his hand, then leaving the three of us alone in this suddenly quiet room.

My mom's heavy inhale is followed by my father's.

"Two or three years," I say. My eyes flit to my mom, because it's her stubbornness I need right now. It's measured. My dad's more likely to call everything, "Bullshit." This is serious, though. There's nothing bullshit about this bed, the surgical collar, the traction devices, the beeping heart monitor.

"Wyatt's here," my father says. I blink a few times at my mom, and she glances at my dad.

"I'll go get him," he says, leaving my mother and me alone. They've perfected their silent communication. He knows I need this minute with her.

"I know," she says before I even utter a word.

"Two or three years." I keep repeating that number. It's how long I've been with Wyatt. I've become a woman in that time span. It's longer than it sounds. And breaking it into months, despite what Dr. Klazmeric says, only makes it feel longer. Thirty-six months!

"We don't know what we don't know, Peyt. And I can tell you from years of experience, there is a whole hell of a lot that none of us know. So let's focus on the now. Wyatt is here, and you're having surgery soon. Those are two things we can prepare for."

"Wyatt . . . what do I tell him?"

I love you. I won't be walking for a few years. Stick around, cool? But focus on football. Because you should. But fuck football. And fuck life sometimes.

"You tell him the truth," my mom says, her words straightforward and plain. Also, probably right.

"I can't." I get those two words out as I hear him moving down the hallway with my dad, and tuck everything else underneath my crumbling bravado the moment he opens the door and our eyes meet.

"Peyt, I—" His eyes well up with tears.

"It's okay." *It's not.* But him crying isn't going to help either of us. And I don't want to watch him break down. It's selfish of me, or maybe it's not.

"You can come close. Sit down, just . . . be gentle." I shift my eyes to my mom, and she flashes a quick smirk.

"One of us was sitting on the bed and making waves," my mom says.

"Let me guess. Reed?" Wyatt says through an emotional laugh.

"Naturally," I answer, throwing my dad under the bus for my mom's sake. I meet her eyes when Wyatt leans over me in search of a way to hug me. My mom winks at me, then backs out of the room to give us a few minutes alone.

"Just kiss me. My lips are about the only thing they haven't put a pin in," I joke. He doesn't laugh, but he does kiss me. Softly. It's sweet, and I lick my bottom lip after he pulls away.

"Your dad mentioned surgery. What do they know? Did you break anything? Is it the spine? And have they ruled out head trauma?" His barrage of questions levels me a bit, and I blink wildly before laughing out the answer I decided to go with for Wyatt—for a little while.

"I don't know."

He shifts gently on the mattress and works his hand into mine. I can't feel it. I can't squeeze him back. He doesn't seem to notice, though, or maybe he simply assumes I'm weak and tethered in so many places that I can't. He doesn't need to know yet.

"Maybe tell me about the second half. It probably seems trivial, but I'd like to hear it. It's a good distraction. I hate that I missed it. Your opening drive, Wy—"

"Peyt." He tilts his head.

"I know. But please. Just, for a little bit. Pretend with me. Call the game as if I were there and you want to relive the good parts."

Wyatt's gaze connects with mine, and we swim in each other's souls for a few long, quiet seconds. I feel his silent plea. I get his sense of urgency. Fuck, I have it, too. But there's literally nothing either of us can do right now, like my mom said. We live in the present, and we resolve ourselves to surgery soon, and answers after that. Followed by questions. And more answers. And more questions.

"I ran the third touchdown in myself," he finally says, and my lungs open with a welcome dose of pride.

"You did?" There's genuine excitement in my voice. I'm not faking this. I needed this news.

His beautiful upper lip rises on one side, all flirty and humble. As sexy as he is, he's also really fucking cute. Just . . . cute. My cute quarterback.

"So, we were about twenty yards out, and Whiskey throws this block, and I . . ."

I close my eyes and smile as he recounts the entire thing to me, and it plays like a movie in my head. Bryce didn't get to take it in—he did. I can visualize his stiff arm, the quick spin he made to break the last tackle, and the cocky growl he let loose in the end zone after he flipped the ball into a spin on the turf. I'm sure there was something extra running through his veins, the game a way for him to channel his worry. Eating the clock to get it over with. Skipping the interview to make it to me. I know all of that. My dad was in Wyatt's head because they're the same, and he told me as much. But that little moment of glory? That's what I'm going to hold on to for now. *This* now. And I'll play the movie in my mind one more time right before they put me under.

Chapter Fifteen

Wyatt

She actually thought I would go to practice today. To film. As if I could sit in a room with a bunch of dudes and watch a two-hour game broken down play-by-play and somehow find any of that serious or worth my time.

I stand up from the thinly padded chair, stretching my arms up as I arch my back and groan. I knew sleep would be hard. I didn't quite think it would be impossible, though.

"I wish I could say you'll sleep better tonight but I won't lie to you," Reed says. Mrs. Johnson's head is on his thigh, her legs bent as she huddles under a throw blanket he grabbed from the truck.

I wander down the same hallway I've walked about two hundred times since I arrived last night. My mom showed up around an hour after me, and she sat with me and Peyton's parents for a little while before heading home. She has a long shift today, so I told her I'd call with updates. I pull my phone out to send her a quick text that Peyton's still in surgery.

This corridor is filled with quiet rooms, the lights still dim as the sun hasn't fully risen for the day. People are all pretending to sleep in cots and in chairs. I don't even think the patients in here are actually sleeping. They're all just drugged to make it seem like it.

I fish my credit card out of my back pocket and swipe it on the vending machine at the end of the hallway, staring at the dismal choices for breakfast for a few seconds before landing on a Payday. I don't even like nuts. I make a stop at the water fountain and fill the gas station cup I've been using since Reed dipped across the street to get us sodas at about two a.m. The ice is long gone, but it's nice to have a straw. *I guess.*

Reed nods toward the candy bar in my hand as I near the seats.

"You like those things?" he asks.

I look at it, clutched in my hand before me, and shake with a short sarcastic laugh.

"No."

Reed laughs hard, but covers his mouth when Nolan stirs at the sound. She rolls her head, briefly glancing up at him, then pulls the blanket up over her face and falls back asleep. I'm glad one of us is getting rest. At some point, we're going to need to take shifts. Hell, I'm still in my sweatpants and football hoodie, and wearing the stench of last night's game.

I plop down in the chair across from Reed, a smattering of magazines on the table—all health-related except for one. It's a two-year-old *Sports Illustrated*, and I've already read it. I'm in that one—just a photo with a caption hyping my junior season. Heisman hopeful, I think it said.

"You know your daughter tried to get me to go to practice today?" I peel open the candy bar and break off half, holding the other half out for Reed. He leans forward and snags it, along with the wrapper.

"She's going to be pissed as hell when she finds out you didn't, you know?" He quirks a brow, then peels the wrapper the rest of the way, biting off nearly a quarter of the Payday.

We chew in silence as we stare at each other, Reed finally uttering, "This is awful," just before he swallows down his bite.

"It's the nuts," I say, choking down mine. We both take a second bite. Fucking gluttons.

"Would you have left Nolan in the hospital during surgery? For practice, I mean?"

It takes him one chew of the jaw to answer.

"Not a chance in hell."

I nod.

"See?" I swallow the rest of my sad breakfast, then pick a caramel-crusted nut from my back molar. It feels like it might pull my filling out with it.

I stand up and take the wrapper from Reed, walking it to the nearby trash to toss away before checking my phone again. My mom texted back for me to *hang in there*. I smirk at her reply. It's the same shit people said to her after Dad died. *Hang in there. It gets easier.*

It doesn't. It never did.

This is different. I know it is, and my mom was simply trying to inject a little levity, I'm sure. But now my brain is correlating these two terrible things, my dad's cancer death and Peyton's injury. I'm sure it's the sleep deprivation, and probably a good bit of anxiety, but I feel a little like I'm the common denominator.

I shake off the nonsense and move back to my seat just as the doctor steps through the doors by the information desk. I'm back on my feet quickly, and Reed rustles Nolan awake and stands with me. The doc crosses the room, removing his cap as he approaches.

"Surgery went well. She's resting," he says.

My legs suddenly feel weak, so I take a step back and land on my heels.

"Good," Reed breathes out, his hand on his chest.

The doctor gives us a second to sit with our relief, and he's also waiting for Nolan to rub the sleep from her eyes and stand next to her husband.

"What did you find?" she asks, suddenly alert and ready to advocate for her daughter. Reed and I exchange a quick glance, and I get a feeling he's also glad his wife is the rested one.

"Well, the scans told the correct story. The fifth vertebra is definitely fractured. The swelling seems to have gone down a bit, which is a good sign. I'm hopeful she'll be able to feel her right side when she wakes up, or at least most of it."

I blink at his words and glance off to the side. *She couldn't feel anything?* She didn't tell me that. Nobody told me that.

"We'll see what our baseline is in a couple days, then go from there. I'd say we could be looking at a spinal fusion surgery within a week, then comes a lot of rehab. She's going to need to find her balance first before she can move on to anything—walk before we run and all that."

The three of us hum in response, and the doctor gives a short laugh.

"I take it she's more of a run first kind of girl?" His right brow lifts above the rim of his surgical glasses.

"She's more of a fly before anything kind of girl," Reed responds.

"Ah, well . . . then you all are going to have to remind her to be kind to herself. It's hard to start back at square one, especially when you're an elite athlete used to operating at one hundred. She's going to be doing things she hasn't done since she was a toddler. Taking first steps. Throwing a ball. Touching her toes. But she'll get there. This is the best-case scenario that we hoped for. I truly believe that."

We all smile at his positivity.

"When can we see her?" I ask.

"A nurse will come get you when she's awake and stable. Not too long." His eyes rest on me for a beat, and I sense he's trying to warn me to prepare myself for a new job. Peyton's number two. Her support. Her ride or die.

"Thank you, Dr. K," Reed says, moving his arm around Nolan and giving her a squeeze. I'm not sure if the shortened name was the doctor's idea or Reed's, but we can all agree we're tired of hearing Reed absolutely butcher his attempts to say the man's last name. This letter system is the way to go.

"I'm going run to the ladies' room, splash some water on my face before she wakes up," Nolan says, stepping up on her toes to kiss her husband's cheek.

"Wyatt, shouldn't you be at film?" She winks at me, having heard her daughter say as much before they wheeled her back.

"I think I saw enough of the game firsthand last night. I'll be fine," I respond. But when Nolan disappears into the ladies' room, leaving Reed and me alone, he questions me a little on the *being fine* part.

"Coach know the full story?" His mouth pulls into a bunched-up, wry smile as he squints.

"I chatted with him for a minute before I left, yeah. I should probably call him or text him with an update. He's good about family stuff. He understands." My worries vibrate underneath my words, though, and I think Reed can sense them.

"You know, Bryce might get the start next week. Road game." Reed's matter-of-fact statement crashes with my paranoia and I suck in some air before nodding.

"I know. I feel it, that it's slipping away a little? That it might happen? But . . . I don't even care," I say.

"Maybe not now. But you will. At some point. When you have time to take stock of it all."

I hike my shoulders up in response and maintain eye contact.

"Perhaps. But right now, everything I care about is in that room down the hall. And I wouldn't be any good to the team if I wasn't present here for this."

Reed nods, then lays his palm on my back, resting it there for a beat.

"And what do you think Peyton will think about all that?"

My lip quirks. I don't have to say it out loud. We both know what she'll think. I need to get my lazy ass back out there, and I need to fight.

Well, pot, meet kettle, Peyton Johnson. I think you're going to need to fight a bit, too. We may as well do this together.

Chapter Sixteen

Peyton

Tasha has called me a nerd a dozen times. It's her way of coping with all of this. Or maybe I am a nerd, what with this massive binder I've made with dated tabs and correlated research articles, and therapies mapping out every single step to get me not only on my feet again, but also on my hands and in the air.

Dr. K calls it a long shot. But he hasn't seen what a Johnson girl can do. *Watch and learn, buddy.*

"My sister is not a nerd," my younger sister Ellie says, lightly punching Tasha's side.

She knows my friend is kidding, but since my injury, she's started sticking up for me against everyone, literally everywhere. My mom said she had to wrangle Ellie out of the grocery store the other day because the local paper had a headline about me she didn't like. QB STAR'S DAUGHTER HAS CLOSE CALL WITH DEATH. My sister started to tear them all in half, but my mom managed to herd her out of the store before she got them all.

"They are free to the public," I said at the time. My mom

wasn't amused and quickly pointed out that most people take one copy, not thirty-four.

"Ellie, come here," Tasha says, pulling my sister up on her lap. She wraps her arms around her and points toward my head, more precisely, the yellow highlighter I've stashed behind my ear.

"You see that marker?"

"Yeah," my sister says, still putting on her tough-girl voice.

"You know who uses markers like that?" Tasha is a snot.

Ellie shakes her head.

Without warning, Tasha tickles my sister's sides and hollers, "Nerd" over and over again until, somehow, my guess is through tickle-coercion, she drags my sweet sibling to her dark side.

"You know, positive reinforcement is supposed to be good for my recovery," I say, flipping to the page I recently high-lighted that proves my point. I hold my finger on it, and both Tasha and my sister sing the word "nerd" at me.

I roll my eyes, but when my sister slips from my friend's lap and runs back to the visitor's room where my way-more-fun Uncle Jason is, I mouth a, "Thank you," to Tasha for making life feel normal.

Just when I think my room is about to sink into some quiet hours, a loud knock on my open door introduces my past, my present, and . . . well, Whiskey.

"I hear there's a party in here. Who's drinking?" Whiskey announces their entrance, Bryce and Wyatt trailing behind, his flair for dumbassery earns him a sharp look from Tasha. That look alone is worth the embarrassment he's drawn to my little corner room.

"Sorry, babe. Was I *too much*?" He puckers his lips and squints at her as if this whole thing is some inside joke. *Shit, they have inside jokes?* And . . . did he call her *babe*?

"Quite the opposite, dick hole. You're not even close to enough," Tasha says with a look of disgust.

Yeah, okay. He called her babe. She hated it.

Tasha gets up from her chair and leans over to give me a one-armed hug. I'm still stuck with only using the left arm for now. But hopefully, tomorrow's surgery will change things.

"I'll wait for your mom to text me. Don't let her forget," she says.

"Ha, as if Nolan Johnson forgets a single damn thing. Where do you think I got my type-A behavior?"

I pat the binder as a reminder, and once again, my friend mutters, "Nerd," before taking off for the day.

"See you at home, honey," Whiskey calls after her.

We can't see it to confirm, but I guarantee Tasha gave him the middle finger just now.

"What?" Whiskey says when he meets my chiding look. "I'm wearing her down. You just wait. That girl, she's in love with me."

My gaze shifts to Bryce, then to Wyatt, and they could not be forcing a more similar wide-eyed smile onto their faces.

Wyatt takes over the chair that my mom has basically been living in since I got here. Grandma Rose has had her hands full while my mom's been away, getting Ellie to and from school, keeping my grandpa from burning the house down, and forcing my dad to stop to eat once and a while. He just kicked off his seventh season as head coach in Coolidge, but between his daily trips to visit me and his evening practices, he hasn't had much time for himself. It shows in his graying beard and baggy eyes.

"So, tomorrow's the big day, huh?" Bryce asks.

I pull my lips in tight for the confident smile I've been rehearsing for days.

"Yep. Seven hours of soldering my spine. Can't wait." I add a jolly punch to the air for emphasis, but none of them are buying my hard sell.

"It's going to go great. You're in the best hands. This place put my older brother back together when he crashed his bike when we were in grade school, remember? And look at him now—he's a motorcycle cop," Whiskey says. I'd forgotten about his older brother's accident. I remember how upset he was back then, a chubby fifth grader who thought his brother Will walked on water.

"Well, if this place can handle an Olsen boy, then they're probably ready for me," I say, reaching my left hand out for Whiskey to hold. He squeezes it, but his eyes shift to my limp right arm.

"Still nothing, huh?" he asks. I wish he didn't.

"Nope," I say, clipped.

The short bout of silence that follows puts that topic to bed, I hope. It was a big enough compromise to get rid of the traction devices and only have to live with this collar brace. Dr. K made the case that sleep was more vital to my healing than keeping my right leg and shoulder suspended in the air.

"So, when do you all leave for Western?" I ask, changing the subject back to the world I left behind. If I remember right, I think they'll be packing up later today. I think their flight leaves early tomorrow morning.

"Yeah, uh . . . about that," Wyatt starts.

I shake my head and whisper, "No."

"Don't worry. I'm going. I'm just taking my own flight. Admin cleared it. I want to be here, though, for tomorrow. I'll take the red eye. It was cheaper. It's fine."

My brow is heavy. I feel it. My face is the one thing that seems to function on both halves. Too bad it's been scowling so much lately.

"Coach knows what you're going through. He's supportive,"

Bryce adds, and I'm not sure whether his words are directed to Wyatt or me.

My gaze shifts back to my boyfriend, my stomach knotting up now that I know his decision. I wish he had talked it over with me. I would have told him to go with the team. My mom can call him first. Or my dad can. He would have known as early as he will being here, sitting in that damn waiting room.

"I know you're upset with me, and I'm sorry. But give me this one win, okay? I need to be here. I feel it." He brings his fist to his chest with a light pound.

Well, fuck. Fine.

"Hey, we're gonna give you two time alone. We'll wait for you in the lobby, Wy. You know, after we visit a few of the candy stripers around this place," Whiskey jokes.

"You know they don't call them that anymore, right? And the volunteers are all high schoolers, so maybe don't do any of that?" Wyatt warns.

Bryce puts an arm over Whiskey's shoulders as he guides him out of the room.

"I'll supervise this one," he says, chuckling on his way out.

Wyatt watches them leave while I study his beautiful face and wait for his gaze to come back to me. He tilts his head, questioning, when it does.

"You and Bryce seem to have found a rhythm." It's cautious optimism. I still don't fully trust Bryce when it comes to Wyatt, but I'm glad to see the stress he was feeling over Bryce being here is morphing into something healthier—dare I say gratitude and a form of friendship?

His lip ticks up.

"Yeah, we have. Not that I've been thinking about football all that much." The weight of my situation hits his voice mid-sentence. I hate that heaviness.

"You should go with the team, Wy. I won't be able to see you when I'm out of surgery, and even when I can get visitors, I'm probably going to want to sleep."

His palm lands on top of my binder.

"You finished it, huh?" Wyatt looks up through his lashes, silently asking my permission to review my work.

"I maybe went overboard," I admit as he pulls the binder into his own hands.

"Walking with help by one month, huh?" He doesn't look up at me for a response, so I simply say, "Yep."

He flips a few pages, looking at the long lists of daily rehab exercises I put together with the specialist at Tucson Strong. My mom works with them periodically, bringing one or two of the horses down to visit with some of the kids who get sent there after illnesses or accidents that impact their motor skills. I've always felt a connection to that place. I trust it.

"Running a 5K by the one-year mark, huh? That one—"

"Yes, I know it's ambitious. But if I'm not going to set bold goals, then what's the point?"

He lifts his head to test my gaze, but I think when he reads in my eyes how serious I am, he accepts the reality I've written.

As he flips through the pages, I feel the urge to shift my position in the bed the closer he gets to the back. I can't move my body, though. I don't have the strength. So, instead, I wait in my physical and mental discomfort as he grows closer to the notes I made in the very back. It's the top question that has me on the highest alert, and it's the one question that I can't seem to push out of my mind.

I watch his lips move slightly with the words, and I read along with him in my mind—*Can I have kids?*

Wyatt's thumb traces that scribbled question, and he chews at the inside of his mouth for a beat before his head pops up and his eyes meet mine.

"You know that doesn't matter to me, right?" He blinks twice, then locks his eyes open, awaiting my response.

"It matters to me," I say, the fear obvious in the vibrato of my voice.

He nods slowly, his eyelashes flickering as his gaze drops to the binder. He closes it and sets it on the side table, then slides to the edge of his chair. Folding my left hand into both of his, his thumb gently draws circles on the back of my hand. I cherish how it feels—*that I feel.*

"It should have been me this happened to, you know?"

I smirk and breathe out a soft laugh, turning it into a joke.

"Statistically? Yeah, football is way more dangerous."

"That's not what I mean."

I mash my lips together and hold his stare, the heavy pit in my stomach growing wider. I give a tiny nod.

"I know what you mean. But I wouldn't want it to be you." I stop short of adding how I wish it wasn't me, either. How scared I am. How angry I am sometimes when I'm with my thoughts alone at night. When I should be sleeping.

The nurse pushes into the room and interrupts by thoughts.

"Good morning, Peyton. I'm Nat, and I'm here to take some vitals and get you prepped for surgery. Mind if I have your visitor wait outside for just a few minutes?" Nat's my age, I think. Probably not, but she wears her hair in braids on either side of her face, and her wrist is tatted with pink butterflies. She has a bubbly personality, which is probably a nice addition to this place most of the time, but right now, I find her upbeat, ready-to-rave-out personality a bit overwhelming.

"I'll go find the guys, then I'll be right back. I want to see you before they take you back," Wyatt says, his hand clinging to mine even as he stands and backs away.

"I'll be sure to tell the doctor to wait for you," I say, trying my best to keep my wry humor intact. It's what's been getting me through all of this.

"Good, glad to hear it," Wyatt jokes back as he slips out of the room.

"You're a lucky girl," Nat says in a sassy, flirty voice, waggling her brows at me as she puts her stethoscope ends in her ears.

"You have no idea," I respond. My voice comes out a bit dreamy, but also, her words sink into my mind, and I ruminate on them as she finishes running through my vitals.

I am lucky to have a love like this, but can it survive what I am starting to come to terms with as my future? I'm resolved to the fight ahead. I know I'm going to get back to a body that might be a little different than I imagined, but just as full of verve and drive. Maybe even more. And sure, it would be easy to lean on Wyatt through it all. But at what cost for him?

"All right, your family can come back in. They'll be up to take you to prep soon." Nat scribbles a few notes on my chart, then updates some numbers in her computer before dipping out of my room just as my father steps in.

He blows out his cheeks, puffing them like one of those fish that kisses the glass of the bowl.

"Gee, you don't look stressed at all," I tease him. He takes over the chair Wyatt left a few minutes ago, flopping back and exhaling.

"Sorry, I've never been good at poker." He pinches the bridge of his nose and squeezes his eyes, almost as though he's resetting his face. His new smile seems less forced, but it's just as worn-out.

"I'm sorry." My words make him laugh, short and hard, and he takes my hand and kisses it.

"You need to stop saying that."

My face eases into a tight-lipped smile.

"I know. I just hate that everyone's world was thrown into chaos because of me. I hate it so much," I choke out. I wipe the tear away fast. I don't need to get emotional before they wheel me back and knock me out. I don't need to carry any of this into my anesthesia dreams.

"Peyton, you are already the center of our world. And nothing about this is chaotic. It's life, and we're here for it. For you." I know people think he was just a dumb jock, but damn, my dad—he says the right things sometimes.

"Hey, I need a favor," I say, pulling my mouth to one side. My dad seems to be reading my face, and he sits back in his chair again, folding his arms over his chest.

"You know I can't make that boy do something he doesn't want to," he says, sensing where I'm going.

I nod.

"I know, but can you just talk to him? He can't shut down because of this. He's already traveling behind the team tomorrow. And Coach probably said he understands, but you know how that world is—you know that coach. Every little thing is one checkmark against him and in Bryce's favor. And Dad, he can't lose his way because I veered off course. With what I'm facing, I can't carry his regret on top of holding up my own resilience. I just can't."

I swim in my father's understanding gaze for a few quiet seconds before he blinks to break our stare, looking down at his legs as he flattens his palms on his thighs. He nods, his jaw flexing, probably because he's in a mental war between what I am asking and what he knows he would do in Wyatt's shoes.

"I'll have a talk with him. And I'll do my best to hold him up, no matter what he decides. I'll make sure he knows how important his success is to you; how much you want it for him. But baby girl, if that man wants to be here, trust me—ain't no defensive line keeping him away from you."

He's right. And it's because of what Nat said. I'm a lucky girl. I just wish I felt like one right now.

Chapter Seventeen

Wyatt

It's been eons since I've had a Happy Meal.

"I'm a little excited about the toy. I can't lie." I carry my box to a booth near the back corner of the restaurant, the only section with tables and moveable chairs instead of booths. McDonald's seats can be a bit tight for Reed and me.

"If we get different ones, maybe we can strike a trade," Reed laughs out.

Peyton's been in surgery for five hours, and I was getting a little stir crazy. Reed was starting to drive Nolan nuts, so she gave him a twenty and told him to buy me dinner. This place is the closest to the hospital on foot.

"Let's open them together . . . ready?" Reed props his elbows on the table and pinches the sides of his box while I do the same. I'm sure we look ridiculous to the few patrons in here during this odd hour that's not quite lunch but definitely not yet dinner.

"One," I say.

"Two," Reed follows.

We both shout, "Three," and pop open the tops of our meal boxes and stare inside like we're looking down a well.

"Yellow Hot Wheel. Sports car. Bam!"

I plunk my tiny race car prize down on the table, and Reed squints as he studies it, his hand still buried in his box. A smirk forms on one side of his mouth, and after a few dramatic seconds, he fishes out his prize and parks it right next to mine.

"Blue Corvette. No trade."

"Ah, man!" I pick up his car and hold it in my palm, admiring it. I pick at the tiny driver's side door, and it opens.

"No fair! I think my doors are fused shut," I say, pushing my inferior mini ride toward him. It rolls about six inches.

Reed holds it up and turns it slowly, eyeing the detail on the mass-produced toy.

"What did I get, a Honda? Toyota Camry?" I think it's just a generic yellow car, to be honest.

"Nineteen ninety-four Ford Mustang. Fastback. Two-door." He pulls his lips in tight, then shifts his focus from the car in his palm to me.

"Trade," he says, palming it and shifting to his side to push it into the front pocket of his jeans.

"Hmm, I still think the Vette is cooler," I say, wheeling my prize back and forth while I lean over my drink and suck Sprite through the straw.

"That's 'cause you're not a car guy. Pops had a car just like this on the lot for years. He refused to sell it," Reed says, pausing to take a bite from his burger. "He ended up driving it for six years. He took that thing everywhere."

Reed smiles through the story, and I can't help but feel the joy emanating from his memories.

"I wish I had known him back then or sooner. He seems like a pretty cool character," I say.

Reed takes a handful of fries and shoves them in his mouth, brushing the salt from his hands.

"Ha, character doesn't do that man justice!" he mumbles

through his full mouth. "He's not so different. Less mobile, but he's still all there. Mostly. I'm lucky."

Lucky. There's that word again. I've been hearing it a lot lately. The doctors have said it dozens of times. Peyton's parents have used it a lot. Hell, Peyton told me her nurse called her lucky for being with me, which I think is bullshit. It's the other way around. But seriously, for all this luck being talked about, I don't feel very lucky.

"So . . . Cal is next week, yeah? Road game."

Reed's segue into football talk is obvious. I finish my bite, then bunch a napkin in my hand to wipe away the special sauce.

"I'll be ready. Just like I'll be ready this weekend."

His knowing smirk probably matches the one I'm wearing.

"I had to talk to you about it. I promised her I would," he admits with a shrug.

"She's hard to resist."

We spend the next few minutes polishing off our tiny meals and slurping down our kid-sized drinks. Reed collects our trash and tosses it into a bin near the kids' play area. I loved those slides when I was a child. I don't think they could hold me now.

"I don't know about you, but I could really go for a beer right now," Reed says, plopping back down in his seat as he rubs his eyes and leans his head back.

"I could go for a few beers, and maybe a week's worth of sleep," I say.

He shakes with his gravely laugh before he sits up straight again, leaning with his elbow propped on our table, his hand covering his mouth and chin. Yeah, I admitted I'm tired. But who wouldn't be. He stares into my eyes and blinks a few times before dropping his hand.

"I think I'll go to the Cal game. I like the drive." He likes making his opinion known on the sideline.

"You know, for the head coach of one of the country's best

high school football programs, you're spending a lot of time away from the field this fall."

He nods, his smirk the look of a man who won't be detoured by my insistence that I am fine—that everything on the field is fine. Probably because it's not.

"Coolidge is a well-oiled machine. I'm basically head coach by title, but more of an assistant nowadays. The staff stepped up the last couple of years, and they've got this season handled. Besides, I can't miss my favorite college quarterback."

"Which one?" I blurt out fast. I laugh it off as the joke it was meant to be, but Reed meets my stare and doesn't crack. I shake my head and blink away, muttering, "Kidding."

"No, you weren't."

I hold my tongue between my molars, my mouth curved with an irritated smile. An embarrassed smile. An ashamed expression. And the helplessness of this entire season—of Peyton's situation—levels me all at once. A breathy laugh slips out as a lone tear gets through my guard, and I quickly wipe it away.

"Son, if you want to see her fight, she needs to see you do the same. That's how it works when you love someone. You dig in when you're going through the shit. It's this relentless battle, and the one thing you know you can count on is that other half. You aren't in it alone."

"Fuck," I utter, pinching the bridge of my nose as more tears threaten to fall.

"Yeah, fucked is right. That's what this whole situation is. And that's nobody's fault. It's not even Bryce's fault. This wasn't his plan from the start. It's where his chips fell. This is what was left on the board to give him the best shot to keep going. And maybe he will. But you're the one driving the bus, Wyatt. He's a mere passenger. Don't quit and give him the keys."

I chew at my lip and let my eyes stare off at the brightly colored slides behind Reed, at the traffic whizzing by out the window, the ambulance bay across the street that has yet to be empty since we've been here. Everyone has their shit they're going through.

"Your analogies are really on point today, you know that?" I huff out in a laugh.

He cracks a wide smile and stands up, offering me a hand.

"Thank you. Nolan's not a fan, but I kind of like them. I learned from that character we were talking about earlier. You know, the one who puts on his Wyatt Stone jersey when he puts your game on the TV every Saturday."

Reed isn't making that up. I've seen Buck's jersey. His wife has one, too. They're all behind me, silently willing me on that field. I'm not big into prayer, but I feel theirs. I feel it extra hard lately.

I follow Reed out of the restaurant, and just before we reach the crosswalk to head back to the hospital, he reaches into his pocket and pulls out the yellow Hot Wheel, handing it to me.

"Nah, trade's a trade," I say, patting my right pocket where the Corvette currently resides. Reed insists I take it, however. So I do.

"Twice the speed. Two styles. Different gears. A little reminder to use all the tools in your toolbox this weekend, yeah?" He quirks a brow as we step into the intersection.

"I maybe see why Nolan told you to cool it with the analogies," I razz.

"Bahhhhh! No way! That was my best one yet," he says, his stride long and his step full of energy. He's heading back into the unknown with fight in his legs, and I think maybe it's the stuff he isn't saying that resonates with me most.

Two more hours pass before the doctor finally pops into the waiting room post-surgery. Reed, Nolan, and I are on our feet in seconds, meeting him halfway across the room. I'm tempted to push past him and rush down the hallway to her bedside, but she's probably still waking up so I pay attention to what he's saying.

"It went very well. I'm really pleased with what we were able to do for her. She'll be in a lot of pain, which is normal from a procedure like this, but with the right regimen, and her stubbornness, I think we'll see Peyton on her feet in few weeks."

"Oh, that's—" Nolan chokes up, covering her mouth as her tears finally rush out. She's been holding a lot in over the past week. She needs this release.

"That's amazing, Doctor. Thank you." Reed pulls Nolan into his side, holding her close as she sniffles and her body quivers.

"By *on her feet*, do you mean she'll be walking next month?" I ask, knowing there are semantics to everything he says.

He nods at first, but the hesitancy in his eyes makes me wait for his words.

"Right, so . . . she'll be able to start therapy. We'll get her fitted for an exoskeleton for her right leg, and that's going to take some time for her to get used to. It's basically like a wearable robot that activates the muscles and helps retrain the brain and nerves how to work together. Balance, however, is something she must find on her own. It can take weeks for some patients. I get that she's going to want to come out of this running, so we need to work with her to set reasonable expectations. At least at the start."

We all exchange glances and nod, and I wonder if Dr. K has seen Peyton's binder. He may want to add a few more sections and steps. But also, he doesn't know Peyton the way we do. She removed those steps for a reason.

"She's waking up, so if you all want to head up to her room, she'll be in there shortly." Dr. K shakes Reed's hand first, then Nolan folds into him with a hug that he chuckles through. I think he's probably used to people's physical relief and gratitude. I'm half-tempted to hug him myself, but I keep it to a firm handshake, though I do cover his hand in both of mine.

Nolan calls her parents while Reed calls Buck and Rose. I can tell when he's talking to Ellie, who is just as focused on the fact that we went to McDonald's as she is her sister's surgery. I send a text to Whiskey and Tasha, as promised. And then we wait . . . *again.*

When they wheel Peyton into her room about thirty minutes later, she's groggy but clearly anxious. I stand back while her mom helps her get comfortable, letting the nurse hook up her fluids along with that annoying heart monitor. The doctor stops in to give an abbreviated version of what he told us in the waiting room, Peyton's mouth locked in the sweetest dopey grin. Now's not the time to tell her this, but she looks the same way after a few too many at Tate's or the Catwalk.

The one thing she seems to really cling to from the doctor's recap, however, is exactly as he warned—*that she'll be on her feet soon.* I don't have the heart to tell her it's going to probably be months before she does anything remotely close to running. But who the hell am I to tell her that anyway? Who the hell are any of us? If Peyton Johnson wants to run sooner than the world thinks she should—*can*—then she's going to. And I am never going to stop her.

She dozes in and out every few minutes, finally settling into her pillow as her gaze sticks to mine once the room clears out and her parents give us a little time alone. I take her right hand in mine, closing both of my palms around it to feel her pulse and keep her warm. I watch her eyes fight to stay open, her lids growing heavier every time her lashes brush the crests of her cheeks. She finally gives in so I lean over and kiss her softly. Her upper lip quivers against mine, pulling up on one side.

"I can feel that," she says, eyes still closed, smile growing.

"There's magic in my lips. What can I say?"

I sit back, ready to watch her for a while, when her right pinky twitches against my palm. My gaze drops to our tethered hands just as her finger moves again, and I nearly leap out of the chair.

"I can feel that," she says again, just before falling fully into sleep.

Suddenly, I think I might be able to run all the way to Western for our game this weekend. All six hundred miles. Then turn around and run right back the moment the clock runs out.

"I feel it, too," I whisper.

I feel it, too.

Chapter Eighteen

Peyton

"**I**'ll make you a deal, Peyton," Dr. K says as he leans on the deathtrap walker at the foot of my bed.

That's my name for it. Deathtrap Walker. It's a ridiculous contraption, and I feel like I would have fewer obstacles to contend with if they simply pushed me out of bed and told me to figure it out. This thing is—a lot. It has brakes, for Pete's sake. *Brakes!*

My eyes shift to my father as he stands in the corner of my room near his handiwork. He went out and bought a bigger TV for the game. Ridiculous. But also, atta boy.

"You should entertain his offer," my pops says.

I exhale, and it hurts a little. Everything hurts a little. A lot of things hurt a whole bunch. But the hurt is good. The fact is, I hurt in most places. Not everywhere, but most.

I level the doc with an impatient expression, my mouth pinched at the corners, my stomach growling finally for real food.

"What are your terms?"

"You make it to the end of the hallway and back, and I'll tell your team to leave you alone until the game is done," he says.

Shit. That's a good deal.

"Gah!" I groan, pushing the thin blanket from my body and nodding toward Steven, my physical therapy assistant. I swore at him a lot just an hour ago when he made me walk with Death Trap. I'm surprised he came back for more.

He quirks a brow.

"Fire her up, Steven," I say, and my father and Dr. K cheer.

Steven steadies my right side as my dad steps in at the left, and they secure the harness that takes some of the weight off my right leg while I attempt to walk. I feel like a zombie, dragging half of my body along the tiled floor while people back away to make room for me, not sure which way I'm going to go.

"Where's Mom?" I ask, kind of missing her words of encouragement right now. While my dad and Steven tend to root me on and praise me with lots of comments like, "You're doing so well," my mom gives it to me like it is.

Suck it up, sunshine.

You already made it this far; you have no choice but to go back now. Unless you want to just lie on the floor.

And my favorite from early this morning, which she directed at my dad when she caught me rolling my eyes at his hyper-positivity.

I wouldn't exactly say she's hauling ass, Reed.

I've never been motivated by soft coaching, and my dad should know that. But I guess this is a special circumstance. It would feel better if everyone talked a little more real, though.

"She may be picking you up a little something Grandma Rose whipped up," my dad reveals. My gaze snaps to him, and I can tell by his smirk and the flicker in his eyes that it's tortilla soup.

"Now we're talking," I say, wrapping my hands around Deathtrap's handles and pulling myself to my feet as Steven tightens the harness to help me stay upright.

My arms shake. I adjust my grip and grimace, but nothing I

try is going to make this easier. The only remedy for this is time.

"Let's do this," I command, and together, the three of us work our way to my door.

"Good work," Steven mutters.

"No, it's not," I grumble.

Dr. K chuckles behind me, clearly having been warned about my attitude. Little does he know this is simply how I'm built. He could be teaching me a tumbling pass right now on the mats, and I'd find fault with my attempt. I set a high bar for myself, and I'm not going to lower it now. In fact, now it's higher.

We get to the doorway, and I shake my head, needing a short break to adjust my grip. My right leg feels as though it's being dragged along for the ride, and I look down to see if I'm even standing on the ball of my foot or just grazing the floor with the tip of my toe. When I see it anchored flat and centered within a square of the tile, I try to lean into it.

"I feel like I'm falling."

"You have to relearn balance. It's normal," the doc says behind me.

"Define normal," I huff out in a pissy laugh.

Nobody answers my request, which is probably for the best.

I nod that I'm ready, and we begin our route down the hallway. There are fewer nurses standing around, and I'm not sure whether it's because they're on rounds and busy or my mom kindly asked them not to. Whatever the reason, I like the lack of an audience. Maybe it's mental, but it makes me feel stronger, and when I make it to the end of the hallway, I nod my head forward.

"I want to go all the way around," I demand.

"That's my girl," my dad says, and I let him have this one because it reminds me of all the times he's uttered that phrase. I let my mind drift through my past as we push on around the nurses' station. My first back handspring in the front yard, and my dad's boastful cheer as if he taught me how to do it himself. The time he took me out to kick field goals on the field in junior high when he was home during the off-season. I doinked two of them. And freshman year, when he insisted I go to his gym with him and learn how to hit a boy hard enough to knock him out.

Fueled by my former successes, I make the lap and am nearly back to my door when my body gives out and Steven swoops in to support me completely. He's a big guy, maybe six-foot-two or three. He's close to Wyatt in height, but his body is bulkier, like my grandfather in pictures of when he was younger. My mom calls it fluffy.

We get back to my bedside mostly on Steven's strength, and my dad helps undo the harness so I can sit on the edge of the mattress while he smooths out the sheets and blanket before I lie back. Everything gets caught on my brace—blankets, cords, even my hair somehow. I think my biggest motivator to build strength is to get rid of wearing this thing twenty-four-seven.

"It's almost kick-off," my dad says as the scent of Rose's soup hits my nose.

"Oh, my God, I need that now," I say, turning to my left where my mom has already set up the rolling table with a steaming bowl. Grandpa likes her pozole, but for me, this creamy bowl of perfection can never go wrong.

"She shredded the chicken a bit finer," my mom says.

The spoon is already in my hand and I'm sifting the broth to cool it enough to devour. My grandma's soup is more like pureed enchiladas, which is probably why I love it so much. Unable to wait, I bring the first bite to my mouth and suck it in, not even caring when it burns my tongue a little.

"Heaven," I say, glancing at the discarded oatmeal bowl from this morning. I glower at it and my dad laughs before clearing my old dishes.

"I'd think he was trying to impress the cute orderlies by helping out so much if they weren't all six-foot-tall men in their fifties," my mom jokes.

"Oh, he's trying to impress them all right. One of them said he was a fan, and you know Dad. Has to show off how he's Captain America," I say before blowing on my next bite of soup.

My father comes back into the room after a few minutes, probably having taken my dishes all the way down to the cafeteria. He ups the volume on the TV, and I settle in, watching for Wyatt between every slurp from my spoon. After a few minutes, my dad's phone rings with a FaceTime call. He smiles at the screen and quickly hands the phone over to me.

"He wanted to watch the game today with his favorite buddy," Rose says, flipping her phone so the camera captures both her and my Grandpa Buck.

"Hey, kiddo. Gonna be a tough one today. You ready?" My grandfather's voice warms me as much as my grandmother's food, and for the first time since I got here, I feel a tiny sense of home.

"I have faith," I say, propping my dad's phone on my table so I can have everyone in my family with me while I watch the love of my life leave it all out on the field.

My little sister pops in and out of the camera every few minutes, wanting to share everything about her last week at school with me, including the bit about the boy who picked her last for dodgeball. I make eyes at my mom as Ellie talks about how gross that boy is—his name's Jacob. *Oh, Ellie. He likes you. And you thinking he's so gross? Yeah, you like him back.*

With Deathtrap parked on the other side of the room and a full belly from real food, I settle in just as Wyatt runs onto the field. Grandpa claps, and I catch him sitting forward in his favorite chair just before Wyatt takes his first snap. He rushes out of the pocket a little early, and I wince, bracing myself for him to pay for it, but he quickly breaks free of a tackle and runs the ball for a fourteen-yard gain.

My gaze flashes to my dad, who insists on standing when he watches Wyatt play. He folds his arms over his chest and rocks on his feet. He may as well be out there on the field coaching him. The sight makes me chuckle softly.

The next play is a pass that hits Keaton in the chest, but he somehow can't hang on to it. And despite Wyatt setting an aggressive tone out of the gate, they end up having to kick after a loss of two on a running attempt and an overthrow out of bounds.

"It's all right. We knew Western was going to come out hard," my dad says. He steps around my bed and takes his phone for a few minutes to swap game plans with my grandfather that nobody can hear or put into action. My mom rolls her eyes, then reaches into her tote bag to pull out a small bag of homemade tortilla chips she smuggled in.

"Don't tell anyone. They didn't want me giving you so much salt but you're not a senior citizen. I think you'll be fine."

My grin spreads wide as I dig my hand into the oil-stained paper sack. I try to mute the crunch from my first bite, but my father's Batman-like hearing hones right in, and his hand scoops out about a dozen chips in one swoop.

"Dammit," my mom mutters. I think she wanted to hoard the chips for herself and me even more than she wanted to hide them from the medical staff.

Our defense does its job, and the ball is back in Wyatt's hands after Western goes three and out. My superstitious grandfather insists that my dad put the phone back where it was, and together, he and I root Wyatt down the field in five plays. But with four yards to go, Coach sends in Bryce.

"Fuck," I say, getting a quick reprimand from my mom, even though I've heard her drop dozens of those over the years while watching my dad. And when Bryce takes the snap and fumbles the ball for a turnover, it's her turn to drop the F-bomb. I glance her way with pursed lips, but instead of pointing out the hypocrisy, I simply agree with her.

My dad groans and steps out of the room. I can't see him, but I'm sure he's pacing with his hands threaded behind his neck while he mentally lists all the things that went wrong with that play. I don't want to be so hard on Bryce, but this one's all on him—he has to hold on to the ball.

The first quarter finishes scoreless, but Wyatt manages to throw deep for a quick touchdown in the second. And by the time the fourth is winding down, we've managed to climb up by four touchdowns, the last one scored by a defensive recovery.

Bryce got in a few more times, mostly to run the ball on sneaks for a yard or two to get first downs. His frustration is obvious on his face, but I'm having a hard time worrying about him in the wake of Wyatt having a breakout game.

My family celebrates the win, keeping my grandparents on video chat for about half an hour after the game ends. Knowing my end of the bargain I made with Dr. K is coming due, I blow kisses to my grandparents and hug my parents goodbye so they can head home for a little rest of their own.

Steven's still on shift, so it's just him and me walking the hallway. I'm less ambitious now, maybe less motivated too, what with no promise of putting off the next round again, like last time. Plus, I'm tired. I've never been tired like this. We make our there-and-back trip down the hallway a little faster than the first attempt this morning, and I settle in for a well-earned nap when he puts Deathtrap back in its corner.

My room is dark when I wake. I'm not quite sure how long I slept, but based on the rounds I've memorized, I'm guessing it was near three hours. The nurse checks my vitals and forces me to stand for a few minutes to keep my body healing. As I shake holding myself up at the foot of my bed, though, I'm not sure how much healing is being done. At this point, maybe sleep would do more good.

She helps me back into bed, and I snag my phone from its charging cord before she leaves. It's only seven at night, but it feels impossibly late. I've also missed a call and a text from Wyatt.

WYATT: You must be sleeping. Flight lands at seven your time.

I reply, letting him know I'm awake, hoping maybe he's gotten in early. I'm staring at my message, waiting for it to say *delivered,* when the phone buzzes in my palm with his call.

"Hi," I say, sinking down as deep into my thin covers as my brace and this miserable bed will let me go.

"Was the game that bad that it put you to sleep?" I can hear the bustling airport sounds in the background.

"Not all of it," I tease.

"Ouch!" His voice is raspy, tired from the game and screaming in the locker room, I'm sure. He's also not sleeping as much as he should. Because of me.

"Hey, I'm about to get my bag, then we get hauled back to campus. Can I FaceTime you when I get home?"

Home. We share a home. Well . . . *shared* a home.

"Of course."

We both say I love you on top of the other's words, and my face warms like a school child with a crush.

Wyatt calls back an hour later, this time on video, and it's nice to see him in our bed. His shirt is off, and he's wearing the red and black plaid pajama pants I bought him last Christmas. It's maybe my most favorite look of his, and his skin looks so warm and smooth. His hair is damp from a shower, and I can nearly smell it when I concentrate. And all those sensory things that I draw on from memory flood me, and my heart hurts.

"Hey, what's wrong?" Wyatt says, holding the phone above him as he falls back onto his pillow.

"Can you put the phone on my side, like I'm lying with you?"

His gaze feels faraway, but his worried smile translates. Guilt and self-pity are harder to fight off at night.

"Yeah, here." The camera focus shuffles around as he flips to his left side and jiggles the phone in his effort to prop it up against my pillow. He folds an arm under his cheek and lies flat, looking at me. I touch my own face, wishing it were him.

"You know I'm not coming back, right?" It's something I've known since I got the news of my injury, and I'm sure Wyatt's thought about it. Still, the reality demands to be said tonight for some reason. *Hard truths.*

Wyatt sucks in his lips and blinks slowly.

"I know," he relents after several quiet seconds.

And I can't help but feel as though somehow this is the beginning of the end.

Chapter Nineteen

Wyatt

I don't like leaning on my athlete status to get through school. It feels like cheating. Probably because it *is* cheating. Every senior athlete gets a no-penalty retake for every test in every class during travel season. In the real world, we should probably be made to plan ahead and set the right priorities—aka put academics first. But football isn't the real world. Not when it makes so much damn money. And I'm tired today. I'm tired every day lately. I know I blew the online test I took this morning for my finance class, so I need to play my get-out-of-jail-free card while I've got it.

Use it or lose it, isn't that how the saying goes?

I rap on the door for my professor's office. It's cracked open, so it squeaks and opens a little more from my touch.

"Dr. Ambrose?"

I've only ever seen this man in a tiny square on my computer, so I'm a little surprised when he swings around in the chair behind his desk and he's not four-feet tall and bald. Well, he is bald, but it appears to be by choice. And he also seems to be quite large. Then there's the Air Force shirt he's wearing that isn't the kind one buys off the rack somewhere, but rather the type of shirt that's earned.

"Ah, Mr. Stone. To what do I owe the privilege of this in-person visit?" He gets to his feet and reaches out his hand for a shake. He nearly crushes my fingers in his grip. Yeah, that's definitely an earned shirt. Also, he's definitely still able to pass whatever fitness test is thrown in front of him.

"I'm not sure if you saw my entry this morning, but the late travel from the weekend caught up with me, and I don't think I did so well on that last test."

Mr. Ambrose sits back in his seat and pulls the gold-rimmed glasses from his face.

"I'm guessing you want to use your travel retake?" He's chuckling as he asks.

He pulls a stack of forms out of his side drawer and flops it down on his desk, along with a pen.

"Must have been some pretty serious jet lag, what your travel being a whole day ago and all," he chuckles.

My brow pinches as I sit down and take the pen in my hand.

"I . . . guess? I mean, we got in late Saturday. But I've had a lot going on, and—"

"Yeah, yeah. You and the other six guys who came in this morning filling out the same form." He laughs to himself, the kind of laugh a person lets out when they're not amused but rather . . . miffed. And if six of us, seven including me, all cashed in our free passes at once, maybe he has good reason to be fed up. Except, I'm not being lazy. If anything, my problem is I'm trying to be too much—too many places all at once. And my head is vacillating non-stop between guilt and paranoia.

I put the pen down about halfway through the form and stare at it for a few seconds while Dr. Ambrose busies himself typing something—probably an email to a colleague about what a loser I am for taking a freebie.

"You know what?"

I stand up, tearing the top sheet in half. I push the stack across the desk, the pen resting on top, and wad my free pass into a tight paper ball in my fist. Dr. Ambrose pushes away from his computer and leans back in his chair as his eyes settle on me.

"You're right. I deserve what I get. I'll keep that score, whatever it is, and if it means I need to be perfect from here on out just to pass, then so be it. That's what I get. Hell, maybe you'll get to mark me ineligible for the grades. I won't even fight it. To tell you the truth, I could use the fuckin' break."

I toss the paper ball into the trash by his door on my way out and walk straight to the weight room where Bryce and Whiskey are waiting for me. I don't remember taking a breath the entire way, though I must have. I'm still standing. And I have enough of a voice left to tell Whiskey to fuck off when he comments on me walking in late. He has a point—I did set the time for today.

But still.

"Fuck off." I say it again.

The silence between him and Bryce while I move plates to the bench press bar is palpable. It's full of judgement. I pop my head up after I put a clip on the right side of the bar, and when my eyes meet Whiskey's, he immediately looks away. I'm like a predator sniffing out weakness. Or maybe I'm the weak one looking for an easy kill.

I grab the forty-five-pound plate from Bryce's hands and push it on the other side, snagging the clip from Whiskey's grasp before he has a chance to help. Without looking either of them in the eyes, I flop down on the bench and center myself under the bar. Perfectly still, I wait for one of them to get in position to spot me, but when it becomes clear neither of them intends to, I drop my hands to my forehead and growl like a wild animal.

"Dude, you're still in your jeans. You want to talk about

what's up your ass this morning?" Whiskey kicks the edge of my shoe lightly after he calls me out, and I lift my head enough to see I'm not only in my jeans, but I'm also still wearing the polo shirt I slipped on for my meeting with Dr. Ambrose.

I might have had a mental breakdown.

"I'm a little rattled today, is all," I say, pulling myself up to straddle the bench. My gym bag is by the door, my change of clothes inside. I vaguely remember tossing it there when I marched in here.

"You don't need to be here, you know." Bryce's observation, however right, eats at the source of my anxiety.

"You're right. I don't *need* to be here," I say, meeting his stare. "But I *should* be here."

We lock eyes for a few seconds while Whiskey looks on. I give my friend enough credit to understand how fucked up this co-quarterback relationship I find myself in is.

"Do you want to know the difference between us?" Bryce finally says.

I shrug and shake my head, my anger and frustration quickly morphing into defeatism.

"I don't know, Bryce. What is it? Your determination to just keep pushing until our roles are reversed? Or the fact that if you blew a test like I did this morning, you'd have no qualms taking the free do-over. Because why shouldn't we take advantage of our perks. Or is it that you sleep fine at night, while I . . . ha! Bryce, I hardly fucking sleep at all!"

My face feels hot, and my chest is heaving with my ragged breath. I'm so emotionally spent that I've exhausted myself. Peyton and I barely got to talk yesterday. And I couldn't visit because of some nerve tests she had, and I needed to watch film to make sure I never throw an interception again. *Ha! Like that's a curable fault.*

"You done now, jackass?" Bryce sits on the bench across

from me and leans forward, his elbows balanced on his knees as he levels me with a hard stare.

I breathe in deeply, then exhale, blinking away the latest rush of rage attacking me. I don't like feeling like this, like life is unfair. I haven't felt this way since my dad died.

"I'm done. Sorry," I say, lifting my hand in gesture.

"You're forgiven. Now, do you want to know the serious answer?" He's reminding me a lot of Peyton's mom right now. Maybe a little bit of my own, too.

I nod.

"The difference between us is I would have picked football. Every time. Tough test I should study for? Fuck that—football. My teammates need attention? Screw them, football is mine. They can get their own game."

I pull my mouth into a wry smile and lift a shoulder, not sure where he's going with this. I mean, it's big of him to admit he's a selfish asshole, but not sure I'm getting clarity from his—

"The best person to enter my life needs my help? I'm busy. With football. She's broken and hurting? Fighting for her self-worth? Her dignity? Her life? That sucks, but man . . . I have football."

Oh.

"I had a gift in my hands. And I fucking chose football every single time. You? You chose her. You chose her over that dumb test that won't matter a decade from now. You chose her over getting on an airplane ten hours earlier for a game you weren't sure you would get to start in."

He stands up and closes the distance between us, dropping his hands into the pockets of his joggers as he breathes out a sad laugh.

"Wyatt, you chose her over sleep, over your own ambition, over football, and you know what? You were right. Every fucking time you made that choice, you were right."

My lungs fill at his words, and my pulse shakes my limbs

back to life. He's right. If he's feeding me bullshit to get me out of the way, then bravo to him for one hell of a performance. Because I believe him. Bryce might have just become the better person he said he wanted to be. That right there—his words? Those were genuine.

My mouth inches up on one side as I reach my hand out for him. He grips it and helps me to my feet before we bring each other in for a real, honest-to-God hug. His palm is heavy along my back, and I mutter, "Thanks, man," over his shoulder.

"Now, go see your girl. If Coach asks, you got in early and put in your work."

We part, but I square up with him, leaving my hands on his shoulders for a beat while I stare into his eyes.

"I'll do better," I promise.

He spits out a soft laugh, then rolls his eyes as he nods toward the door. I pull Whiskey in for a hug on my way out, apologizing for taking things out on him. He waves me off, but I can tell by the way he struggles to meet my gaze that I hurt him.

I snag my gym bag, which never got used, and sling it over my shoulder.

"Hey, Wyatt?" Whiskey stops me before I pull open the weight room door.

I turn and nod.

"I don't know about that test you failed or whatever. But you should know that you don't ever have to worry about choosing football. You put in the work because that's what they tell you to do. But you're better than the work. Fuck, Wy. You're better at this game than all of us put together. So, just go fix your girl. This will be right here. The ball will wait for you."

My lip curls, and damn that big man, but I think I feel the burn of teary eyes coming on.

"Thanks, Whisk," I say, just before I leave them behind and go do exactly as they said.

I'm going to fix my girl.

Chapter Twenty

Peyton

I'm starting to come around on the death trap. This thing and I have a complicated relationship, but now that I'm moving a little faster, I understand it—and its brakes.

"Peyt, you're doing so good, kiddo."

I might be coming around on my dad's pep talks, too. Though, I could do with fewer of them. I've been counting the tile squares in the hallway, and he's averaging a motivational prompt every eight to ten tiles. That means twenty of them by the time I finish a lap.

"Hey, you look like you need a break, old man. Mind if I take over?"

The smile on my face at the sound of Wyatt's voice is almost immediate.

"Yeah, he definitely needs a break," I say, shifting my upper body awkwardly to glance behind me so I can catch a glimpse of my boyfriend.

"Wow, you two team up to sideline me?" My dad shakes Wyatt's hand but steps aside to let him take over spotting my right side.

"Last I heard, you were having a hard time keeping up," Wyatt teases. He winks at me—*the wink*. I've missed it.

"Ha ha." My dad kisses my cheek as he pulls his cell from his pocket. "I could use a minute to check in on Coolidge anyhow. We might be starting a freshman this week. Seems our quarterback climbed some fucking tree out at one of those parties and fell out. Broke his arm."

Wyatt chuckles, but shuts the laughter off quickly when my dad's glare hits him.

"Hey, even Bryce stayed out of trees. And I never liked the parties," Wyatt says, straightening his spine to show off good posture on top of his weird brag.

"You all had plenty of your own dumb shit, so don't even." My dad points with one hand and holds his phone to his ear with the other. His slight smirk keeps it playful as he walks away.

"Your dad still scares the shit out of me sometimes," Wyatt admits.

"Good." I smirk. "Now, let's finish this lap and get back to my room so we can cuddle."

"Girl, you're just trying to get me killed," he laughs out. He slides his hand along my lower back anyhow, just below my brace, and together we make it back to my room at the fastest pace I've traveled since my surgery.

Once my various contraptions are put away, Wyatt helps me lie back down before he nestles himself along my side, tucking his arm under my pillow to keep my neck cushioned while he trails his fingers up and down my body. I've missed his touch so much.

"You want to tell me why you're here instead of hitting film or the weight room? And don't forget, I can see right through you because you lie about as good as my father does."

Wyatt winces at my scrutiny.

"I am a shitty liar, huh?" He's avoiding my question.

"Yeah, and an equally terrible dodger. Spill it. Shouldn't you be somewhere else?"

I hate to complain because I've missed him so much. Over the two days or so since I saw him last, I feel as though so much has happened to both of us. I want to tell him about every single win, like the way I held a fork last night and was able to feed myself with my right hand. But I'm willing to save all those stories up, to keep a journal if I must, if it keeps him from bailing on football just to get to me.

"Today was optional. No coaches, and Bryce and Whiskey will cover for me."

"*Hmm.*" I'm quick with my skepticism, my mouth a flat line.

"No *hmm*," he insists, scooting in close and pressing soft kisses into my neck. His face still looks guilty when he pulls away, so I give him side eyes, at least as best I can. My mobility is improving, but my movements are still stiff.

"And what's to keep Bryce from ratting you out?"

"He won't." His insistence is genuine, but still . . . my trust with Bryce is thin. It's based on a lot of history, and maybe the scales are tilted because of how much I want this season to be perfect for Wyatt. He deserves it.

"I don't want you to think I don't want you here. Because I do. But Wy, you can't keep this up. You can't be in two places at once. And as much as I am glad to see you—"

His fingertips brush my lip, and I lose my momentum. Also, I forgot how nice it feels for him to touch me softly. We haven't been alone much lately. And when we are, I haven't exactly been in a condition to *be* touched.

"I am willing to bet on Bryce. Because seeing you is everything to me."

He shifts his arm under my head, bracing himself enough to lift his body and bring his mouth just over mine. His eyes pause on mine before dipping to my lips.

"Okay?" he prompts.

"Okay," I whisper back, my lips suddenly buzzing with desire. I haven't ached to be kissed this intensely since the first time I kissed Wyatt Stone.

His gaze flits up to mine one last time before his eyes close and his lips brush against me with a feather-light touch that sends goose bumps down my arms. Both arms. I feel it.

"More," I utter, my mouth forming a smile against his.

"You can have as much as you want," he laughs softly against me. His mouth sucks in my bottom lip, the rough edge of his teeth grazing me as I slip loose of his hold.

"You taste like lemon," he muses.

I lick my lips and squeeze my eyes shut tight before popping them open.

"I had a sucker! I earned it for throwing a ball."

Wyatt sits up a little, a proud smile taking over the sexy one for a moment. I like them both, but right now, I'm really craving the seductive side of him.

"You threw a ball? That's amazing!" He lowers his head until it rests on mine, our eyelashes tangling as we blink. It makes me giggle, and that . . . that feels good.

"I didn't throw it hard, or anywhere near the target. But it was the motion. I squeezed it. And then I sort of dropped it as my arm fell. So, it counts as a throw."

His free hand cups the side of my face, his thumb brushing against my cheek as he pins me with his awe-struck stare. From anyone else I might feel placated, maybe even patronized, but from Wyatt? That look means everything.

"It absolutely counts. They should see what you'd be willing to do for a T-shirt," he teases.

I laugh, and the sound is strong and loud, alerting the nurse just outside my room. She steps in to make sure I'm okay, but when her eyes meet mine and she sees Wyatt embracing me, she backs out of my door and closes it nearly completely.

"You know, there are other physical things I would really

like to test out. And only you can help me," I say, my overt come-on mincing no words.

Wyatt sinks back down beside me, his fingertips grazing along my collarbone, then down the center of my chest, along the soft cotton shirt I've basically lived in for the last two days.

"I'd really like to change," I say.

His mouth tugs up on one side, and his dark lashes mask his eyes as his focus drops to my chest. His palm hovers between my ribs, his index finger drawing a soft line down to my navel before his fingers curl under the hem of my shirt.

"I can help with that," he says in a soft voice, lifting his head to meet my eyes and level me with a devious smirk before shifting to press a soft kiss against my bare stomach.

"These are cute," he remarks, teasing my skin along the band of the soft white cotton boxer shorts I'm now obsessed with.

"The incision is a little tender still. Besides, I kind of like them," I say, wishing I had the muscle strength and ability to wriggle my hips and lure his hand lower.

"I kind of love them," he says, moving back to the hem of my shirt. I suppose all touch is good at this point. My body is aching, and not from laps around the fucking nurses' station.

Wyatt glances behind him, probably checking the door, then returns to my body, bringing my shirt up until my bare breasts are exposed, and his mouth covers one almost instantly.

"Do you feel that?" His tongue flicks against my left nipple, and I whimper.

"That's a yes." He chuckles. "How about this one?"

He moves to my right side, and while my hand and leg have been slow to cooperate with me, my tits seem to be completely on board with feeling everything.

"Oh, fuck," I mutter. I suck my bottom lip in hard as my eyes flicker toward the door.

"Should we test . . . other things?" His mouth covers my

nipple again, suckling it as he looks up at me through his lashes.

"We definitely should," I say, my voice full of want.

In my mind, I'm lifting my hips, and I very well may be the tiniest bit, but it would be impossible to tell. Wyatt's soft breath tickles my hard nipple, driving me wild as his palm slides down my stomach and underneath the band of my boxers. His fingertips brush along the trail of hair above my pussy, then slip between my legs. I throb instantly at his touch.

"Oh . . . oh, yes," I stutter.

I'm going to come, and I'm going to come soon.

"Wyatt," I say, his name more of a plea than anything.

"Come for me, baby," he says, kissing my nipple as his finger slides against my soaking wet skin.

My lips part, and I lay my left arm over my eyes, wishing I could arch my body into him. He dips a finger inside of me, then two, hooking them as he pushes deep into me, then slides back out, coating me in my arousal.

"Fuck, you feel good, Peyton. I can't wait until it's my cock in you again," he says, his dirty talk making my pussy swell against his touch.

He flicks his tongue against my nipple again, then teases my clit before pushing two fingers back inside. The pattern continues, and it gets faster as my breathing grows out of control. I let out a tiny cry with every pass of his hand against me, my pussy soaking wet as I get closer and closer to the edge. I can feel the wave coming as my core tightens; I turn my head and lift my gaze just enough to catch Wyatt's eyes.

"Please," I beg.

He sinks his fingers in deep, pressing his thumb against my clit and circling it as his teeth pinch my left nipple into a sweetly painful ache. My body wants to convulse, but every single bit of my orgasm is concentrated where Wyatt's thumb is circling between my legs. It's nearly torture taking every wave of pleasure that courses through me, and I have to bite my fist to keep from crying out loud.

By the time the last surge shatters me, it's all I can do to open my eyes in the light of the room. I can barely breathe. And my smile will not leave my face.

Wyatt slips from the side of my bed and moves to the small suitcase my mom brought with extra clothes for me. He pulls out his favorite shirt—the one he gave me after our freshman year when he led the Wildcats to a conference championship. It has his name on the back, along with a whole lot of other football players, but it's his I care about.

"Let me help you," he says, supporting me as I sit up tall in the bed. I raise my arms one at a time, the right needing assistance from Wyatt as he slips one shirt from my body and replaces it with the new one.

When he nestles back into the bed beside me, I bend my left leg, nudging his thigh as my left palm teases his side. He takes it in his hand and brings it up to his mouth, pressing a kiss on my wrist before meeting my gaze and shaking his head.

"I don't need anything besides your pleasure."

The massive hard-on in his sweatpants says otherwise.

"Are you sure?" I really want to touch him, but also, it's not something I can do easily just yet.

He nods.

"I'm going to wait for when it's time to put my cock in your pussy again. And then, I'm going to fuck you senseless."

And right on cue, my nurse knocks at the door to announce it's time for my vitals. I'm sure my face is bright red. It's hot, but also, my entire body is now hot. Wyatt can't seem to temper the massive smirk on his face. I think he rather enjoys seeing me rattled. And he basically seals that deal when he makes a bet with the nurse that my blood pressure may be a little elevated.

I want to die. But also, what a happy death.

Chapter Twenty-One

Wyatt

I've only seen Bryce's dad a handful of times, but the last occurrence made such an impression on me that it must have imprinted his profile deep into my brain. There are a dozen or so visitors in the stands watching our open practice today, mostly reporters speckled around the front two rows behind the training staff and coaches. From across the field, though, I recognize one man—one profile. Alex Hampton, Bryce's sudden number one fan.

I flip around, knowing Bryce is a few yards behind me, and try to distract him on our way onto the field.

"Hey, did I tell you Peyton threw a ball yesterday?" He's been supportive of hearing every little accomplishment I have to share about her, and at the news of this latest one, his brows lift high.

"Could she do that before?" he jokes. For being the daughter of a legendary quarterback, Peyton's athletic talents take a different form. She's more power, speed—strength.

"Maybe it's like when Spiderman got bit by the radioactive—"

"Fuck me, what's he doing here?" Bryce cuts me off.

It was a good attempt by me, but the second Bryce glances over my shoulder, he has a clear shot of his dad.

"Try to ignore him." I know it's an impossible bit of advice the second I utter it, but it had to be said.

"Yeah, you mean the way he always ignored me. Got it." His heavy brow and soured expression drop a weight into my chest. I'm not sure he's going to make it through today's practice without causing a scene.

We drop our gear on the sideline and meander out toward the center of the field along with Shad, Coach Skye, and the receivers group. We do some stretching as a team, then run a few sprints, warming our legs up. Bryce's attention seems to be pulled away every few seconds during warmups, even as he and I toss the ball to prime our arms for throwing drills. Finally, Coach Skye steps in front of Bryce to block his view of his father.

"Do we have a problem we need to address, Hampton?" Coach Skye is about as warm and fuzzy as our head coach, meaning he's sharp as a knife and cold as a steel blade.

Bryce's nostrils flare in response, and I can tell he's fighting to keep his cool. The student managers for our team are talking the group of visitors through today's run-down for practice, and Bryce's father claps louder than everyone else anytime there's a reason to applaud.

Not wanting Bryce to get himself in trouble, and maybe because I feel I owe the guy, I step in front of him and press my hand on his chest.

"He's fine. Just anxious to work some new routes today." Coach's gaze flashes to me, and he nods with a short laugh before leaving us to finish our long toss.

"I know this sucks, and I'll tell him you don't want him to show up here anymore once we get through this practice, but you have to show you can handle yourself without being a hothead in front of Skye and Byers, okay?"

Bryce's eyes drift to mine, his gaze still hardened, but he nods with a faint exhale.

Somehow, over the last couple of weeks, I've started to root for Bryce's success. Not that I want him to surpass me, but I see the changes he's making, and I'm seeing the legacy I could maybe leave behind by handing the team over to him next season. Maybe it's a little selfish of me for wanting the credit for mentoring him too. But it turns out I *like* mentoring. And I might just be damn good at it.

"Gentlemen," Coach Byers says, pulling us into a tight circle. "That tough schedule I've been promising? It starts this week. You thought Western put up a fight, but Cal is going to give us hell. Bryce, Wyatt? I know you guys spent some time watching their defense yesterday. Did you see the same weaknesses I did?"

Shit. I did not watch their defense. Granted, Cal has had the same defensive coordinator for eleven years, and they're known for one thing—shutting down the passing game.

I glance to Bryce, waiting for him to take the lead, but he seems stalled—either panicked because he knows I wasn't there watching with him, or he's still distracted by his father, who has started to wander down the row toward the end zone.

"I think we need to open with the run, really hammer it, force them to change up their defense. It's the only way we're going to get our receivers involved," I say, taking a gamble.

"Good. I agree," Coach says.

Bryce exhales along with me, our shoulders relaxing for a breath.

"So, Bryce, you're gonna get the start," Coach says.

And my shoulders tighten right back up. *What the fuck?*

"Oh, yeah. Okay," Bryce rambles, his gaze shifting to me,

maybe looking for permission. I'm too stunned, and angry, regardless of how unjustified it is.

"Wy, I'd like you to work on the deep routes with the receivers today, and Bryce . . . we're going to mix in some running plays this weekend, maybe even a double hand-off with our backs, some extra sneaks behind the O-line. You ready?"

Coach's questions aren't really questions. They aren't even suggestions. That's the plan, and we're off to execute it.

Mentally spiraling, I find my way to the other end of the field, where I begin with a few warm-up routes to Keaton and Nick. I can tell they're thrown by the split in practice today, too, their attention constantly diverted to the middle of the field, where Bryce is rushing the ball in every possible direction, practically wearing paths into the grass while Coach Byers looks on.

"What's the deal with that?" Keaton finally asks me when Coach Skye is out of earshot.

"He's getting the start," I say, my answer clipped and flat.

"Fuck! Seriously?" Keaton's loyalty feels nice, but his response gets him in trouble, when Coach Skye hears what sounds like a complaint and quickly sends him to sprint to the opposite pole and back.

"Anyone else mad about today's drill?" He stares Nick in the eyes for a beat, then Shad. He never gets to me, though, and for whatever reason, that's the thing that pushes me over the edge.

"I'm pretty fuckin' pissed about it," I let out.

Oh, shit.

"Excuse me?" He's in my face before I can blink twice, his fingers looped through my helmet's mask to hold my head in place.

May as well take this as far as I can now that I'm in it.

I meet his stare and make a promise not to blink a single time no matter how loud he gets when I finish saying my piece.

"Coach, I've worked my ass off for three years, and I know I'm just coming off an injury, but I feel proud about my performance so far this year. I think it's fair to say I'm not holding back out there, and I'm certainly not playing scared and nursing my break. Bryce is a good quarterback, and I think he'll be ready to step up when I graduate. But I'm not happy that he's getting the start Saturday to do something we all know I can do better—run the ball and score. So, yeah. I'm pretty fuckin' pissed that I'm doing this drill while he's over there doing that one. I'm pissed we're not all working on the same page, on the same skills, growing as a team. And I'm mad that something I've earned is being toyed with on a whim. Now, if you excuse me, I'm pretty sure I have sprints to run. I'll be right back."

I place my helmet on the ground, my heart beating so fast I can feel my pulse in my eyeballs. I turn and begin a slow jog that I turn into a sprint, passing Keaton on his way back. He lifts a brow at me, but my only response is a quick, "Don't."

When I get back to the receivers, Coach Skye doesn't as much as glance up from his clipboard. I pick up my helmet and fasten it back in place while he taps his pen on the paper a few times, his tongue poking into his cheek. Finally, he swirls the pen in the air, drawing a tight, invisible circle.

"Run the routes again," he says.

I purse my lips and shake my head, but I do as he says, clapping twice and nodding to Keaton before lining up to drop the thousandth pass I've thrown to him this month.

"Blue, forty-two!"

Keaton takes off as I slap the ball, and I fake a scramble before sailing the ball down the field and hitting him midstride about forty-five yards out. I turn to my right, waiting for Coach Skye to glance up after writing down his notes, and when our eyes meet, I blink slowly and chew at my mouth guard to keep from spilling out my rage again.

He circles the pen in the air once more, opting for hand

gestures over words. Probably for the best. I can't imagine what my hand gesture would have been, though I have an idea.

Nick lines up for this one, Shad watching off to the side, getting ready for his turn. Maybe, if I work hard enough, I'll be able to knock myself down to third string today.

Fucking goals, I guess.

Regret for my actions sinks in about an hour into practice. My arm grows tired from overthrowing to prove a point, my jaw aches from clenching my teeth, and my stomach is so tight I think I might throw up when I hit the showers. *If* I hit the showers. I kind of just want to leave today without talking to anyone else.

Whiskey busts up that plan quickly, though, knocking my cleats from the bench where I set them as I peel off my practice gear.

"Don't fuck things up, Wyatt." His glare is pointed, and the hard look on his face is easy to understand.

I sigh and lean back against my locker. My eyes scan the team room, our defense just now dressing out to hit practice hard, the second-string offensive players peeling tape from shins and worming out of pads so they can shower and get to the student center before the good food options shut down. Everyone does their job, no matter what that job is for the day. Why did I have to get so bent over mine being different for once?

I run my palm over my face and pull down on my cheeks, stretching my eyes as I meet my friend's stare.

"Could you hear me out there?"

Whiskey, who was in the opposite end zone hitting pads and practicing snaps for most of the day, shakes with his laughter.

"Fucking Cal heard that temper tantrum, dude! You lost your cool. You completely threw your cool out the window. No fucks given."

"Gah," I groan, landing the back of my head on the locker door again with a little thud, self-punishment style.

"I should fix this," I say, stripping off the rest of my practice clothes and zipping up my bag before heading straight to Coach's office. I stop short of marching through the door, instead hovering outside when I hear him having words with Coach Skye on the other side. It's hard to make out everything they're saying, but my name sure seems to come up a lot. And when the door flies open, revealing me in all my tail-between-my-legs glory, Coach Skye basically confirms my hunch that my behavior is the big topic of the day.

"Speak of the asshole. He's all yours," he says, waving a hand to usher me in as he steps out. I'm not sure if I'm the asshole by his statement. I don't think it matters.

"Go on and shut the door, Wyatt."

"Yes, sir," I say, finding my manners again, it seems. I close the door and take the seat across from coach's desk, my gym bag straps wrapped around one fist as I clutch it between my knees. I'm in ready-to-go position, half expecting to be kicked out as soon as I get comfortable.

"Wyatt, I don't know if you know this about me, but my wife and I . . . we lost our daughter about twenty-two years ago."

My gut fills with instant rocks. His gaze meets mine, and I can tell by the way his pupils widen he's not letting go. I *am* the asshole.

"I'm sorry, Coach. That's terrible." My mouth waters at the thought of such a loss. Losing my dad broke me—broke my mom. I can't imagine what it would have been like for them if it had been the other way—if they'd lost me.

"It was. She had a pretty aggressive form of leukemia. It happened fast, and there's not a day that goes by that I don't wish for one more hour with her. Playing with our family dog in the front yard, acting in her school play while her mom and I cram into the last row of seats because I was always late, tearing away Christmas paper to get at her gifts. That girl, she sure loved art supplies. That last Christmas . . . that was the year we got her an easel."

He leans back and chuckles at the memory, but his focus sticks to me. I force my upper body to relax but keep my bag held tight. This story has a point, and it could be that I'm not worthy of wearing this jersey with an attitude like this. I'd get it. I'd deserve it.

Coach leans forward, folding his hands together on his desk as he blinks slowly. I adjust my grip on my straps, my toes curling inside my shoes as if trying to grip the ground and ward off being sent away.

"One of the things I loved most about you when we had our recruitment meeting was how you talked about your father. And the way you talked *to* your mom. You had this sense of right and wrong, this deep understanding of priorities, that just . . . well, it's rare for young people. Let's just say that."

His lip ticks up and I find mine doing the same.

"Thank you, I think?" I eke out.

"You're welcome. And no thinking about it. It's a huge compliment."

I nod and the silence stretches out between us for a few seconds. I fight to hold his gaze, not wanting to look down—to cower.

"I'm starting Bryce Saturday, Wyatt," he says, and my fist tightens even though the straps are cutting into my skin.

"Yes, sir." My mouth waters.

"And I know you don't like it," he adds, pulling his hands apart and lifting one palm along his desk, urging me to hear him out, I think.

"It's not that—"

"Wyatt, I got an earful from Coach Skye. He doesn't like my decision either. But he doesn't like you very much right now, so maybe just shut up and listen, okay?"

My muscles slacken and I drop the bag to the floor as I nod.

"You have a resilience that is far too mature for your age, young man. The things you can handle mentally . . . emotionally? Most of us ancient creatures have a tough time with that stuff, but you . . . you take things as they come and compartmentalize and trudge forward. It's admirable, but it's not always healthy."

I mash my lips, wanting to argue with him but not really having a good one. He's right.

"You are my guy, Wyatt. You are my number one, and you are going to be the face of this program this season as well as long after you are gone. I believe you are that good. I believe you are that type of a man. But we have a chance to give you a little breathing room this weekend, and it's an opportunity to see what Hampton is made of. It's not some sort of test for you, but it is a bit of a test for him. If I'm wrong about it, course correction will happen fast, and you'll be in the game trying to fix my bad decisions. It's a risk I am taking as the head coach. It's not just what's good for the whole of this program looking ahead to possible playoffs and then next season, but it's also what's good for you."

I work my jaw, uncomfortable admitting to feeling weak but recognizing that lately, I have been running on fumes. I'm tired. And I'm worried. All I can think about is Peyton and whether she's going to be able to meet her own wishes and expectations for herself. I want to fix everything for her, to right the wrongs, reverse time. But I can't. All I can do is be there. And there's no way I'm not showing up. I don't care what it costs me, or this program.

Coach sees that. It's why he's making the call.

"Thank you, Coach," I say, standing up and snagging my bag from the ground.

I reach across his desk and take his hand, and before I pull away, he holds on to me extra tight, forcing me to look him in the eyes.

"You're strong enough for this, Wyatt. For all of it. Even standing to the side and letting someone else do the work for just a little while."

My mouth pulls into a tight smile, and I nod. It's nice of him to say. It still hurts. And I'm not entirely convinced it's true.

Chapter Twenty-Two

Peyton

These pancakes are the best I've ever had. Jack's never misses, and I've been craving these suckers since the day my doctors cleared me for solids. This trip to Jack's does not disappoint.

Nothing about today disappoints. I'm grateful to the team that got me this far, but I'm so ready to go home. Jack's is the only diversion I'm allowing. I can't wait to hear my grandfather's laugh echo down the hallway, to feel the sun beam in through the skylight in our living room while I rest on the couch and watch *SportsCenter* with my dad, and to walk with the help of Otis, the oldest horse in our barn and the literal best therapy a girl could ask for.

It's a damn near perfect day. The only thing off is Wyatt. Something's wrong, and I wish he would quit pretending it's just stress leading up to the game against Cal. It's something more than that. I think it's me. Not *worrying* about me, but balancing time with me—it's wearing on him. And I wish he would let go of something. I'm okay.

"If you're not going to finish those . . ." I poke my fork in the half pancake Wyatt has left on his plate. He grins and pushes the plate over to me.

"Go ahead." His smile doesn't quite reach his eyes.

I lean to my left and kiss his cheek, then dump a little more syrup on the plate and dig in.

"If you're carb loading, does that mean we get to walk extra far when we get to the house?" My mom smirks at me, and I wink and utter, "We'll see."

She has spent the last two weeks setting up our downstairs guest room with everything I'll need to rehab at home. I'll still make the trip to Tucson to work with Dr. Garmish at Tucson Strong. He's been friends with my mom for years, and she was able to get his help, making sure I could stick to the aggressive schedule I made for myself. Even more, he believes I can accomplish everything on my list. He even added an item—a marathon. Five years from now, but still.

Me. A marathon.

I like it.

"You said to let you know when it was three. It's just a few minutes before," my mom says to Wyatt. He shakes out of his trance, which he's been in a lot today, and meets her gaze with a quick smile.

"Yeah, I hate to miss the homecoming, but we leave for Cal tonight and I've been told I should always travel with the team." He swivels his head and quirks a brow, bunching his lips in a cute but accusatory way. For a moment, he's himself.

I touch my fingertip to his nose twice.

"Whoever told you that was right. Now, off you go. Get me one of those touchdown things," I say as his lips hover an inch away from mine. He breathes out a short laugh, then kisses me.

"I'll do my best," he says, snagging his phone and wallet from the counter and moving toward the end of the counter where my dad is talking with Jack's owner, Maggie.

"Something's wrong," I say to my mom, and she follows my

gaze to where both men seem to be having a quick heart-to-heart.

My dad puts a hand on Wyatt's shoulder, then pats it a few times before saying, "Good luck."

My dad settles our bill with Maggie, who always tries to feed us for free, then carries my walker to me from behind the counter so I can steady myself and make the slow but steady trek out to the parking lot.

I'm still getting used to the exoskeleton brace, but I am moving faster with it. My balance is improving too. It's just the strength part, and then of course, working my way to making these journeys on my own, without a guide. And eventually, without the walker.

Quit racing yourself.

My mom said those three words to me a few days ago, and they really stuck. I've been racing myself my whole life in one way or another. Life came along and made the race unfair, though, so now I need to pace things. Finish strong.

It feels as if it takes us an hour to get to my parents' vehicles, though it's probably ten minutes. I lean into my dad while my mom collapses the walker to put it in her SUV. I stop her before she lifts it from the ground.

"Actually, I'd like to ride with dad. I need to ask him a few boy questions, things only another boy would get."

About Wyatt.

My mom nods with a soft smile, then shifts her body to boost my walker up and into the back of Dad's truck.

"No goofing off," she says, eyeing her husband first but including me next in that warning.

"No promises," I say, an answer typical of my dad.

She shakes her head and laughs before getting into her driver's seat.

"I love you two. See you at home."

We wait for her to pull out so my dad can open the

passenger door all the way, giving me plenty of options of where to hold on to. His hands go to my hips, but I shake my head.

"Let me try on my own first."

"Okay. I'll be right here," he says, the reservation obvious in his tone. It's not that he doesn't think I can do this, it's that it's hard for him to see me fail. That's something I've learned over the last two weeks. It's where my father and I crossover the most—we're competitive to a fault. With ourselves.

Quit racing yourself.

I take a deep breath and bring my right leg up, having to guide it part of the way to ensure my foot is flat on the running board. I search for the perfect holding spots, feeling good about my left hand clutching the grab bar, and settling for my other hand wrapping around the open window frame. My father stands at the door's edge to keep it from closing on me, and I grunt my way into standing on the running board on my bad leg.

"Holy shit!" My eyes are wide with shock, and my body feels wobbly, but I lifted myself a foot off the ground.

"Atta girl!" My dad's celebration is warranted this time. I'll allow it.

Twisting my body proves to be a little trickier than I expect, so I call my dad in for a boost to get my hips moving in the right direction. Soon I'm in the seat, buckling myself in, and excited about getting out on my own when we get home.

My dad fires up the engine, his radio blasting that twenty-year-old rap he loves so much. I giggle and rap a few of the lyrics with him as he pulls out of the Jack's lot. He turns the volume down when we hit the road, and after about a mile, he looks my way, ready to get serious.

"Is this going to be one of those talks where I should pull over? Or if we take the long route home, will that be enough?"

He slows the truck a little, and I hike my shoulders up, not sure how this is going to go.

"I think you're going to have to tell me. I know you know what's going on with Wyatt. What's wrong? What happened?" I know it's football, and there's no way my dad isn't all up in that business.

My dad's chest rises with his deep breath. He looks back to the road, then glances into his rearview mirror before looking back at me.

"Long route should do. But how about we make a little stop at the high school? It's the JV game tonight. They'll be warming up." He tilts his head, urging me to say yes. He hasn't been around much for the high school boys this season. Part of that is because of me, but mostly, he planned to spend this year supporting Wyatt.

"I'd like that," I answer, my response pushing my dad's grin up into his cheeks.

He flicks the turn signal on his truck and makes a wide left turn toward the towering light poles in the distance. It's early yet, so by the time we pull into the Coolidge High lot, most of the guys are just getting dressed out and making the walk from the locker room to the field.

My dad helps me out of my seat so I can stand outside the truck with him while a few of the players jog over to shake his hand.

"Remember to watch for the long pass tonight, Davis," my dad says to one of the smallest kids on the squad. He suddenly stands taller after getting my dad's tip, then nods to him and says, "Yes, Coach," before pushing his helmet onto his head and rushing out to the field.

"He's small," I mutter when Davis is out of earshot.

My dad sighs.

"Yeah, it's a small few classes we've got. They're fast, though.

Looks like we might have to get sneaky to win our division this year."

Or start illegally recruiting.

I don't say that thought out loud. It's a dirty topic but one that every single coach in this state does. The parents participate, shopping for playing time guarantees and recruitment looks before filling out waivers to get their kid into some school several miles away from their home. And the hard truth is my grandfather worked that system for my dad years ago.

"You want to get back in, or you want to sit on the tailgate a little while?" He leans his head to the right and I grin.

"You know that answer." I hold out an arm so he can help support me as I wobble my way to the back of the truck.

There's no easy way to hop onto the tailgate, so I let my dad lift me up. I attempt to swing my legs, and it works . . . sort of. I use my left one to push my right. For a minute, I'm a kid again. The only thing missing is a strawberry shake from MicNic's.

"So." I stare at him, wearing my worry, I'm sure. My stomach rattles with butterflies, but the nervous kind.

"Oh man, I kind of hoped he'd say something, but I get why he didn't. Why he won't." My dad rubs his palms into his eyes, then drops them to his lap while my stomach takes a trip on an invisible roller coaster.

I already know before the words leave his mouth. But hearing them . . . they still make me cry.

"Bryce is getting the start."

"Fuck."

I blink away the tears and stare out at the field where kids half my dad's size—half Wyatt's size—count down jumping jacks in unison. It sometimes feels so pointless.

My dad leans into me for a second.

"I won't tell your mom about the F bomb." He chuckles, and I roll my eyes.

"I mean, since you taught me, that makes sense."

He feigns offense.

"Fuck that," he jokes.

I laugh a little harder, but it dies out quickly.

"I hate that he didn't tell me," I say, even though I understand it.

My dad doesn't have a response, so he simply sits quietly with me for a while, listening to the distant whistles and cracking voices of boys becoming men out on the field.

Chapter Twenty-Three

Wyatt

I'm taking it out on Bryce—though he clearly covered for me. It's not his fault that Coach is following his instincts on this move. After my heartfelt chat with Coach in his office, a part of me gets his reasoning, though I don't think this decision is totally for my benefit. He's thinking about winning as much as he's thinking about my mental wellbeing.

Maybe I'm jaded.

Part of what attracted me to this program was Coach's no-nonsense, zero-tolerance-for-bullshit approach. I'm not sure why I expected anything else when it came to me.

"He feels like shit about this, you know?" Whiskey says as I stuff myself into pads I probably won't even use tonight.

I don't answer him. I'm not sure what to say. The best I can do is give him the look, the same expression I wore with Reed when I gave him the news—a face pulled in two directions, guilt and disappointment.

I had to let Reed know I wouldn't be starting since he was planning to drive out for the game. He stopped in for a little pep talk with the team a few minutes ago. Part of me hoped he'd give me some motivational speech that would amp me up enough to get my head in the game and to be the leader Bryce deserves. It's not his fault. Hell, he hasn't even played that well. A true team player would hype him up right now, but instead, I can't even look at him.

"He'll probably fumble the first play," Whiskey says, and I chuckle, but shake my head.

"I hope he doesn't. We need this win." I need this game too, though. My stats are good, but I haven't exactly had that showy breakout everyone's been waiting for. I can't seem to find my game. It went missing the second Peyton was loaded into that ambulance.

She's my reason.

My phone buzzes deep inside my travel bag, and since there's still a lot of time before I need to head out to the field, I fish it out to check the message. It's a photo from my mom, of me on my dad's shoulders, hoisting my Pee Wee football trophy. I must be seven or eight in this picture, but I remember the feeling like it was yesterday.

My phone buzzes with another message from her as I exit out of the image.

> MOM: Remember who you are. You're Todd Stone's MVP!

Her words do enough to edge the corners of my mouth up.

> ME: Thank you, Mom. I love you.

I'm about to put the phone away when it buzzes again. I wake my screen back up to a new photo from my mom, and it takes my brain a few seconds to realize what I'm seeing. Peyton is sitting on a horse. Her mom's hand is on her thigh, and I'm sure it took teamwork for her to get up there, but she's doing it. She crossed one thing off her list.

ME: Are you with them?

It looks like the right color of sunlight for this to be happening right now. I hate that I'm missing it, but I feel so alive seeing it.

MOM: Yes. Nolan invited me over to watch the game. Rose made carnitas.

ME: Tell her I love her.

MOM: Rose?

I snort out a laugh and the sound surprises me. I haven't laughed for real in a while.

ME: Well, her too. But you know what I mean.

I wait for a minute while my mom appears to be typing, then suddenly my phone buzzes with a short video that appears to be Peyton on the horse. I glance around to make sure I'm alone enough then press play, turning my volume up just enough to hear. I tear up instantly.

"Wyatt, I'm doing it. Can you believe this?"

Peyton's body sways with her horse's slow steps. Her mom's hand is still on her leg. And it looks as though Rose is out in the arena with them. She's surrounded by support.

"I wanted to do something hard today. For you. I know you have to do something hard soon, and I want you to know that I believe in you. Your greatest gift isn't how you throw a football, Wyatt. It's your spirit. You make people believe they can. Now, go have the game you deserve."

I press my finger to the player for the video and drag it back a few seconds to hear her say that last part again.

I put my phone away and stare for a few long seconds at my

closed locker door. Teammates are shuffling around behind me, locker doors slamming shut while the scent of pre-wrap spray filling the air. It's college game day. My last season in this uniform. The last time I'm going to take on Cal, the school that said they weren't interested in me when I was a junior. The school my dad said didn't deserve me.

They're going to lose today, and it's going to take two of us working together to get it done. Peyton's right. So is my mom. It's time my father's lessons make an appearance.

"Let's go!" I shout, turning around and drawing the attention of the few players still in the locker room with me.

"Hell, yeah!" Shad shouts, pushing his palms into my chest. I give it right back to him, hyping him up for a game he has even less of a chance of getting into. Yet look at him—ready to show up for us. However. Whenever.

I lead the dozen players left in the locker room down to the tunnel. The roar of a sold-out stadium rings in my ears, and I mentally convince myself that those screams are for us. *For me.*

I make my way through the team to the front, where Bryce, Whiskey and Keaton are all holding hands. I break into their line and take Bryce's hand in my right, Whiskey's in my left. Turning to face Bryce, I press my face mask against his, both of us breathing like two bulls ready to be cut loose in a town painted red.

"You get that ball; you don't let it hit the ground. You get your ass in that end zone. And then you do it again." I grit out the words with so much force I spit.

"Yes, sir!" His fire matches mine.

He unfurls our grip for a second, grabbing the back of my helmet and holding me to him as his eyes lock on mine. It's a silent thank you. A masculine show of affection. A football love letter.

"I believe in you," I say.

Just like that, everything clicks behind his eyes. Confidence colors his irises, power flexes his jaw. I grab his helmet back and growl as he does the same, and in a blink, we rush onto the field as a team—all of us and both of us. The boos fuel us. The fireworks fill our senses with the need for destruction. And the brass horns blaring our fight song set a new rhythm in our hearts.

I hype up the team along the sideline as we receive the kick, stopping at Reed long enough for him to see the clarity in my eyes. His heavy hand on my back as I walk away lets me know he's proud, and when I reach the end of the line for our team, I close my eyes for a moment to see my dad, too.

I feel his shoulders holding me up. I hear his voice telling me he's proud. I see my mom smiling at both of us. I feel their love. And suddenly, Peyton's there, sitting tall, kicking the sides of her horse before it sprints off into the sunset as she rides.

Rushing back down the line, I hold my helmet up to fire up our student section too. I can always count on our drunk frat boys to get things going, and their painted, shirtless bodies jump wildly as Miguel Montoya, the best kick returner in college football, gets the ball to the fifty-yard line.

I run over to Bryce, taking up his other side while he gets his orders from Coach. I slap his back a few times to bring the blood to the surface and waken the lion within, and he turns to me just before running backward onto the field.

"This one's for you, Stone."

It's not a taunt. And it's not him showing off and being arrogant. It's my friend, my brother, doing something to get me into the game. He won't fumble. He's going to score. In fact, he's poised to score a lot until Cal is forced to put a stop to him. And then, it's my turn to carry us home.

With three minutes to go before the half, we're up twenty-seven to fourteen against a tough Cal team. Bryce has taken a beating, and he exits after getting stopped on the third down, his nose bleeding and the bruise on his right bicep already a deep purple. They've closed the gaps, and if they keep that up in the second half, I'll get my turn.

"Stone, get in there!" Coach shouts.

Or maybe I'll get my shot now.

My pulse ratchets up as I slam my helmet on my head just before Coach pulls my face in close to his. It's a fourth and long, and there are three minutes left, which means if I fuck this up, Cal gets the ball in a pretty good spot with plenty of time on the clock. But if I pull this off—

"You're my guy," he says, his gaze locking on mine, his mouth a stoic straight line. "Get it done."

"Yes, Coach!"

I rush out to the field, half the stadium losing their minds in my favor, the other half wishing nothing but my total demise. I'm about to fucking ruin their day.

"Hey, look who's back!" Keaton punches my left shoulder pad, and I give him a nod.

"Time to let it fly, boys You know what to do."

We break and hit the line, the Cal defense scrambling at our quick change in plans. I count off the snap and my world turns to slow motion. The ball in my hands, I fade to back while the line holds the pocket to buy Keaton time. My eyes are like military target locks, my arm the missile launch, and Keaton the destination. He's not as deep as I want him to be, but the pocket is collapsing around me. I spin out, avoiding a tackle, and run to the opposite side of the field, but Keaton's in lock step with some pretty good coverage. It's too risky.

I don't panic. There isn't time. Instead, I chart my path and run. It's not what Cal is expecting, not from me, so I easily manage the first down. But then a hole breaks wide open in front of me, and I turn up my speed. In seconds, I'm in the end zone, spinning the ball right before Keaton lifts me up.

"Hell yeah, motherfuckers! Hell yeah!" Whiskey rushes at

me, bumping my chest with his, and I ricochet a few feet back. It's the best feeling in the world, even if it hurts.

Coach grabs my arm when I hit the sideline and pats my helmet a few times, meeting my eyes.

"There's my guy! There he is!" He sends me off with praise, and I head right to Bryce, who blasts into me the same as Whiskey did.

We end up holding Cal until the half, and I finish out the game with two touchdown passes and two flawless quarters.

I use my game MVP status to get my own seat on the bus, tucked in the back, away from the rowdy linemen and the annoying loud country music being played by one of the assistant coaches. Peyton texted me her own play-by-play reactions throughout the game, and I've read them at least a dozen times. My favorite is when she sent the tongue-out emoji for some reason. I'm going to need clarification on that. I promise her I'll call when we get through the mountains, but by the time most of the guys on the bus are either passed out or watching videos on their phones, it's close to midnight.

I chance that she's awake, sinking low in my seat as I press call. I pop my earbuds in so I can keep the volume low. She answers in a groggy voice after about three rings.

"Hey, how late is it?"

I feel bad. She was asleep.

"It's almost midnight. I'm sorry, I just got a signal. You go back to sleep. I'll see you in the morning." I'm talking in a hushed tone, but it feels loud on the quiet bus. I maybe should have called during the country music binge. Of course, then I wouldn't have been able to hear her.

"*Hmm*, okay. Hey, Wy?"

"Yeah, baby?"

"I'm so proud of you."

I smile to myself, wishing I video called her instead so I could see the sleepy look on her face. I love it when her eyes fight to stay awake, and I love it even more when she gives in. Her lips always part with the sweetest breath, her nose crinkling whenever it's tickled. *Sometimes that's my fault . . . on purpose. Because it's cute.*

"I'm prouder," I say, knowing she's already fallen asleep and hasn't hung up. I listen to her sleep for a few minutes, the buzz of the fan in her room, the soft hum she makes when she nuzzles into her pillow. She's had to train herself to sleep on her back, and she's still never rested enough.

Since I'm still wired on the high from my game, and from hearing her voice, however brief, I decide the moment we get off this bus, I'm heading right to my truck and driving the sixty-five miles of desert to hold her through the rest of the early morning hours. I want to bring her breakfast in bed.

And then, I want to help her ride a horse again. Because I hate that I missed it, but I love that she can.

Chapter Twenty-Four

Peyton

At first, I think it's a dream. Wyatt's fingers sweep my hair from my face before moving to my arm, painting it with a soft touch that lulls me into a deeper dream.

But this isn't a dream. This is real. He's here, in my bed. And his hair is wet as if he just stepped out of the shower. I force my eyelids open for proof and am hit with the faint outline of his jaw. His lip tips up, the room softly lit from the bathroom light through the cracked door.

"Hi," he whispers.

"*Mmm*," I moan, wanting to shift to my side.

"Here, let me help," he says, moving the bolster pillow from under my knees to between them so I can lie straight on my side.

I can't do it for long, but I can long enough. His hand moves to my face, brushing my hair away again before his thumb traces along my cheekbone, down my jaw, and over my lips.

"It's still nighttime. Go back to sleep. I wanted to be here when you woke up," he says, pressing his lips to my forehead and holding them there.

"You were here when I woke up. Now I'm awake," I muse.

"*Shh*, no you're not. This is a dream. Go back to sleep."

Wyatt's soft chuckle draws me deep into his chest. I ball my hands up against his heart, my left hand holding my right. I've learned to let the left lead.

"I can't believe I didn't hear you shower," I say, breathing him in. He smells like the lavender soap my mom put in the guest bathroom, and his hair is soaking the pillow.

"I tried to be sneaky."

"You are very sneaky," I respond. "Now, play "Sandman.""

My nose grazes along his neck as he breathes out a quiet laugh in response to my latest nickname.

"Yes, ma'am."

"That's yes, Cheerleader," I correct. I never stopped being one.

His lips kiss my forehead again.

"Yes, Cheer Captain," he says, one-upping my request. I smile against his body, glad he slipped into my bed without a shirt on so I can taste his skin with my kiss.

"I'm not very good at lullabies." His fingers weave into my hair, the massage to my scalp making my eyes fall shut again. He's right. He's a terrible singer.

"Then, do what you're good at," I hum, already drifting thanks to his warmth and touch.

His body shifts a little, and I feel the heat from his breath at my ear.

"I'm good at this," he says, his tongue peeking out to sample a taste of my earlobe. His teeth nip at it next, and a shower of goose bumps trails down my neck all the way to my toes.

"You are," I sigh out, my eyes heavy but not so drowsy that I'm willing to turn any of this down.

My breath hitches when his palm slips under my T-shirt, and his cool fingers walk up my ribcage until his hand curves along my breast. I moan softly as his thumb rubs over my nipple. His mouth shifts to mine, his lips closing around my bottom one and sucking it in. His teeth graze along my skin as he brings his finger to his thumb under my shirt and rolls my nipple into a hard pebble.

"Sandman," I say, my voice dreamy, my lips a drunken smile.

Wyatt kisses my chin, trailing along my jaw, until his mouth stops at my ear again.

"Roll over," he says, his hand shifting to my hip, ready to help me.

I move to my back, bracing myself on my right shoulder as Wyatt adjusts the body pillow for me again. He swoops my shirt up my body, helping me slide my arms out one at a time before nestling my head into the pillow as he holds my back against his chest. He's so warm, and I can feel his cock pressing against my ass through his boxers.

"Close your eyes and go to sleep," he says, surely knowing that won't happen. I listen to him anyhow, shutting my eyes so I can't see what's coming.

I revel in the foreplay as his right arm curls around my body and his palm covers my left breast. His fingers graze along the hard peak, his touch featherlight, teasing me into a precious ache. If I had the strength to push my breast into his hand, I would. I can, however, press my ass into his cock, so I torture him just as he is me until his fingers pull my nipple into a raw bud as he grinds into me from behind.

"You're supposed to be sleeping," he utters, his voice quiet but heavy at my ear.

"I am sleeping," I lie. He presses into me again, pulling on my nipple until I gasp.

"Liar."

A quiet giggle escapes my mouth.

Wyatt continues to tease my breasts, at one point rolling both nipples between his fingers and thumbs then pulling them away from my body and letting his fingers snap with the pinch. I love the sting and instantly want more.

His right hand goes back to the tender touch, his thumb grazing the raw pink skin while his left palm inches down my body, pausing at the waistband of my cotton boxers. A low growl leaves his mouth as he presses his lips into the back of my neck.

"Fucking love this new fashion of yours," he says, his hand slipping into the shorts and trailing between my legs until his fingers slide through my wet, swollen pussy. I bring both of my fists to my mouth, stifling the cry I have to let out.

"You talk in your sleep," he says, continuing to rub his palm between my legs while his other hand kneads my breast.

"Uh huh." My voice is faint. Those are the only sounds I'm capable of.

I want him to push inside of me so badly, but also, the long, teasing strokes are almost better. My breath starts to match his rhythm, my chest filling with a deep inhale as his fingers rub against me, then I slowly exhale as he threatens to pull his hand away. His touch, however, never leaves. I'm not sure if he teases my pussy for minutes or hours. I'm not even sure if I dream throughout it. But eventually, it all becomes too much, and I clench my thighs around his hand, trapping him to me as his finger flicks my swollen clit and I break out into shivers and my body convulses with the best orgasm of my life.

"Now, go to sleep, or I'm going to take my hand away," he scolds, teasingly.

I move my hand down to cover his, pressing his palm into me, wanting to feel him against my still throbbing pussy. I could easily come again right now. In fact, I might. I may come all night. But first, I better get to sleep so he doesn't make good on that threat.

I awaken to the smell of bacon, and it pulls me out of the best dream. Wyatt and I were swimming in the ocean somewhere, laughing. We raced, and naturally, I was winning before this heavenly scent woke me up.

"Breakfast in bed. Full day ahead, so fuel up," Wyatt says, sliding the tray over my legs and sitting on the side of the bed next to me.

I rub the sleep from my eyes then pick up a crispy piece of bacon. I can tell Wyatt made this for me. It's his standard fare, lots of meat and scrambled eggs.

"Good?" he prompts.

"*Mmm hmm,*" I say, nodding and chewing.

My body aches, reminding me of my interrupted slumber last night. It pulls a smirk to my lips, and my cheeks warm with a blush. I tuck my chin and inhale the scent of Wyatt's shirt. He put it on me at some point last night. I'll wear it all day so I can remember everything.

"I let you sleep until nine. I figured that was only fair," he says, leaning into me and pressing a kiss to my cheek.

"*Mmm,* since it was your fault I was up late, yeah. That seems fair." I stuff another piece of bacon into my mouth and crunch down with extra bite as he glowers at me teasingly.

"Next time I'll let you sleep."

My mouth falls agape.

"Don't you dare!"

His mouth tightens into a sinister grin—dimples and all. I'm so far gone for this man.

He snags a piece of bacon for himself, and I try to swat his hand away, but he gets up from the bed before I can.

"You have fifteen minutes to get to the arena. Your mom is getting Otis ready."

Shoot, fifteen minutes used to feel like a lot, but now it sometimes takes me that long to get to the front door. Heeding his warning, I shovel a few more bites of egg into my mouth, then nudge the tray in his direction so he can move it to the dresser.

I push my blanket down my legs and twist so I can sit with my legs hanging off the side. My walker is near the bed, so I use it to brace myself as I attempt to stand. Wyatt hovers close by, and I can see him gesturing to help me in my periphery.

"I'll call an audible if I need you," I say, putting it in language he can understand. I did the same thing with my dad. Wyatt laughs.

"Fair."

I wrap my wrists into the straps I've started using to help me get a better grip on the walker. It keeps my hands from getting tired. Grip strength is a new goal for me. It takes me a few seconds to situate myself to a decent standing position before making my way to the dresser, where my mom has put most of my clothes into the top two drawers. I pull out a soft sports bra and a clean pair of undies, along with some loose joggers. I could spend a few minutes working my shirt off myself, but since it's Wyatt in here and nobody else, I look him in the eyes and nod.

"The thing about audibles is they're usually audible," he teases.

"Yeah, well, I didn't want to shout, 'come strip me' in case my dad's close by."

Wyatt's mouth forms an O and he's at my side in half a second. He's gentle, taking his time to pull his T-shirt over my head, and though his gaze lingers on my bare breasts, he shows restraint in touching them. I'm a little disappointed, but also, my fifteen minutes is dwindling. There's time for that later.

Once my bra is on and the shirt is back over my head, Wyatt helps me balance myself as I shimmy out of my shorts. Again, his eyes scan the length of my body, and he bites the tip of his tongue at the sight of my bare ass.

"You should see the front," I tease, stepping into my cotton panties one foot at a time.

"Fucking hell, that's not fair," he groans.

It feels nice to be seen that way, as something sexy. I've struggled a lot with my self-esteem the last few days. Not that I need to feel beautiful, but I do need to feel seen. Wyatt gave me that last night. And just now.

Once I'm dressed, shoes on my feet and my leg brace in place to shock my nerves and muscles into the right routine, Wyatt helps me navigate the hallway into the living room. It's empty, which means my father probably went to the high school this morning to make up for how much time he's missed with his players, and Grampa is probably at an appointment with my grandma. Wyatt gets the front door for me, and I slowly drag myself through it, staring at the temporary ramp my mom put in to make it easier for me to get up and down the few steps that lead to our driveway.

"Wow," Wyatt says as he walks beside me along my parents' ridiculously expansive driveway.

"Don't gawk," I say, frustration building in my stomach. I get that this feels impressive to him. I admit that it *is* impressive—that I've come this far and have gotten this strong. But I want to run. And this . . . it isn't running.

"Wouldn't dare," Wyatt says.

I swallow down that guilty feeling I get whenever I snap at someone. I open my mouth to apologize, but when I meet his eyes, he shakes his head and utters, "Don't."

I bite my lower lip and nod, focusing instead on the pathway ahead. Getting on the horse is the easy part of this. It's the trek over various terrains to make my way to the barn that's the biggest challenge. I'm sure we've gone over the fifteen-minute mark, but I've definitely gotten faster. My leg feels steadier, too. I can tell that the exoskeleton is working to improve my sense of balance, but I'm not naïve enough to think I don't need this walker.

My mom pulls Otis out as we step into the dirt near the barn. He's our oldest horse, practically an uncle to me at this point. I grew up with him, and his gentle soul seems to be exactly what my heart and body need to heal.

"You ready?" My mom holds the reins out for me to take.

"Yes," I say, glancing to Wyatt for help. "Just sort of spot me. You'll know where I need you most."

"Okay."

I take the reins in my left hand and brace my body weight on the walker with my right hand. It takes a few attempts for me to shift my body so I'm facing Otis's side. I grip the saddle as my mom pulls the walker out of the way, and my focus drops to the stirrup.

"Take your time," my mom says.

Quit racing yourself.

"Can she pull herself up?" Wyatt mutters his question to my mom, probably not wanting to break my concentration, but it still pokes at my pride that he asks her when I'm right here.

"Yes, she can," I respond. I take in a deep breath, then add, "Sort of."

"Do you want Wyatt to do it? Or me?" My mom wants me to want Wyatt to do it, probably because I've been a little snippy. She's right. He's trying to help. And I want him to see me do this. He needs to. For me, and for him.

"Wy, can you help place my right foot in the stirrup?" My gaze flits to him for a second, and I catch the brief panic that widens his eyes and opens his mouth. It kind of fires me up, makes me want to show off a little, which is good, because I'm going to need every ounce of upper body strength I've got.

Wyatt moves one hand under my knee, lifting my leg to waist high before taking my foot in his other hand. His mouth is pulled tight with concentration, and it takes him a few seconds to figure out how to maneuver my foot into the stirrup. I fight the urge to hop on my left leg. I know better now. I tried that last time and fell on my ass. Instead, I give myself a moment to feel all the places I'm connected to a base —the ground under my left foot, the stirrup on my right, even if it feels strange, and Otis, my wall directly in front of me.

"You ready, boy?" I run my palm along his body, and he dips his snout, tucking his head enough to see me. He loves me.

"I'm right here. Wyatt's got your leg." My mom steps into the left side of my body, her hands bracing my lateral muscles and my upper back while Wyatt's hands move back to my right foot and my right thigh.

"On three," I say.

"One. Two. Three!" I grunt the final number out and pull up on the handles my mom fashioned on Otis's saddle. The straps wrapped around my left hand dig into my skin, and my right arm shakes from the weight of my body. I don't quit, though. The more it strains my healthy muscles, the harder I work to climb higher. My mom helps with a small boost under my left thigh, and finally, after what feels like several long minutes, I'm high enough to swing my left leg over and embrace Otis from the saddle.

"Good boy," I say, rubbing his neck and falling forward to kiss this beautiful animal. My eyes tear up, just like they did yesterday.

"Good boy," I repeat, feeling the warmth of Otis's neck and the flex of his muscles under my chest and hands as I hug him.

"Wyatt, you want to drive?" My mom holds the reins out for my boyfriend, his smile a work of wonder. I can see the pride etched into the creases at the sides of his eyes, and I know he's fighting off happy tears, too.

"You can cry a little if you want to," I say, maybe teasing him a little but mostly giving him permission to feel. This is big. I've done this twice now, and this time? It was easier. As hard as it was to get up here, it was easier.

"Ha, yeah. Maybe a little," he admits, running his forearm over his eyes as he sniffles away his reaction.

He takes the reins from my mom, who walks alongside him in case something goes wrong. Otis is the horse my mom uses for her most delicate clients. He is also the horse of choice for all the autism families who come here. He has a way of bringing out joy. And as he takes long, slow steps across the dirt pathway that leads to the arena, he gives that joy to me.

"Is this right?" Wyatt glances over his shoulder to my mom, his eyes locked in an open position, his body rigid. It's funny, because for a man who flings his body into other men and into the air just to move a ball a few yards, he's being awfully cautious.

"It's perfect, Wyatt. You can go a little faster," my mom says.

Wyatt's eyes flit to me, and I smile and nod.

"I'm comfortable. And Otis doesn't really run anymore." *I don't run so much anymore, either, Otis.*

Wyatt picks up the pace a bit, and we make loops and figure eights around the arena, the warm Arizona sun stinging my cheeks with welcome heat. Otis's tail flaps at flies, and the ends tickle my legs—both of them. I've started noting everything I feel, like a mental journal or list for me to appreciate. There are still things that don't quite feel right when I encounter them, like certain motions and pressure against my bones. But I get hints of my old self coming back. I miss her. I can't wait to blend her with this new version of myself. She's stronger.

She can do anything.

Chapter Twenty-Five

Wyatt

I've never been great at interviews.

I know it's part of the game, at least at this level and beyond. The media side of things is what drives the train, so to speak. Celebrity begets TV contracts, and advertisers bring money to programs, which, in turn, brings more talent. It's a vicious cycle, the business of sports. And it can get nasty.

While I like to be honest and transparent about everything, I also try to be private. When my dad died, there was a lot of local press about it. He was a big voice in the cancer community for firefighters. And our battle to get him care and coverage was an important story. I just hate that we had to tell it. It was hard on my mom. Hard on me.

I'm coming off the best game of my career, though. And we're looking at taking on a tough Texas Valley at home this weekend. I'd like to remain Coach's "guy." So here I am, at practice an hour early to talk with the guy from *Althetico* about who knows what. Coach asked, and I said yes. Running away is no longer an option, either, because he's here now. Coach Skye is walking him up to the press box in the stadium. We thought he might like the view. I hate that I'm in a glass box with only one door out.

"And here he is," Coach Skye says. He eyes me for an extra beat, the tension still very much present between us since I blew up at him last week. We never discussed it beyond him calling me an asshole as he stormed out of Coach's office. On the field, it's been business as usual. I'm kind of bracing myself for him to call me an asshole now.

"Wyatt Stone, meet Kelly Brooks, *senior* college football reporter for *Athletico*." The senior thing must be important, I guess, since Coach Skye leaned into it.

"Kelly, nice to meet you," I say, standing up from the swivel chair I've been spinning in for about ten minutes. I reach out a hand toward the stocky man who appears to be in his forties. He grips my hand back, his shake firm. There's a certain former-coach vibe emanating from him, from the short-sleeved plaid button down to the nylon cord attached to the temple tips of his glasses.

"Likewise, Wyatt. I really appreciate your time. I'll try to keep this to the hour they set aside."

We smile at each other, and I hope like hell he can't read through mine, because *we set aside an hour for this?*

"It's fine," I lie. My chest is tight, but I'm sure I'll relax when we get into it.

Coach Skye pulls up a chair, and it helps having him in the room as we run through some of the nitty gritty stuff for his story. We cover my background, my love for the game, high school, and my dad. Turns out Kelly's the son of a firefighter, too. When we start to nerd out over firefighter culture, Coach Skye excuses himself, I think feeling a little awkward and left out. Of course, the second he leaves the room, *senior* reporter Kelly dives into the hard stuff.

"So, whose idea was it to run two quarterbacks this year?" He sits back in his chair, his phone recording everything from the table between us. He jots down my key comments in a small notepad propped on his knee.

I smirk and turn my head a tick to give him a sideways glance. He chuckles.

"Yeah, I've been doing this a long time, and I know the best answers come when the stiffs leave the room."

"Stiffs, huh?" I glance through the window to where Coach Skye is jogging out to the sidelines, waving a hand and blowing his whistle.

"Yeah, very few coaches make for good interviews. I mean, there are exceptions, of course. I interviewed Bobby Knight back in the day, and he was colorful. Had plenty to say, most of it unprintable."

We both laugh. Also, he's got some good street cred.

"And I've given a good interview or two in my time, back when I coached in Texas." *Ah, yes. I heard that accent.*

"I had a feeling you coached. Call it instinct." I leave out the clues I got from his fashion. I need him to like me, at least until this story goes up.

He smiles and shakes his head, holding up a hand.

"I was probably one of the worst coaches in Texas high school football history. My record was . . . abysmal. But I doubled our wins in the five years I was there."

"You go from one to two?" I joke.

"Ha!" He points at me, squinting one eye. "You're funny. And close. I went from four to eight. Even made playoffs the final year. Got our asses handed to us from Permian."

I chuckle.

"They're legends."

"Indeed, and for good reason."

He taps the end of his pen on his notepad and glances at his phone before looking back at me. I think he senses my paranoia, or hell, since he's been at this so long, he's probably inciting it. After a few awkwardly quiet seconds, he reaches for his phone and pauses the recording, flipping the screen and showing me.

"Sometimes the recording makes people nervous," he says, laying the phone back down on the table.

I smirk at it, then meet his gaze.

"I'm not sure that's the part that makes me nervous."

His lips pull into a tight smile and his eyes flit to his notepad. He taps the pen on the paper a few more times, then pops his gaze back up to mine.

"You weren't on board with two quarterbacks, were you?"

I shake my head and pull my brow in.

"I didn't say that." I don't want him choosing my words for me. I nudge his phone toward him and lift my chin.

"Go ahead and turn that back on." I'm uneasy either way; may as well be uneasy but quoted accurately.

Kelly restarts the recording and licks his lips, seeming to choose his words strategically.

"The two QB thing—it seems to be working out well for you guys so far."

I lift my brows, waiting for the question, and eventually realize I'm meant to agree with him.

"We're three and oh." That's confirmation enough.

He nods and jots that killer quote down.

"You've been running the show here since you were a freshman, though."

"Ah, I've been throwing the ball. Coach Byers runs the show. He's been at the helm for a long time. He deserves the credit." I may have learned a few things in my PR and messaging classes to keep me out of trouble after all.

"Spoken like a loyal quarterback who loves his coach. But it had to sting a little, no? That he wanted to change things up?"

He pokes his tongue into the inside of his bottom lip as he waits patiently.

"There's no room for egos out on that field. It's a team sport, and Coach saw potential in switching things up to start the season."

Shit, I slipped.

"Start, huh? So, are you moving back into the starting role this week? Have we seen all we'll see of Hampton this season?"

I shake my head.

"I don't know. I'm not the coach. I can tell you that Bryce and I are both ready to do what needs to be done, to answer Coach's call and help lead this team into a playoff position. That's always the goal."

Phew. Back on point.

"So, that potential you mentioned . . . you think he had a reason to think Hampton had an edge that you didn't when it came to the start against Cal?"

He waits me out as I mull that question over. I know what he's trying to fish out of me—he wants me to say I was mentally distracted because of Peyton's injury. He wants to make this a story about us rather than simply the game. I won't pull her into it.

"I can't speak for him, and you know that would be a foolish move. Coach Byers speaks for himself."

His mouth pulls into a knowing smirk, and his eyes stick to mine for a few extra seconds while he waits me out. I'm not breaking, though. That's all he's going to get on that subject.

"Okay, well, I had to try. You know Coach Byers is a man of very few words." He glances up from his notebook, and once again, I merely shrug. Nope. Not falling for it.

"Let's move on to your future, then. Heisman talk is something that's been bandied about with your name in the past. It was a different kind of start to this season, but your game against Cal has people talking. Are you feeling that pressure?"

I relax a little, laughing off the compliments.

"I'm glad I put up good numbers last week. We need all the yards and big stops we can get with this schedule. And while the chatter about me is nice, it's not what I'm focusing on. I want to win games. Make the playoffs. Leave this place on the highest note possible. Anything after that is—" I shrug, not wanting to get into my future right now.

"So, the combine. We might see you out there?"

"You might," I say, purposely vague.

I'm having a harder time masking my impatience, and I think Kelly can feel it. I glance out the window and wait until Coach Byers looks in my direction. I hold up a finger, and he nods. It's a show for Kelly's purposes, to hurry this along and get my ass back down on the field where I'm far more comfortable.

"Well, thanks for your time, Wyatt. I'm rooting for you. I think you're an exciting player to watch. And my best to Peyton."

My mouth tinges with his overstep, and a sneer creeps along my lips.

"Thank you," is all I utter. And I don't shake his hand a second time, instead getting up to hold the door open for him as he tucks his notebook away and drops his phone into his bag.

I follow him down the steps toward the field, one of the reps from the university's athletic director's office waiting to walk him out.

"Good luck, again, Wyatt," he says, holding his hand out to me in front of everyone, probably to see what I'll do. It kills me to give in, but if I meant what I said—that this place is about the team and not the individual—then I have to get over myself and shake hands with this piranha to leave a good impression. His grip is as firm as before, and I try to forget the feel of it by slinging the football as hard as I can for the next hour.

It seems Bryce is ready to work out his own tension, because he fires the ball back with the same amount of zest. When one of his passes nails me in the diaphragm, knocking my breath away for a brief second, I tuck the ball under my arm and level him with a stare.

"You have to talk to that ass face too?" I ask.

"Nope. Not that ass face," he says, holding his palms out and snapping for the ball. I toss it back as his jaw flexes and he works through his own shit. I don't have to press him for details, though. Because his headache is related to him. And that kind of ass face is a whole lot harder to shake.

Chapter Twenty-Six

Peyton

I didn't think I would be up for a house full of people, but it turns out having my other grandparents fly in and pairing my Grandpa Rich with my Grandpa Buck was a gamechanger.

"What exactly is this thing?" Tasha pushes the makeshift "speed walker" that my Grandpa Rich put together with a little engineering help from my Grandpa Buck. The two were out in the shop working all day yesterday, and they refused to let anyone in. It pissed Grandma Rose off because she was sure they were smoking cigars and drinking brandy, both major no-no's for Buck. Instead, the two handiest men in my life were inventing me something to help get me not just walking but hopefully running sooner rather than later.

"I named it Josh," I say, pulling myself up to stand between the balance bars.

"*Hmm*, Josh. He's cute," Tasha says, tapping the front where my grandpas built in a headlight.

"Yeah, they envision me taking this puppy out at night sometimes. I'm not there yet, but maybe. Eventually." I move my hands to the more comfortable grips, ones at a natural height rather than at my armpits, which is what I've been dealing with.

"So, how does this thing make you . . . faster?" Tasha quirks a brow.

A deep chuckle gurgles in my throat before I press the button for the small motor that kicks on.

"It drives." I grin, squeezing the two-handed clutch system lightly, which starts Josh in motion. The all-terrain wheels roll slowly, thanks to a regulator—Grandpa Buck's idea. I move along the kitchen floor with the device, focusing more on the movement of my hips and legs than how to move a hunk of metal straight ahead.

"Josh, you badass. Look at you navigate that engineered hardwood surface." Tasha pats the headlight like she's petting a dog's snout, and I unfurl the clutch and kill the engine.

"The hope is I start doing more of this outside. I'm sick of the house, and I can only ride and walk Otis in circles so many times."

Tasha nods in understanding, then holds her arm out for me to hold for balance as I work my way back to the kitchen chair. Wyatt loaded Tasha up with most of my school materials, along with my laptop, and she came over this morning to help me set a few things up. The university offered to give me a medical withdrawal, but I still want to graduate, even if it won't be on campus or I won't be walking across the stadium field with my graduating class. *That pomp and circumstance is over-rated anyhow.*

"Are you going to be able to make up the month you've missed?" Tasha asks.

"I mean, writing papers is the only other thing on my daily agenda at this point, so I think the odds are on my side," I answer as I fire up my laptop. It instantly flashes a low battery warning, so I dig into the tote filled with various chargers that she also brought me. I hold up the one for my reading light along with the one for my e-reader.

"Your boyfriend didn't know what went with what, so you got 'em all." She shrugs and takes the tote by the bottom, tipping it upside down so everything spills out on the table. Something clanks off the tabletop and onto the floor, so Tasha drops to her hands and knees in search of it while I spot my laptop cord and untangle it from the mess.

My screen reboots, bringing up the university home page along with the various news links, including one headline that catches my eye in the athletics section—TWO QUARTER-BACK SYSTEM WHEN THERE'S ONLY ROOM FOR ONE.

"Fuck," I mumble.

"Yeah, fuck indeed," Tasha says, her head popping up from under the table.

I furrow my brow, wondering what her reaction is for.

"You know what this is?" She pinches a delicate ring, holding it in front of me, and my eyes jet open so wide I think they might fall out.

"Is that—?" I take it in my hand to study the intricate pattern on the band woven into a setting that holds an impressive princess-cut diamond. The ring is old, but it's polished to perfection. My gut says it's probably a family heirloom. My heart wants it to be for me. And then my fucking head is screaming all the reasons that ring should be put away and saved for later.

"Girl, that's an engagement ring!" Tasha's voice is loud, and my head spins around while I scope out every corner of this house within my sightline to make sure we're alone. There are a lot of people here right now, people who would lose their minds if they saw this ring.

I pocket it and glare at Tasha.

"We don't know what it's for—"

"Peyt, yes we do."

"Gah!" I drop my shoulders with my sigh.

"Look, all I'm saying is you need to find a way to get that ring back in Wyatt's possession, or you need to bring it up. And then let whatever comes next . . . happen." She's grinning like an idiot, and there's a part of me that's ready to jump up and down with her, screaming with glee. Except, I can't jump up and down right now. I can't take my classes on campus. I can't fucking get around this kitchen without some whack invention my grandfathers put together.

"I'll figure it out. In the meantime, can you maybe . . ." I shake my head, knowing my best friend is shit with secrets. My guess is she'll text our friend Lexi about this by the time she hits my driveway. Regardless, she crosses her heart and pulls her lips in tight.

I hug my friend goodbye after she helps me organize the mess of cords, and she doesn't bring the ring up again, though she does waggle her brows as she leaves. She just wants a wedding with an open bar.

The weight of the ring in my pocket feels heavy, and I'd swear it's burning into my thigh, like one of those hobbits with the magic ring. I do my best to push it to the back of my mind while I return my attention to starting some schoolwork, but I'm quickly diverted by that headline I saw before.

Like a glutton, I click on it. I try to simply scan it at first, not letting myself get caught up by the opinion clearly woven into the *Athletico* piece. But then a quote from Alex Hampton, Bryce's dad, catches my eye.

"All I'm saying is they brought my son here for a reason. Maybe it's time they go all in and let him do the job."

My blood boils. I read the line again, parsing together the only facts I know—Bryce hates his father, the man isn't intimately knowledgeable about his son's anything, and there isn't a single quote from Coach Byers in this story.

I click on the tab that offers more from the story, including podcast bits recorded from the interview Kelly whoever this guy is did with Wyatt. It doesn't help me feel any better. Wyatt is clearly irritated by his questions, and when asked about his name being tossed around in Heisman conversations, Wyatt shuts it down completely, claiming all that stuff doesn't interest him.

It must interest him. Heisman? The combine? The draft? What's happened to his plans?

Me. I happened.

I'm in a pretty good spiral by the time my mom comes home, ready to haul me to my check-in with my neurologists and then Dr. K She's intuitive, so I get away with about five minutes of silence during the car ride to Tucson before she pulls off on an exit with nothing but a Wendy's and a gas station.

"You craving fries?" I ask, my moody tone not masked very well.

My mom whips into the gas station parking lot with her full tank and pushes the gearshift into park before twisting in her seat and leveling me with one of her threatening glares. I let my head fall sideways against the head rest as I match her urgent gaze with my despondent one.

"I'm not going to coddle you like Dad does. What's up your ass, Peyton?"

She holds her eyebrows high, her nostrils flexing with her quickening breath. I get my impatience from her. I roll my head along the passenger seat, turning my focus to the old pick-up truck parked about a dozen yards away. An older man is filling the back with water jugs.

"You think he's prepping for the end of the world?" I joke.

I feel my mom's gaze stick to me.

"Yeah, I do. He senses it's coming by the energy you're giving off. Now, spill it."

I shake my head and flit my gaze down, feeling the sting of

tears. This has all been a lot. And I don't want to talk about the ring that is now tucked in my underwear drawer, but I do want to talk about Wyatt and how I feel as if he's giving up and picking the wrong thing.

"There was this story in *Athletico* that made it sound like they were replacing Wyatt with Bryce. And I can't help but feel he's giving up things for me, and I don't know—"

My mom punches out a hard laugh, and I roll my eyes to look at her.

"I feel guilty about it. He spends so much time going back and forth, and I know Bryce and him have worked a lot of their shit out, but you know he wants to take the starting job. Bryce is ambitious, Mom."

She opens her mouth to respond but quickly snaps it shut, I think tempering her snap-judgement a little. She breathes in deeply through her nose, holding her mouth in a faint, closed-lip smile as her head tilts a little.

"Your dad and I, we've told you before why you're our little miracle," she begins.

I nod softly, biting my lip. I know my mom had a pretty traumatic miscarriage. They weren't sure they'd be able to have me. I've been thinking about that a lot lately, too. About how maybe I won't be able to have kids. And Wyatt, he deserves to be a father. He was born to be one more than he was born to play football.

"What I never told you was how I kept it all to myself when it happened. I didn't tell your dad. I didn't tell Grandma or Grandpa. The only one who knew was Aunt Sarah, and that's because she was there when I lost—"

My mom's eyes glass over, and I reach across the center console to squeeze her forearm. She covers my hand with hers.

"I have very few regrets in life, Peyton. I believe things happen in life for a reason, and there are lessons to be learned. But that moment, it wasn't a lesson. I made a choice. A really bad choice. I swallowed my trauma and let it break my heart over and over again without asking for help from the one person who cared the most. Instead of asking questions, I made assumptions. I pushed him away when, really, all he wanted was to be there for me. To be with me. And I regret that I missed out on his support. I could have used it."

I hold my mom's stare for a beat, her message pretty clear. I keep swearing to myself that I'm not pushing Wyatt away, but really—I am. Not forcefully, but subtly. A little at a time. And if I'm not careful, that may be my biggest regret.

Chapter Twenty-Seven

Wyatt

I don't want to call my mom. When she gave me her ring, the one my dad gave her when he proposed, it was a pretty emotional moment. It was over the summer, and I was telling her about my plan to ask Peyton to move in with me, and then the conversation sort of rolled into future plans and me proposing soon.

She gave me the ring to hold on to for when the time was right. Well, it's about time. I've been thinking about it a lot lately, even before Peyton's injury. But to be honest, the last month has only made me want to ask her to be mine for life even more. I want her to have a symbol of my promise to her, to know that I'm not going anywhere. That I'm in this, with her, for it all.

And now I can't find the fucking ring.

Anywhere.

My finger hovers over my mom's contact info on my phone, twitching. My stomach feels sick even though I know she'll tell me not to worry and we'll look together. But I've already searched everywhere there is. I'm afraid, somehow, I've lost a token from my dad, something so important that, wherever it is,

I'm sure it's glowing bright. One would think that would help me find it, but nope. Nada.

"I can't," I mutter to myself, shoving my phone in my back pocket before grabbing my keys and heading out to my truck.

The sun is setting. My body is exhausted. Practice was killer today. We all felt it, Bryce more than me, because even though that boneheaded comment that hit *Athletico* wasn't his but his father's, Coach took it out on him all the same.

So much running.

My legs quiver as I lift my body into my truck, and I halt once I'm in my seat, hands gripping the wheel as I imagine what this is like for Peyton. This is how everything feels to her. Exhausting.

That thought wedges into my mind as I rush to Whiskey and Tasha's apartment, hoping like hell that I somehow put that ring in something of his. We moved a lot of things last month, and I ended up giving him some of our shared appliances and electronics. Boxes got muddled. It's possible. Not likely because I'm pretty sure I kept that ring in the watch box in my sock drawer, but since it's not there, well . . .

I take the stairs two at a time when I get to Whiskey's. I pound on the door, but the music is blasting on the other side. I know he's home because I parked next to his truck, and that music? That's not Tasha music. He's probably dancing around in his boxers or showering with his beer, a weird thing he likes to do. He saw some dudes doing it on social media and decided to make it part of his brand, whatever that brand is. I think it's basically loud, drunk, and obnoxious. I'm probably being judgmental, though, because *he won't answer the fucking door!*

On a whim, I twist the handle, and when the door pushes open, I exhale, glad I won't have to go all Chuck Norris on it and kick it down. It takes me a few seconds to come to terms with the reality on the other side, though.

Whiskey's naked. And so is Tasha. And they are . . . *connected.*

"Oh, my God!" I slap both hands over my eyes, and the last thing I glimpse is my friend's very white ass pumping into Peyton's best friend from behind.

"Ahhh, what the hell! Wyatt, get the fuck out!" Something crashes against the open door as Tasha screams. I peel my fingers from my face as I glance down and see pieces of a remote.

"I'm out. I'm out!" I flatten my palm over my face again and spin around, feeling for the door and quickly stepping outside and flinging it closed behind me.

What the fuck?

My heart racing, I pace back and forth on the small landing outside their door. The music stops inside, and I move to the stairs, my wobbly legs now a whole lot worse. I step down one stair then sit on my ass, digging my thumbs into the corners of my eyes while I nervously chuckle. The door creaks behind me, and someone shuffles in my direction. Whiskey's sock-clad feet eventually come into view. I refuse to look up.

I cover my eyes with both palms again.

"Dude, I'm not looking."

Whiskey's deep belly laugh makes me join him.

"What the hell, man?" I say, cracking an eyelid open and glancing up when I feel him move into the space next to me to sit down. He hands me a beer and I take it, popping the cap off and swigging down half.

"I told you I was wearing her down," he says.

Smug fucker is grinning wide. I shake my head at him and take another sip of my beer before setting it down and leaning back on my palms.

"You're going to have to fill me in. Is this . . . new?" I point over my shoulder as my friend shrugs.

"It's been a week or so. We had a competitive Wii game of

ping-pong, and then one thing led to another, and well—" He smiles through his dip of beer and winks.

"You smooth motherfucker."

We sit side-by-side for a few minutes, finishing our beers while I pepper him with questions he can't seem to answer. He's not sure if they're dating, but they are *definitely* fucking. And he likes her a whole hell of a lot. That I knew. He has for a while. I just hope this means something to Tasha, because if she's simply messing with him to pass the time, it's going to break this big man into so many pieces.

Eventually, I explain why I barged in on the two of them, and after getting permission from Tasha to let me inside, Whiskey and I search through the few boxes he still hasn't unpacked by their entertainment center. Tasha forbids me from entering the bedroom, where she's locked herself inside and swears she's never coming out again.

"I can take a look through there, but it's mostly her clothes and makeup shit. I took my stuff straight from drawers and my old closet to the new ones," he says.

I wave off his offer, pretty sure I lost the ring on my own somewhere else. I give him a hug on my way out and ask him to keep the ring business between us for now. If Tasha finds out, then any element of surprise I may have planned down the road is off the table. There are a lot of things Whiskey isn't good at, like saying no to freebies and not escalating conflict. But keeping secrets for his friends? He's got that on lockdown.

Back in my truck, I let the last thirty minutes really set in, and decide rather than calling my mom, I'll give my place one more toss. I didn't check the washer, and maybe the ring hitched a ride somehow and ended up in there. Plus, the only thing I can think of doing now is sharing this massive revelation I just had with Peyton.

I buckle up and sync my phone, pressing call while I back out of my spot next to Whiskey's truck. When the phone goes right to voicemail, I press END CALL and give it another try. After three attempts of nothing getting through, I grab my phone at the stoplight and check our shared location app to see if maybe she's out in the arena. When her icon shows the University Hospital, I panic.

Flipping the car around, I dial Reed, and call him relentlessly until he finally picks up.

"Wyatt, she's fine. Everything's okay," he says, knowing I must have seen her location since I'm calling him.

I roll to a stop, my body tingling with adrenaline. My head is sweaty, so I pull my hat off and toss it into the passenger seat and rub my forearm across my brow. I put on my hazards and wave the line of traffic around me when the light turns green, ignoring the honks from assholes who don't know what a panic attack is.

"She and Nolan were at her neurology appointment, and they were concerned about something they saw. It's a small blood clot, and they wanted to deal with it right away rather than risk having it travel up her leg."

"Okay," I say, not fully understanding what Reed said. I'm still trying to let the part about her being okay settle in.

"We'll probably be here overnight. It was a quick procedure. But she's going to need to heal from this. I'll call you when—"

"No, I'm coming. I'm already five minutes out. I have to come, Reed. I need to be there."

He doesn't argue, likely knowing it's the same thing he would do if our situations were swapped. He gives me vague directions for the room Peyton's in, and I jot down what I can using an old golf pencil and my last oil change receipt from my glove box. I hit one-ten on the highway to the hospital, and I'm parked next to Reed's pickup in minutes.

I sprint past the information desk to the bank of elevators, repeating the room number—sixty-five-oh-one—until the elevator doors open on the sixth floor. I'm hit with an intersection of hallways that all look the same, so I ask for help when a nurse pushes through a set of doors and heads my way. She sends me down the right corridor, and by the time I make it to Peyton's room, her original doctor, Dr. K, is leaving. We make brief eye contact as we pass, and I try to dissect meaning from his dour expression. I know everything I need to, though, when I slide the curtain back a hair and find Peyton weeping in her mom's arms. And like a useless dumb jock, all I can do is stand here and feel helpless.

Chapter Twenty-Eight

Peyton

An entire month's worth of accomplishments, gone. Wiped out.

Pointless.

Wyatt has been sitting with me in silence for an hour. I think he can sense I don't want talk. It's not only that I'm disappointed, but rather that I feel completely defeated. And unworthy.

"Peyton?" The nurse who's been taking my vitals today pops her head into my room, and both Wyatt and I lean forward, awaiting her words.

"Yeah?" I croak.

"Your parents are pulling around. It's time to head home. We'll bring the wheelchair in a minute."

Such succinct instructions. Nothing about them makes me feel empowered. Someone else will push me down the hall. Someone else will drive me home. I won't be going to my apartment at school or waking up the next day to take a new step forward. I'll be working on getting out of bed again and straightening my leg, forcing it to feel the ground beneath it.

"*Groundhog Day*," I utter.

"Huh?" Wyatt breathes out.

I shake my head.

"It's like that movie, the one where he lives the same day over and over? *Groundhog Day*? Until he can figure out the magic thing that lets him move on to the next day." My parents love that movie. That movie and everything Adam Sandler has ever made. When other kids watched cartoons, I watched *Happy Gilmore*.

"I remember that one," Wyatt says, moving his hand along my back. His fingertips touch the scar on my spine. It feels different, and I shudder.

"Sorry," he says, pulling his hand away.

I shake my head.

"It doesn't hurt. I just . . . hate it."

His eyes drop and he slides off the bed.

"Oh."

"It's not you. I mean, I hate what that scar represents. And I'm going to hate the new one, too. And then next month, ha! Probably something else." I flap my arms at my side, and Wyatt's gaze stays on my hands for a beat.

"You know, last time you couldn't move your arm all that much at the start. So, it's not all gone." His eyes flit up to me, but I can't meet his stare. I can feel the flat line of my mouth.

Wyatt helps me move to the edge of the bed when the nurse comes with the chair, and he follows along as I'm pushed to the elevator, then down to the lobby where my dad takes over, guiding me out to my grandmother's car. They decided to swap out my mom's SUV today for something with a lower profile. It's easier to climb into a sedan.

"I'll see you at the house," Wyatt says, taking my hand briefly as my mom helps me straighten my legs in the passenger seat.

"Oh, you don't have to—" He's gone before I finish, and when I turn to face my mom, she levels me with look of pity.

"Don't," I say, not wanting the lecture about pushing people away.

"I'll stop if you stop," she says, and as pissed off as her retort makes me, it also makes me puff out a tiny laugh.

My dad climbs into the back seat and we make the long drive home. The driveway is packed with cars, which means everyone is here—both sets of grandparents, Aunt Sarah and Uncle Jason, and Wyatt's mom. My parents had planned on having everyone over for dinner, and I guess they didn't change the plans despite, well, fucking *this*.

We pull in and park, Wyatt coming to a stop behind us, and my dad rushes around the car to open my door. In seconds, it's nothing but hands reaching in for me. It overwhelms my senses, and nobody seems to be able to figure out the best way to get me out of the car. What's worse? Nobody seems to be asking me—the one needing out of the fucking car!

"Just . . . stop!" I slap my thighs, and the sting on my skin of each leg hurts equally. I blink for a second, registering that fact and putting it in my new book of wins. If I'm going to do this all again, I need to do it my way. And people need to listen.

"Wyatt, help me get out of this low-rider. Mom and Dad? Go inside. Get dinner going so we can all eat, and then everyone can go back to where they came from, and I can go to bed."

My dad's jaw flexes, his instinct to dig in and fight me warring with wanting to make his daughter happy. My mom meets my stare, and I mouth, "Please." She gives me a soft nod and turns into my father, pressing her hand on his chest to urge him inside.

"They've got this," she says.

Wyatt hangs outside the car, his hands balled into fists at his sides. I think he's waiting for me to tell him what to do, which is why I wanted it to be him. Of everyone in my family, he's the most likely to hear me. To listen. But I need him to hear it all. Even the part he's not going to like.

"I just want to sit in the air with you for a little while. Help me to the back of the car?" I look up at him and he nods.

Kneeling, he scoops a hand under my thighs to help me twist in the seat. I loop my hands around his neck and hang from him as he holds my hips and helps me into a standing position. I feel like I'm choking him, and my body feels heavier than it did before.

I prompt Wyatt to brace me under my right arm, and he holds me tightly against his side, my feet barely needing to work as we slowly make our way to the back of my grandmother's car. I lean against the bumper, not quite sitting but not standing either. It will have to do. Wyatt mimics me.

"Until the sun sets, yeah?"

"Okay," he answers.

I close my eyes and inhale the desert air. There's a thread of coolness running through it, like fall wants to happen. It's different out here. The heat has levels, and when it's football season, it's still hot in the desert, but not *as* hot as it can be. But this ribbon of coolness isn't warm at all. It has a chill. I'm ready for it.

"I don't want you to come for a while," I say.

"Peyt—"

I hold up my hand, unable to look at him.

"I'm not being a brat or trying to be dramatic. I'm just being real, Wyatt. I know Bryce had nothing to do with the story that guy wrote—"

"*Pssh*, that was just bullshit press, Peyt. That's nothing."

I give in to the temptation to look him in the eyes, and when I do, as hard as he's trying to hide it, I can see his reservation. There's a weight pulling them down. His upper lip twitches. He feels the pressure.

"You said the Heisman talk wasn't important," I point out.

He shrugs.

"It's not."

I laugh, then lean my head back to look at the sky when my eyes water.

"But it is, Wyatt. You've known for years that this draft class is going to be tough. You've put in so much work. It's the finish line. You cannot take yourself out of the race. Not when you're this close. And I . . . I have to go back to the starting line. It's going to take me years to get back to something close to what I was. At least a year to walk on my own."

"So, I'll help you," he says.

My gaze snaps to his.

"But I don't want you helping me. I want you fighting for your dream."

We stare into each other's eyes for several long, quiet seconds while the sun drops below the mountain crests. It paints us with a hue of orange, then violet. It's beautiful. Wyatt's beautiful. I love him so much. But I can't be the thing that pulls him away from his dream.

"I don't want to be the reason you have resentment in your heart," I finally say.

"Peyt, I couldn't. Not ever."

I shake my head because I know he means it, but I also know it isn't true. Nobody plans to be resentful; it simply creeps in over time.

"I'll be right here. We'll talk every day. Even after the draft. And I'll memorize whatever time zone you're in when you get there, to whatever team is lucky to score you. And then, maybe . . ."

"Fucking *maybe*? Peyt, there's no maybe. There's us. This isn't going anywhere. You're being—"

"Real. I'm being real, Wyatt. And I agree. I believe in us. But for now, I need to know that you are giving football your all. And I promise I'll give this my all too."

He shakes his head again, his gaze drifting off to the side before he steps in front of me and cups my cheeks with both hands. He licks his lips, then closes the short distance to press his mouth to mine, taking his time to suck in my top lip before my bottom. It's a deep kiss, his tongue tangling with mine until he pulls a soft moan from my body, and my hands move to clutch the front of his sweatshirt on instinct.

When he pulls away, he holds my stare, his mouth a hard line, his eyes devoid of tears—but nothing about his expression is happy.

"We'll talk about this more later. I'll let you have your way for now, but . . . uh uh. I'm not done with my argument just yet."

I sigh and he quickly retorts, "Sorry, but I'm not."

He glances down to our feet, and I follow his gaze. Our toes don't match up, his left foot pointing at me while mine veers off to the side. I can't feel it doing that. I feel the shoe over my foot, the compression sock that squeezes me all the way up to my knee. I even feel the chill in the air bringing my skin to pebbles. But I can't tell that my foot isn't ready to move forward. And I was just on the cusp of being able to try a step on my own before one blood clot, and not even a long procedure to remove it, ruined everything.

"Let's get you inside. If you don't mind, I'd like to stay for dinner and then I'll let you have your way . . . for now. I'll go back to campus and get up for weights in the morning, then prep for our game Saturday. But this conversation is only on pause."

I breathe in through my nose and finally give him a little nod. When he feels free of the weight of having to care for me, he might realize just how much it's been dragging him down.

Together, we shuffle our way forward, Wyatt knowing me well enough to understand I want to make this awkward walk without anyone's help but his. I don't want the walker—the old one or the new one. And though he's doing most of the walking for me, I'm doing a little. It's that little that gives me hope that next week there will be more on my own. And then next month, yet even more.

We make it to the door, and Wyatt holds my right side while I brace my body on the railing that my dad had installed to go along with my ramp. I'd like to take the stairs, but that's way too ambitious. I was just starting to work on the transition from dirt to concrete before this setback. I'll need to get back up to speed.

While Wyatt moves to my other side to help guide me up the ramp, we're hit with the spot of headlights, and we both turn to squint to see who it is. The rumble of Whiskey's truck stops, and when he kills the lights, I'm able to make out both him and Tasha inside. Wyatt chuckles just then, and I glance his way.

"What's funny?"

He bunches his lips, staring at Whiskey's truck for a beat, then moving his gaze to me.

"I was on my way to tell you about it before your hospital trip. But you should know, for your own amusement tonight, that Tasha and Whiskey? They're fucking."

"They're . . . what the fuck?"

"Hey, girl!" Tasha shouts, dropping from the passenger side of Whiskey's lifted truck onto the driveway with a *clomp* as her boots smack down.

I'm still in shock, and no matter how loud my inner voice tells me to pull my shit together, my face doesn't get the message. When Tasha steps in close enough to make out my features, her eyes instantly flash to Wyatt and her face turns a new shade of red.

"Wyatt! You told her?"

"You two are . . . fucking?" I say, moving my finger between both of our best friends just as my Aunt Sarah opens the front door.

"Hey, everyone! Peyton's friend and Wyatt's friend are fucking! Now we all know," she announces, poking her head out the door and meeting Tasha's incredulous expression with one only the queen can wear. Nobody does a mic drop like my Aunt Sarah.

Whiskey moves between us, carrying a case of beer as he steps inside. He glances at me on his way, and the smile on his face says it all.

Fucker wore her down.

Chapter Twenty-Nine

Wyatt

I haven't thought about the ring since Peyton set these stupid rules in motion a month ago. I mean, I've thought about it because I hate that it's lost, but I haven't thought about the moment I'll show it to her—how to give it to her, the words I'll say, her response.

It's her response that scares me most. I thought I knew. I took that *yes* for granted, I suppose. I didn't think anything could break us, but I get that her spirit needs every ounce of her strength right now to heal. It doesn't mean I like any of this. I do respect it, though. I respect her wish, but I'll be damned if I'm not going to keep working to change her mind in those little in-between moments when she'll let me.

Like now.

Her text asking me if I want to come help her ride was waiting on my phone after practice, along with a message from my finance professor letting me know that the test I blew will be the one I get to drop. Lucky for me. That's a near quote—he told me I was a lucky SOB. I fought the urge to write back that I'd rather be a lucky SOB than just an SOB like he is. Probably not the best way to finish a semester.

"We're going out for happy hour at Tate's. You want to jump in with me and Tasha?" Whiskey asks.

I chuckle, still blown away that they're now six weeks in on this thing and somehow growing more and more comfortable with the concept of being a couple.

"I can't. The boss wants to see me today, so—"

"Yeah, I get it. You should go."

Whiskey's the only one I talked to about my latest relationship challenges. I needed someone to throw my frustrations at, and I didn't want to lay this on my mom. It's bad enough that I can't find her ring. And I knew it wasn't time to put up a fight with Peyton. I would have just come across as defensive. Besides, she's the one who said our situation needed time— that I'd come to realize I need to prioritize and focus. Thing is, though, I think she needs this time, too. And my priorities, they've only grown more set in stone.

I love this game. I plan to play it for as long as I can. But I plan to be with Peyton forever. That's my priority. And the sooner she sees I'm firm about that—the sooner she lets me back in—the more whole I'll be. And I think she'll be whole, too.

I head down the corridor from the locker room to the student athlete lot, holding up a hand to wave to Tasha when she spots me through the windshield of Whiskey's truck.

"Hey!" she shouts, dropping the feet she had propped on his dash.

I walk over to the passenger side, the stench of nail polish strong despite the rolled-down window. I wave at the air.

"Whoo!" I say.

"Yeah, yeah. Like your gear bags don't smell ten times worse," she says.

"Yeah, but that's sweat. That's natural. You're wafting around chemicals."

Her lips purse.

"You think you guys smell natural?" She punches out a laugh, and I have to give it to her.

I tilt my head.

"Fair."

"Did Whiskey find you? We're getting Tate's."

They've been including me on a lot of date nights lately. "Paying it forward," Whiskey says. I'm pretty sure that's Tasha's doing, though. While I haven't opened up to her the way I have to Whiskey, Peyton's probably filled her best friend in on how our relationship is going. Part of me would love to dissect everything Tasha knows, but I'm not ready to believe just yet that Peyton and I have secrets. I'd like to believe everything is as I know it to be, and that when Peyton's ready, she'll say so.

Like she did today, inviting me to come out to the arena.

"Peyton asked me to come over," I say, my cheeks tightening the way they did when we first started flirting years ago. It's like getting those first glimmers of attention all over again.

Tasha's expression softens and she sits up higher in her seat.

"Yeah? That's good. I think she could do with a dose of affection. She's been—" She stops herself, though I know Tasha well enough to know she let slip exactly the amount she wanted to. She won't break her friend code, but she wants me to know Peyton misses me.

"I miss her, too," I say.

Her mouth quirks up.

"Yeah, I know. You threw two interceptions last weekend."

"Ouch!" I shake my hand out like she bit me.

She lifts a shoulder.

"Call it like I see it. You're better when you've had your Peyton fix."

"Fix? Is that what you call it?" I smirk, partly teasing her for getting involved with Whiskey when she swore it would never happen. She holds my gaze for a beat, and for a tiny moment, her eyes are very serious. She never answers me. We both know nothing about either of our hearts is casual, and she's in deeper than she'd like.

"Hey, maybe this is a little intrusive of me to ask, but . . . since when do I give a shit about things like that. You ever think about proposing to our girl?" Her head falls to the side, and she bites the tip of her tongue, a knowing smirk tugging up one side of her mouth.

"Uh, yeah. I have. Why?" My eyes squint a little, trying to sort out her expression and see if I can read her thoughts. Tasha is like one of those Rubik's Cubes after the stickers have all been rearranged, though, so I'm not going to get anything out of her she doesn't intend on telling me.

"Just curious. I like to dream about weddings I might be in one day. The dresses, the hair—riding in on a horse and carriage." She bats her lashes.

"Isn't that the kind of thing the bride and groom do?"

She drops her chin a tick.

"Wyatt, let me be clear. When you all get married, I better get my own damn horse and carriage."

I punch out a hard laugh and back up a few steps, giving up on learning anything new. I lift a hand in goodbye.

"I'll make sure that's in the binder," I tell her, then turn around.

"Oh, and hey, Wyatt?"

I spin on my heels but keep stepping away as I lift my chin.

"If you're looking for the ring, you might want to check her sock drawer."

I stop dead. My mouth opens.

"I thought you were getting out of here?" Whiskey shouts as the exit door slams shut behind him.

I blink a few times, and Tasha wiggles her fingers in a wave as she rolls up the window. My gaze bounces back to my friend, and my agape mouth forms a shocked smile.

"I'm leaving now!"

I don't know how it ended up in her possession, and I am positive she would fight me on it if I brought it up right now, but the fact the ring found its way from my sock drawer to hers is some sort of sign. I have zero doubt.

Pausing for a second as I get into my truck, Tasha's words run through my mind, and I decide to toss my gear bag in the back rather than on the floor of the passenger seat. She's right. That shit smells bad. And if there's a chance I might get to take my girl for a drive somewhere tonight, I'd like to put my best foot forward.

I hop in, crank the engine, and peel away, grabbing the hat from my passenger seat to squash the wild hair left from my shower. When I got Peyton's text, I pretty much forgot about everything else. It's a miracle I remembered to put my pants on. In fact . . . I glance down.

Yeah, I have pants.

The sun is starting to go down a lot earlier, so it's dusk by the time I pull into Peyton's driveway. There are a few extra trucks parked to the side, and I'm guessing from the Coolidge Bears stickers on a few of them that there's a coaches' meeting happening inside.

The arena is lit up, but as far as I can tell, Peyton's not out there, so I head to the front door and knock before pushing it open.

"Hey! There's our state record holder!" Reed's father shouts as I step into a room full of people. About a dozen men, some of whom I recognize, crane their necks and look in my direction. Buck likes to give his son shit for losing his record to me. I think he likes to stir the pot, too, and get Reed worked up at me.

"Yeah, yeah. He didn't break the college ones, though," Reed fires back, holding up his half-drunk beer as a toast to my failure.

"I mean, I'm still gonna make out with your daughter later, so—"

"Ohhhhhh burnnnnnn!" someone shouts, while a few other guys chirp. Reed, ever the classic, holds up a middle finger, then smirks.

"She's waiting out back. And for the record, I've got cameras everywhere." He winks and I chuckle, but as I leave the room, the laughter still roaring behind me, I mentally catalog all the times Peyton and I have done things around this house.

I step out the back door to the walkway that winds around to the stone patio. Peyton's waiting for me, braced on the new walker her grandfathers built for her. She's wearing black leggings and an oversized sweatshirt, her hair pulled back in a braid, and one of those knitted headbands covering her ears. She's so cute in the winter.

"Did you know your dad has cameras everywhere?" I ask, startling her. She smiles big at seeing me, and my heart kicks wildly.

She shrugs, a devilish grin playing at her lips before she looks away to situate her hands on her handlebars.

"Peyt, that's not funny." It's a little funny.

"Relax, Wyatt. I disabled anything that would have caught something incriminating." She flits her gaze up through her lashes, teasing me. Something's changed. It's a glimmer of her old self, a taste of the gritty wild woman who pushes bound-aries and breaks barriers.

"I'm not sure if that makes me feel any better." I chuckle.

"Come on. We gotta get a horse," she says, tilting her head toward the barn.

I hop close, my hands ready to help her, but before I can hold up some of the weight on her right side, she steps forward with nobody's help at all. I stand still and let her get about a dozen paces away before she notices, stopping and glancing over her shoulder.

"Wow," I say.

Her mouth tips up on one side.

"You talking about my ass or the walking part?"

My lips pull in tight, and I fight off the laugh.

"A bit of both, I guess."

It takes us a while to get to the barn, but when we do, Peyton moves from holding her walker to holding onto Otis by herself. I flatten a palm to one cheek and cross my other arm over my body as I watch her in wonder.

"I'm not sure what you need me out here for," I admit.

Her cheeks push up, a bashful expression touching her face before she looks down and bites her lip. When she lifts her chin and meets my eyes, her smile isn't quite as big, and I step in close on instinct a second before her bottom lip starts to quiver.

"Peyt, what's wrong?" I pull her into me, holding her head to my chest as she sniffles. A faint and nervous laugh leaves her mouth.

"I'm sorry. I didn't think I'd fall apart like this," she says.

"*Shh*, it's okay. You're allowed to be human, you know?" I kiss the top of her head, happy to have her warm body against mine, in my arms. She looks up, her chin pushing into my chest as I tuck a few loose hairs into her headband. Her cheeks are red from either the cold or from her abandoned emotional mask. I run my thumb along her cheekbone, cherishing the soft skin I missed so much.

"Don't say I don't need you. Because I need you, Wyatt. I need you so much."

My hands cup her face, and my lips move to hers before the next cry hits her lips, and I kiss her so long that I worry I may be starving her of air.

"I didn't want you to think I didn't need you. Every call we've had, all the videos, the photos, the little hearts you send —that's why I'm able to do this." She gestures down to her feet, her toes pointed directly at mine, her balance almost there.

"I never thought that," I lie. She doesn't need that weighing her down. Not now that she's just learning to fly again.

But honestly, I always knew deep down she needed me as much as I need her. For a while, I was hurt at the thought that she didn't want me. But then I realized she simply wanted big things *for* me more. And it's hard to resent someone for that. No matter how wrong they are.

Otis neighs, stomping his right foot into the loose hay.

"I think he wants to go for a walk. What do you say?" Peyton says.

"I say, lead the way," I respond.

And without my help at all, she does.

Chapter Thirty

Peyton

Wyatt went back to our apartment, and I let him. Every fiber of my soul wanted him to stay, but with two losses and a tough game coming up, I want him to focus for Saturday.

We might miss the playoffs. It's a hard year, and the system still has its flaws. The number of times my dad has gone on a rant about the weight of our schedule versus the SEC school that will get a bid no matter what their record is rivals only the number of conversations I've had with Tasha in the last twelve hours while I panic-search my room for the ring.

I've tossed everything from all my drawers, even going so far as to sit my ass on the floor and feel inside the bottom drawer and then take a flashlight to look underneath the dresser. The whole ordeal took me an hour, and it hurt like hell because I did it by myself. But there's no way I'm bringing anyone else in on my dilemma. I still have no proof that ring was from Wyatt and meant for me, let alone that if it was, I probably shouldn't be hiding it.

I'm chewing at the inside of my mouth, sitting on the end of my bed as my eyes scan every possible hiding spot, when my mom knocks softly at my door.

"Come in," I say, folding my hands on my lap and doing my best to look nonchalant. My hair is sweaty, though, from the recent aerobic activity. My mom clearly notices, drawing her brow in as she looks me up and down.

"I was trying a new exercise. It was hard."

"Ah," she relents. "Well, you have a visitor."

There's a slight edge to her voice, so I grip the side of the bed as I do my best to sit up tall. Or rather, taller. Tall is really the only way I can sit now. I hold my breath, not sure who to expect, and when Alicia's eyes meet mine, a sudden lump forms in my throat. I haven't seen her since the accident.

"Hi," she says, bunching her hand up nervously. She stays behind my mom for a moment, almost like she's hiding, but eventually steps into my room.

"Hi. I . . . I'm sorry, I didn't know you were coming," I stammer. My gaze moves to my mom, and I'm sure the panic on my face is front and center.

"I'll give you guys some privacy." My mom gives me a reassuring nod, then backs out of the room.

Alicia moves in for a hug, then stops suddenly, her arms bent as she leans awkwardly. "I'm sorry, can you—can I give you—"

"I'd love a hug," I reassure her.

Her body relaxes immediately, and she moves in to embrace me. Her touch is gentle at first, so I make sure to squeeze her tight so she can feel my palms on her back. She closes her arms around me a bit more before stepping back.

"Have a seat," I say, nodding next to me.

She sits on the very edge of the mattress, her legs flexing like she's doing a wall sit, and I can tell she's trying to tiptoe around me.

"You're allowed to sit normal."

"Oh, yeah," she laughs out, moving deeper into the bed and eventually tucking one leg under the other. I make a mental note to put that on my goals list.

"Your mom said you've been making a ton of progress," she says, her gaze moving slowly over my body. I kind of think she's searching for scars.

"I am. I had a little blood clot issue a few weeks back that was sort of like a hard reset, but I feel like I've progressed again. I'm walking on my own with a walker. It's slow and looks a little bit like that dance Coach Kane does—"

"Oh yeah, the robot!" Alicia hops to her feet and does a decent impression of our coach. We both laugh.

"I'm glad," she says, her gaze drifting away from mine as the pregnant pause grows into an extended silence.

I'm about to fill it with more pointless banter when her eyes snap to mine.

"I'm so sorry, Peyton. About . . . hurting you. I didn't mean . . . I wasn't . . ." Tears well up in her eyes, and I feel them threaten mine as well.

"Alicia, it was an accident," I say, holding my arms open again. She falls into them, almost knocking me back.

"I'm so, so sorry Peyton."

Her body convulses with sobs, and I can't help but cry along with her. My mom steps in, hearing us wail, but I quickly hold up a hand to let her know we're okay. We're more than okay. We're healing.

Alicia and I cry it out for what feels like an hour, and as painful as it is to relive some of the things I've been through, I share every detail when she asks. I hold back the part about my future of having kids. That's a question that will linger for a while, and a conversation I'm going to have to have with Wyatt one day. Probably soon.

There's this huge gap in my memory of the accident, which Alicia is finally able to fill. I remember seeing her body lurch forward above me, and then I felt the drop in my stomach as my base collapsed. But I never fully understood when the impact happened. Alicia, however, was alert for every millisecond. Her knee landed on my head just as my bottom hit the ground, and the impact from both ends was too much for my middle to absorb. That's when the fracture happened.

"I dream about it sometimes," I tell her, wondering if I'll see it happen differently next time.

"I dream about it every night," she admits, her mouth souring as her gaze drifts away.

I know from the text messages with other teammates and emails with Coach that Alicia hasn't been back out since the fall. She was cleared a couple of weeks ago, having been on concussion protocol. She's one of the best flyers I've ever seen.

I can feel us both slipping back into the hurt. I'm so done feeling sorry and resentful, so before Alicia falls apart again, I reach for my walker and lift myself to a stand. Even though I've ridden Otis a lot these last few days, one more trip to the arena is in order. This time, I'll lead while she rides.

"You ever been on a horse?"

Her eyes are already wide, I think from watching me pull myself up. It's probably jarring for someone to watch when they haven't seen it yet. I suppose it either looks like a miracle or a struggle, depending on the perspective. Rather than label it either, I waggle my hand in front of her zoned-out gaze and snap her attention back to my face.

"Horse? You been on one?" I flash a tight smile, and we've been friends long enough for her to know that means I'm ready to change subjects.

"Uh, maybe? When I was little?"

I chuckle and urge her to follow me.

"You're still little," I joke. She's under five feet. It's why she's our flyer.

We pass through the kitchen, and I bend my head down a little to catch my mom's attention at the stove. She's trying to learn how to make some of her mom's recipes. They practiced a lot of things when my grandparents were here, and I get a feeling my mom wants to be able to teach me what she learns. I'm more of a buy-the-cookie-dough-ready-made kind of chef, but I admit there's a big difference between the shortcut and my grandma's way. Both grandmothers, truthfully. Though my Grandma Rose has a few secrets she says she won't share until it's her time to go. That's her way of being competitive, my mom says.

"Taking Alicia to meet Otis. Wanna come?" My mom nods and sets whatever's on the stove to simmer, wiping her hands, then rounding the counter to join us. I want her expertise in case Alicia gets nervous. It's near impossible to startle Otis, but nothing is ever a total impossibility with animals.

The three of us get Otis out of his stall, and my mom fits him with his saddle then leads him out to the arena.

"Go ahead. I'll catch up," I say, wanting Alicia to head in with my mom rather than watch me struggle over the rough terrain. I know how far I've come making this trek, but she doesn't. I know what it looks like when I guide these big wheels through the rock and dirt.

My mom is just about wrapping up her walk-through of the various steps to mount Otis by the time I step up to them.

"You ready?" she asks.

Alicia glances to me, her eyes buzzing with reservation but also excitement.

"You can do this," I reassure her.

"Okay," she says, sucking in a breath and grasping all the places my mom showed her. She pulls herself up as my mom gives her an extra boost, not because she isn't strong enough, but because she's tiny.

"Oh, wow, it's high up here," she says, her voice vibrating.

"He's got you. This is Otis," I say, holding my hand against his side. "Otis, tell Alicia you've got her."

He neighs, shaking his head as he knows to do on command. My mom has spent years working with him on small things like stomping his foot, sidestepping, and nodding and shaking his head. He's great with kids because of it. Turns out, his tricks also work well on freaked out twenty-somethings getting over trauma.

"You ready to ride?" I let go of the walker and lean on Otis for my balance.

"You're coming with?" Alicia asks.

I nod.

"Yep. We both have you," I promise.

I click with my tongue and Otis takes a slow step forward, his body swaying like a hippo. Alicia laughs as it swings her from right to left, and I move my left hand to her calf to give her extra support.

"He's got hips, and he knows how to use them." I look over my shoulder to give my mom credit for her joke I just stole. She's been saying that for years.

"Yeah, he does. Oh, my God, Peyton! I'm riding a horse!"

We meander around the arena at a snail's pace, slower than my usual rides since I'm the one guiding. But this walk is good for me. I've tried it a few times with my mom or dad right at my side, ready to dive in and take over if I start to lose my balance. This is the first time I've been totally on my own. There's not much Alicia would be able to do to help me from way up there. And while I'm a little nervous, I'm also liberated. Dare I say, I'm fucking impressed with myself.

"Hey, Alicia?"

She looks down as I slow Otis to a stop. I scratch his neck and hold her gaze for a moment while I search for the right words. And then it hits me.

"Quit racing yourself," I say.

Her face puzzles briefly. Those words hit different for her. While I tend to aim too high and struggle when I fall short, Alicia is just the opposite. In her race, she won't get out of her own way.

"You can still fly better than anyone. And it was an accident. Stop racing yourself and get out of your own way."

She holds my gaze for a few long seconds, then looks up and stares off into the skyline.

"I'll try, Peyton. I promise you I'll try."

And that's good enough.

Chapter Thirty-One

Wyatt

It was a tough loss. And it may have been the game of my life.

We have two games left, but they're basically meaningless. Bryce will probably get a lot of time, though—and we'll still want a bowl bid of some sort—but at this point, it's about looking toward our future. The extra cash for the school is nice, and it's a boost for the players going into next year.

Those of us kicking around the draft, though? It's not worth getting hurt for the Cotton Candy Oreo Cheese Puff Bowl.

I'm anxious to get out of this press conference. I've never been a fan of them, but now that I have my mother's ring in my pocket and a plan in my heart, sitting through questions about whether I'll be at the combine or not feel empty and pointless.

I won't announce anything here, that's for sure. I'll want to think through the messaging because while I plan to postpone the draft for a year, I'm not pulling myself off the table entirely. I'll get in some workouts and spend the year bulking up and gaining speed. Maybe I'll gain some more smarts while I'm at it. I've been thinking a lot about grad school. I feel as though my education has been on cruise control, and I regret that. I'd like to learn something and get good at it, maybe even teach. I still want to run a business one day or maybe take over parts of the Johnson Ranch business that rescues horses for therapy. Honestly, it's been nice letting my mind wonder at the possibilities. I took football off the table mentally, and it's made space for so much more.

But before I do any of that, I need to get down on one knee in front of Peyton and ask her to marry me. I'm still a little anxious about her answer, even though I know her heart will want to say yes. It's her head I need to convince.

Believing me has never been something she's shied away from. I'll simply have to remind her of that.

Naturally, Kelly Brooks from *Athletico* is the first to ask me about the draft. I know he'll push even after I answer, but I stick to my plan.

"I'm not thinking about that. We have two games left to play. I want to help position this team for the future. I intend on being there for Hampton and showing him what I can. That's as far as it goes for me right now."

I glance to my right, meeting Bryce's eyes. He knows my plan to sit out a year, and while he's not thrilled at the prospect of entering the draft with me, there's a little piece of him that's also fired up because of the competition. Who knows, maybe our rivalry will push me to be better next year as well.

"Okay, so is Hampton getting the start next week?" Kelly presses. *What a pain in the ass this guy is!*

"As we've said before, these are questions you'll have to ask Coach Byers when it's his turn," Bryce answers, repeating the same words I used a few questions ago. "Neither of us is dumb enough to speak for him."

I shoot Bryce a lopsided smirk, then roll my wrist over to check the time on my watch. I want to get to Peyton's house before the sun goes down, but that window is narrowing.

"Go on," Bryce says, covering his mic and leaning into me.

"You sure?" I whisper.

"Yeah, I'll just answer for you the same way I do for Coach. And then maybe they can haul my dad in here for more questions since he's eager to talk." We both laugh while the press members lean in, attempting to eavesdrop.

"I'm sorry, y'all, but I have somewhere I need to be. Thanks for understanding."

I push my chair back amid the flashes from still cameras and a few shouted questions that I've either answered or dodged already, and after a short lecture from our media manager, I slip out to the back parking lot and hop in my truck.

I make it about five miles before my phone rings with a call from Peyton. I smile, laughing silently as I answer with a voice command.

"Yes?"

I know she watched the press conference. They all did. It was part of the deal that everything went along as normal. The only wild card in the situation was Buck, but Rose promised she'd keep his mouth shut until after I proposed.

I asked Reed for his permission after I snuck the ring out of Peyton's sock drawer. As terrifying as facing the Ohio State defensive line is, it's nothing compared to asking Reed Johnson for his daughter's hand in marriage.

He had his reservations at first, like his daughter's worries that I'm giving up on my own dreams—being impulsive or desperate. But I have an answer for everything, and I know what I want—I want my life with her. I want to be the one she leans on for the hard road ahead. And I would hate myself for missing a minute of it.

Peyton's uncle helped me parse out my options, having spent years as Reed's agent. He knows the game well, even the seedy part behind the scenes where negotiations and trades get ugly. He kept Reed out of a lot of bad contracts, and when I do go pro, I want him in my corner. After looking at his projections, I was pleasantly surprised. By holding out a year, my draft number improves, assuming I perform well at next year's combine. I'll get an automatic bid for deferring. And Jason will make sure that promise sticks.

"You want to enlighten me on where exactly it is you have to be, in the middle of a damn press conference?" She's only a little serious. Mostly, she's sassy.

"Yeah, well, it's somewhere important," I say, stringing her along.

Her sigh comes through my speakers, and I laugh.

"I hear you," she chides.

"Oh, I don't doubt you do. You hear everything."

"That's not true," she says, but quickly backpaddles. "Besides, you're bad at sneaking up on people. And you *do* snore a little. And whose toes crack that much when they walk around at night."

"Wow, you're getting it all off your chest," I muse. Man, is she going to feel bad when my knee pops as I drop down to propose. I'm sure she'll hear it.

I toy with her for a few more minutes, until I can tell she's genuinely getting irritated, and then I tell her to wait for me outside with Otis.

"I already took a shower. I don't want to get dirty," she argues.

"Well, you'll have to take another one. I'll help you."

"*Hmm*, I'm not sure you deserve to. But fine. I'll meet you outside."

She ends the call, and my heart races with what comes next. I'm really doing this. And I've let everyone in on it. My football brothers are going to have to settle for Tasha's video, as are Peyton's out-of-town grandparents and her Uncle Mike. But as for having an audience, I feel like I really stacked the bleachers, so to speak. If she says no, at least a dozen people are going to witness it. My mom. My dad's old fire captain. Tasha, Jason,

Sarah, Reed and Nolan. Buck's reaction is the one I am bracing for most, no matter which way this goes. That man's wit knows no bounds, and when it comes to taking his fellow man down a peg, he's rapid-fire fast.

I'm starting to sweat, so I pull my hoodie off as I exit the highway and make my way toward the Johnson home. It's fifty-five degrees outside, which for Arizona is basically freezing, but my chest is burning up. I think I might be scared.

I pull into the driveway, having passed my mom's SUV and Tasha's car parked off the side of the road by the main gates. I'm not sure where everyone is hiding, but I know they can all see. And as Reed mentioned again when I was planning all this, he has cameras everywhere.

I get out of my truck and pat my pocket, feeling for the ring. I've probably worn the diamond's edges dull at this point. The thing has become a worry stone of sorts.

I drop my hands in my joggers and embrace the chill in the air. Peyton is walking in slow circles with Otis out in the arena, a slight fog of dust from his foot-stomping glowing with the yellow lights. The sun is almost down, and I curse Kelly Brooks under my breath for asking too many questions. I hope Tasha will be able to film enough in the dim light.

Glancing around as I make my way into the arena, I drop the suspicious look when Peyton spots me. She halts Otis and puts a hand on her hip. I stop to take in the sight, wanting to remember her just like this—a movement that she said she worked on just so she could deal with me. Well, woman? You may as well pull it out now because if this goes as planned, you're going to have to deal with me for a long time.

"This is not an important place you had to be, Wyatt Stone. It's a dirt farm. And you've been here before. Now, fess up. What is that all about?"

I glance to my right, figuring her family is probably tucked away in the barn by now, looking through windows and cracks in the door. I shake my head, then close the distance between us so I can kiss her, partly to shut her up, but mostly because *my God, do I love this woman.*

Before she has a chance to catch her breath—and somehow ruin this—I drop to my knee and fish the ring from my pocket.

"Peyton Johnson, I've been thinking a lot lately about what's important to me. It was sort of your mandate when you grounded me to our apartment, so that bit is your fault," I say, mentally working out the meaning behind her frozen, wide-eyed expression.

"I know you found this," I say, holding the ring up and smirking.

Her head tilts slowly and her lips part, but dare I say, there's a smile in there somewhere.

"It was Tasha's fault," she finally utters, and I drop my head with laughter, hoping her friend caught that on video.

"Okay. That doesn't really matter. I want you to know I've been thinking about this for a long time. Longer than you probably think. And when you made that speech about me chasing my dreams and focusing on my future, you were leaving something major out of the conversation."

Her brow furrows.

"You."

She sucks in her bottom lip, and my pulse finally settles. I think she might just say yes.

"I know you have a long journey ahead, but Peyt? I want to be on that journey with you. I want to hold your hand at every doctor's appointment, to work in the garage with your grandfathers on the next great gizmo they come up with to help in your recovery, and to clap louder than anyone when you cross goal after goal off your list. That, Peyton Johnson, is my dream. *You are my dream.*"

"Wyatt, you can't possibly fly back and forth when you—"

She shakes her head and tears up. I shake my head, stopping her before she goes down that road.

"I'm not giving up on football, so don't think that. I'm simply putting it off for a year. I'd rather spend that year growing with you, becoming a better human, letting you inspire me, holding you accountable, and letting you get angry at me when you need someone to blame. I want that more than I want some draft dream that might send me to Oklahoma, or Jacksonville, or Buffalo."

"They won't take you in Buffalo. They're kind of set," she teases, her mouth tipping up on the right.

I roll my eyes and get to my feet, taking her left hand in mine while her right holds on to Otis. I can't think of a better witness.

"The game may have picked me, but I pick you. You're my everything. My beginning, middle, and end. All the things in between. Marry me."

I hold my breath, about ninety percent sure she's going to say yes but a small sliver worried she'll give in to her doubts.

"You promise you won't give up on the game?"

I nod my head and let it fall against hers, closing my eyes as I let my fragile smile spread.

"Baby, that game gave me you. I can't imagine what else it's got in store. And if you write it on your list, then I won't be able to cross it off without you knowing. So yeah, I promise. Marry me, Peyton Johnson. Make my dreams come true."

She shifts, her lips brushing against mine, and I feel them morph into a tight grin just before her head nods.

"Yes, Wyatt Stone. I will marry you."

I slide the ring on her finger, relieved that it still fits after all these months. I figured out her size through lots of sleuthing.

I cup her face, not wanting just yet to break our small bubble and announce her answer to the hiding family and friends. She lets go of her hold on Otis and relies on me, her hands moving to my biceps as I widen my stance to help her feel steady.

"One request," she says, leaning back enough to look me in the eyes.

"Anything," I say.

"We don't set a date until I can walk down that aisle."

I can see the fire in her eyes with those words, and I nod immediately.

"You pick it, and I'll move heaven and earth to make sure you get everything you want that day." Apparently, I'll be lining up multiple horses and carriages.

"Then yes, Wyatt Stone. I will let you marry me." Her mouth puckers with her smug grin, and I press my lips against hers, loving every bit of who she is.

"She said yes!" I shout finally, backing away and turning toward the barn as the doors fly open and everyone spills out.

"Seriously?" Peyton says, covering her face while I hold her up against my side.

"You honestly think I would be allowed to do any of this without inviting them?" I point out.

She waggles her head, but then her eyes flash wide, and she covers her mouth.

"Yeah, Tasha probably heard you throw her under the bus," I say.

And as her friend marches toward us through the thick arena dirt, her face all twisted with disgust as mud chunks cake to her fancy boots, Peyton and I bite our lips and brace ourselves for the storm that is Tasha. After all, what's one more tornado on our walk through the impossible?

Epilogue

Wedding Day

Peyton

It was important to my mom that I wear her dress for my wedding. We tailored it to fit me and updated the style a little, turning the skirt into an asymmetrical style so I could wear my favorite boots with it. The bodice, however, stayed the same, and I can't help but think of how beautiful my mom must have been back then as I look at myself now.

"You look so much like her," Grandma Susan says, hugging me around the waist.

She's misty-eyed, and I think a little tipsy. My mom and I got a good cry in about an hour ago, before my make-up was applied, so I need to hold it together—at least until pictures.

I still need to get my feet into my boots, so I send my grandmother to check on my dad and see if he's been able to polish them. I practiced wearing them a lot over the last two weeks, getting used to the new brace being shoved into leather, and it left them a little banged up. It's a tight fit with my brace on, but I always wanted to wear these down the aisle. I'm determined. Besides, I already relearned how to walk for this thing, what's one more skill?

"All right, I think I got the scuffs out—" My dad steps into the small tent we set up by our barn, and his words stop the second I turn around.

"Damn it, Daddy! I can't cry anymore," I blurt out in a half-laugh-half-choke.

I tap my fingertips below my eyes, hoping the liner and mascara hold. My dad sucks up all the air in the room and adjusts his belt, clearing his throat and burying what promised to be a pretty good-sized blubber.

"You're beautiful, Peyt. Beautiful."

My body quakes with emotion and nerves as I fan my face with my hand and give him a tight-lipped smile.

"Thank you, Daddy."

This whole wedding thing has turned me and him into two sappy motherfuckers. I've been a daddy's girl my whole life, but lately, I've been extra. Wyatt and I will be living with them for a while, at least until we figure out what the plan is after the combine and draft. And even then, I'll see them all the time. But this day still feels like a severance in some ways, like that final snip between my youth and adulthood. I have my suspicions that my father might simply start traveling with us as an assistant. Who knew my mom was the independent one?

My father kneels at the foot of the wooden bench, and I take my seat, holding out my left leg for him to slip my boot onto my foot, and then my right. This is the tricky one, and it takes a little maneuvering to get the fit just right with my brace. Once they're on, though, I'm able to stand and even jump a little bit.

"I can't believe how far you've come," my dad says.

I shake my head as I hold my skirt up a little and gaze down at my feet. It's been exactly one year. I'm not great at running yet, but I have relearned how to walk. There have been setbacks and some dark days when I wasn't sure I'd be able to do it, but through it all, Wyatt was there.

My steady.

My one great thing.

The love of my life.

The soft guitar music shifts into something more here-comes-the-bride, so my dad straightens his jacket and adjusts the Johnson Ranch buckle on his belt before holding his arm out for me.

"Let's get you hitched."

I nod and take in my last deep breath before everyone I've ever known turns around and stares at me. My dad pulls the curtain open, and together, we make our way along the stone path that leads out to the gazebo my grandpa built with his own two hands years ago. We had it repainted and covered in lights. It's perfect.

My cheeks hurt from the instant smile that stretches the width of my face seeing my sweet sister drop white petals on the ground before us. I nod silent hellos to the overflow of friends we pass through before we get to the aisle and even more people seated in rows to witness me and Wyatt seal our lives together. When I clear the final guest before the aisle, I stop and squeeze my father's arm tightly as my soon-to-be husband turns around and takes his first look at me, in boots, in this dress—walking toward him.

Wyatt's hand covers his mouth, then comes to rest on his chin for a moment as his eyes glisten and his smile beams at me. He looks so proud, but more than that, so in love with me. I am not sure what I did to deserve him. I even tried to ward off football players to avoid men like him one day. Fate had other plans, I guess. And now that I've grown up a lot, I see just how incredible those big ole football hunks can be. My dad made his own mold, and Wyatt did too. Similar yet unique. Both the best men I've ever known.

Whiskey pats Wyatt's back, chuckling at his friend, who is quickly losing it at the altar, and when I step up next to him, he shakes with a very loud sob and immediately laughs.

"Sorry, y'all. It's just . . . Peyton, you are beautiful."

I wave my hand at my face again, feeling those tears prickle my eyes.

"Thank you," I mouth. My father unlocks our arms and transfers my hand to Wyatt's, squeezing both of ours together and taking a moment to look us both in the eyes.

"I love you both," he says.

And I know he does.

"You may be seated," says Charles, our minister who was the chaplain at Wyatt's father's fire station. It was the one thing Wyatt truly wanted for our wedding, and I couldn't think of a more meaningful person to bless our union.

We chose to keep the prayers simple and light, focusing on our commitment to do good for each other and everyone we touch. For a girl who wanted to avoid repeating her parents' marriage, I sure have switched up my opinion. Now, I hope we're just like them.

Charles prompts us to say our vows, then hands us each a sparkler. This was my one request, well, besides every other little detail I demanded for the wedding. I wanted to use sparklers to honor my grandfather and my tradition with him.

Whiskey helps us light them and then passes the lighter down the row so the rest of our wedding party can join in. I look up at Wyatt, a strand of hair curled over his right eyebrow, his dimples deep, his blue eyes as clear as the sky, and we nod.

"On the count of three, guys," he says. "One . . . two . . . three!"

Wyatt and I form a heart by each painting half in the air repeatedly while the members of our party spell out the word love or at least come as close to it as they can. Our photographer took a long-exposure shot, and if it comes out right, it might just become my most cherished picture ever.

"Just one more thing, you two. We need some rings," Charles says. I glance to my mom, who has already slipped from the front row and moved down the aisle to walk Otis up as he carries the small basket with our rings in his mouth.

"What if he eats them?" Tasha whispers, rather loudly.

"Then you'll have to go in and get them," Whiskey jokes back.

The two of them stick their tongues out at each other, and anyone who doesn't know better might think they're siblings who hate each other. But Wyatt and I know better. Those two have been dating for more than a year now. And they're both employed. Miracles do happen.

My mom takes the basket from Otis, and Wyatt and I both rub his nose and thank him. She unties the rings from the small ribbon on the pillow inside, then hands them to us.

"With this ring, I thee wed," we both say, pushing the black metal bands with today's date engraved into the insides onto our fingers. I wanted to keep his mother's ring safe and used for special occasions, and with his football and my work with the horses, sturdy and meaningful made sense.

"Can I kiss her now?" Wyatt quirks a brow to Charles, and he nods.

Licking his lips, Wyatt pushes the few stray hairs from my face, the desert breeze working its magic as the sun goes down. With one hand on my back and the other on my cheek, he bends me back slowly and kisses me for what feels like hours. His mouth clings to my upper lip, and my teeth tease his lower one. I've waited so long for this day, to be able to move like this, to wear a dress like this, to call him husband.

"I give you Mr. and Mrs. Johnson-Stone," Charles says, revealing our plan to honor both of our family names.

He holds my gaze as he stands me up, and we can't stop staring at one another all the way down the aisle. With every hug we give, each handshake and smile, his hand always comes back to mine. The small touches send goose bumps over my skin. The whispers in my ear making sure I'm doing all right warm my heart. But it's the butterflies that hit my chest when we finally finish our couple photos and his fingertips glide along my bare back that really send me over the edge.

"Are you sure we need to take group photos *now*?" he whispers in my ear, his body behind mine, his hand sweeping the hair from my neck. Our photographer just left to gather everyone.

I giggle. "I am pretty sure if we don't take photos with your mother and mine, they will disown us."

"*Mmm*, probably true. But what if—"

His hands begin to gather the back of my dress, and my breath hitches as I stand in the middle of the small bridge crossing the wash. It's the perfect desert landscape, the greenery rich, the desert blossoms a deep violet and orange. This old bridge serves no purpose; the wash barely holds water except when it storms. But I always wanted photos done here. I thought it would be my college graduation pictures, but this— this is better. It's also a little private.

"With Rose and Buck having to take the motorized cart, we'll hear anyone coming. And I just have to know what you look like under here," he says in a husky voice that only comes out when he is really—*oh*. I swallow as my hand finds his hard cock pushing against his jeans.

"You have to be fast," I warn as he drops to his knees and presses his mouth against my ass cheek. His hand flicks the white satin garter belt against my thigh before he takes a small nip of my skin.

"This is happening," he says, pulling my dress up as he stands. I hear his zipper lower, and I lean forward against wooden rail, now needing this as badly as he does.

"I can't believe I get to fuck my wife now," he moans, sliding my lace panties to one side and pressing the tip of his cock into me.

"Your wife really needs to be fucked," I whimper, my eyes

fighting to stay focused on the trail ahead and the tents and party in the distance.

"Spread your legs," he orders, and my devilish grin comes out to play.

I've missed being wild with him, being rough and sweet all at once. We've had sex as I've healed, but he's always been so cautious with me, as though afraid to hurt me. When I told him I want our wedding night to be all of the things, I was afraid he'd still hold back. But now, it seems I may need to hold him back. But not now. Definitely not now.

I widen my stance and bend forward more, arching my back as much as I can as he pushes his cock inside of me.

"I own this pussy," he says, his dirty talk in my top ten favorite Wyatt Stone characteristics.

"You do," I moan as he slides all the way out. I cry, needing him back inside, and he delivers with a hard thrust that pushes my belly into the railing.

We're on a tight schedule, and he wastes zero time, picking up his pace and pumping his hips as his dick slides in and out of my soaking wet pussy. He leans forward, his chest covering my back as he reaches his hand around the front and gathers my dress up even more. His fingers find my clit, rubbing circles against the swollen wet skin while he fills me from behind. The tension builds just as I hear the first rumble of the cart hitting the trail in the distance.

"People are starting to arrive, Wyatt."

"Well, then, I guess you're going to have to come faster."

His hand presses harder as his cock sinks deeper, and I cover my mouth as the first wave hits me and renders my entire body numb. Wyatt's hands grip my hips, pulling me back into him with each thrust as he orgasms and fills me completely. His cum soak my panties as he slides them back in place.

"You'll know I was there all night," he says, biting the edge of my ear, then kissing my neck as he zips up and buckles his belt.

We straighten my dress, and I pace a little, mostly to get the blush that I know is heating my cheeks under control. Tasha is the first to arrive, and she eyes me skeptically—or maybe I simply feel guilty.

We start with the family photos, then peel away one at a time to take pictures with our separate families and then with all of us together. I love that Wyatt and I are always at the center. I love that we're surrounded by love. But more than anything, I love that we have a lifetime to look forward to. So many days of food, friends, dancing, and dirty little secrets out in the desert where I'm just Peyton, and he's Wyatt, the boy who will always own all of me.

Bonus - Epilogue

Bonus – Preview of Final Down - Book 3 in the Waiting on the Sidelines Next Generation Series

Wyatt

Twenty-eight doesn't feel old. Not until I get dragged by a bunch of footballers ten years younger than me. Then? Then it feels ancient.

"Arm sore, captain?" Reed catches me rotating my shoulder on the sideline after showing the Coolidge quarterbacks how to throw the cross route.

"I'm fine, old man. You keep your arthritis cream to yourself. I don't need it yet," I tease. Honestly, though? I could maybe use a little.

Spring ball at the high school is always a shit show. We get a lot of the hopefuls out, guys who probably shouldn't be in the game of football but always wanted to try. or their parents want them to play. We play touch in the spring, then seven-on-seven in the summer with flag rules, but tackles happen. Only the solid guys come out for that. We travel, so it's not worth the expense for guys who aren't serious about the game. It's where guys get the early college looks, too. It's what got me my offers.

"Hey, Coach Stone? Does this look broken?" Brady, a sophomore who should *not* come out for summer or fall, holds up his elbow. He's got a good raspberry. It's not even bleeding anymore.

I pat his helmet and smile.

"I think you'll be fine, Brady. Maybe check out the summer track program, though. You're fast as hell." He's decently fast. He's better at running than he is at throwing and catching. And at a buck-twenty, maybe, he's not built to take a tackle. I wouldn't feel right encouraging him to be out here.

"Yeah, I was thinking about it."

I'm glad to hear him say that.

"Well, if you do, I'll come to your meets."

"Okay." He nods and smiles.

I keep my promises to the kids. There are a few players I've encouraged to go other directions for safety reasons or their own mental health, and I always support their new paths. Kai, a guy who had one hell of a foot but was jittery under the pressure of Friday night lights, found a good home guarding the net for our soccer team. I've been to all his starts since he was a freshman. He's a senior now and looking to play in college.

"You're good with them—the young ones." Reed squints from the sun. It's hot out today.

"Thanks. Hey, maybe I'll get the head coaching gig when this old fossil retires," I jest.

He glowers at me, then snags a full cup of cold water from the bench and tosses it at my face.

"Ah, fuck. Okay, yeah. I deserved that," I say, wiping the droplets from my eyes and smoothing back my hair before pushing my hat back on my head.

The spring guys are running laps, so Reed and I start to pick up. I've been coaching with him for five years now, since the combine came and went when I was twenty-three. I really thought I had it. We all did. But it wasn't my year. I'm not sure I would have been ready right out of college either. I have zero regrets, even though Peyton always asks if I do. I understand where she's coming from, but my life's work is making sure she never feels an ounce of guilt for anything. I made my choices then, and I'd make them again. Spending the year with her— every follow-up surgery, the work she put in? It was inspiring to the human spirit. Ain't no game of football that would give me that. And now that we're trying to have kids—man, I'm a lucky has-been, and I'm good with that.

But the competition? Yeah, I miss it a little. It's what makes coaching so satisfying. And I feel like I have a lot to teach. Hell, sometimes I learn more out here than the young guys do. The things I've added to my football IQ over the last five years sure would have served me well in college. Maybe would have helped my combine showing too. Who knows?

"Well, I'll be damned. They'll really just let anyone on campus, won't they?" Reed says.

I follow his gaze to the gate by the track. I haven't seen Bryce Hampton since he got drafted. I probably should have stayed in touch, but it was awkward, him getting the call and me not. And then he washed out in two years, and that felt *extremely* awkward.

"I guess that former Coolidge High QB title carries a lot of weight," Reed says, pulling his hat off and swinging an arm around Bryce.

Bryce rubs Reed's balding head, and I laugh, having done it myself a few times. Once today. Reed sneers at us both, then pushes his hat back on. He shaves what hair he's got up there, which is a good look on him, but it's harsh in the sun. At fifty-two, I'm glad he's not so proud that he doesn't take care of himself. Mostly. He still drinks too much beer for having a family-history of heart problems. His dad is still kicking, though, which is the point he always brings up when Nolan warns him off the red meat.

"Bryce, good to see ya, man," I say, pulling him in for a hug.

His beard is thick, but it's patchy in places. Mine is better. I'll always be trying to one-up this dude.

"You're actually the reason I'm out here. You got a minute?" he says, glancing at Reed in a way that makes me feel as though he wants to chat with me alone.

"You know what? I'll get these little shits to finish picking up the field, then head in. Stop by the office before you leave, though. I want to catch up and hear all about what you're doing now."

Reed shakes Bryce's hand.

"For sure. I'll see you in a few minutes," Bryce says.

He drops his hands into the pockets of his slacks. He's wearing a deep gray polo and sunglasses that look expensive as shit.

"You look more like a golfer every day," I tease, leading him over to the bench. I offer him a paper cup of water, and he chuckles as he takes it.

"I'm probably a better golfer than NFL quarterback, so that's for the best," he says, tipping the cup back and gulping the water down.

"What's up?"

I take a seat on one end of the bench as he sits on the other, pulling his sunglasses off and tucking them in his collar. Leaning forward and balancing his elbows on his knees, his gaze swings in my direction. He breathes out a short laugh, his mouth pulled into a tight smile that I can't read.

"You talk to Jason lately?" he asks.

My chest tightens a little, and I shake my head.

"Not this week, but, I mean, yeah. We've talked."

Bryce nods slowly, and I start to feel a little uneasy.

"What . . . Bryce, what's this about?"

He leans back, stretching an arm out along the back of the metal bench as he squints into the sun.

"You played that semi-league a few months back, with the Rattlers?"

I nod, then utter, "Yes." How does he know that? Is he stalking me? It's a minor, minor, minor league. I did it for fun, to hang out with Whiskey and see if I still had it. We won the league, but that meant five grand, which mostly went to taxes.

"Portland noticed," he says.

I stare at him until he turns his head my way and repeats his words slowly.

"Portland. They noticed." His eyebrows lift.

I tuck my chin and gurgle a belly laugh.

"Yeah, they're all up on the Tyler, Texas news, I'm sure. I bet they've got a whole list of QBs staring down thirty."

"Not a list. A name," he says, and I realize he's fucking serious.

"Bryce, I'm . . . I can't hang with that anymore."

Can I?

He stands up and pulls a card out of his wallet, handing it to me. It's the same firm Jason's at. He's an agent now. He's dead serious. This conversation is really happening.

"Think about it. Give me a call in a couple of days."

He slides his sunglasses on and turns halfway, gazing out on the field as he nods at distant memories.

"Those were some pretty great games, weren't they?"

"Which ones?" I ask, feeling the sharp edges of his card press into the pads of my finger and thumb.

His head swivels back to me, his lip tipping up on one side with a faint laugh.

"All of them, Wyatt. All of them."

He holds up a hand, and I do too.

"Call me," he says.

I think I answer, "I will." I'm not sure if that was out loud, though. And I'm not sure I told the truth if it was. Will I? Do I even want to entertain this?

I glance to my right where Reed is pointing toward the storage shed, directing the gangly group of freshmen to stack the pads neatly. I chuckle silently as I watch—they're too short to stack them. Reed knows it, too. He's fucking with them.

I stand up and stuff Bryce's card into the pocket of my joggers and rotate my arm a few more times. It's not sore. It's just . . . out of practice. Especially for throwing so many passes in a row. I wave to Reed as he looks my way, gesturing that I'll wheel in the cart full of balls. He gives me a thumbs up, then holds out an arm to sling over Bryce as he walks up beside him. I pick up a few stray balls and drop them into the basket, but I keep one in my hand, rotating it with a short toss in the air repeatedly, until Bryce and Reed turn the corner and are out of sight.

Portland noticed, huh?

I had a good summer. It was a lot of fun. Mostly, it was a nice excuse for Peyt and I to get away with Tasha and Whiskey. Since they got married and had twins, double dates have been hard to manage, and getaways are impossible. But with the rental house in Texas and the summer off, it was a nice chance to escape and pretend we were young again.

And the lights. The night games under the lights felt . . .

I walk down the field, stopping at the ten-yard line, and toss the ball in my hand a few more times before scanning the landscape for witnesses. Joey, the seventy-year-old guy who works in maintenance, is swapping out a trash bag by the bleachers, but he's not looking up.

I dig the toes of my shoe into the turf, seeing how well my sneakers grip. These things are orthopedic, so not great. But they'll do.

With my eyes focused on the way the ball fits in my hand, I tune out the world around me and mentally put myself there—in the game. It's a clean snap, and I fall back a few yards, checking the pocket, spotting my receivers, nodding to Keaton

Jones as he turns at the sideline and sprints to the fifty. The defense is rushing so I have to spin and run wide right to buy more time. There are three seconds left. This is it—game on the line. One final play.

I sling the ball with all I've got and fall back a few steps, imagining the blow I'd take if this were real. The ball spins tight, cutting through the air, on track to hit Keaton mid-stride. Nobody's guarding him. It's a clear shot to the end zone.

My ball crashes into the middle of the cart, knocking it sideways and spilling the fifteen balls inside it in all different directions. My gaze pops up a tick to Joey, whistling with his fingers in his mouth.

"You still got it, Coach!" He waves, and I wave back.

I rotate my arm a few more times, expecting to feel something. And I do. I feel . . . good. Better than good. I jog to my mess and pick the balls up, tossing them in one at a time, but I keep one out and tuck it in under my bicep as I push the rest into the shed. I hold onto it as I hike across the parking lot to my truck, and I keep it nestled safely in my grasp as I stare out at the high school field of my old rival, where I now coach.

Portland noticed.

If you enjoyed this book, you might also like:

The Varsity Series

A New Adult Sports Romance Series

Begin Your Binge with Varsity Heartbreaker

Lucas Fuller is a lot of things.

He's the boy next door.

He's the first crush I ever had.

He was my first kiss.

He's also the only person who has ever broken my heart.

For two years, I've wondered what happened to the us I used to know.

We were best friends, and then suddenly...we weren't.

I tried to run away from it. I even changed schools just to make the hurt disappear.

But no matter how hard I tried to not think about Lucas, I just couldn't stay away from the high school quarterback with perfect blue eyes and so many secrets.

I'm back. We're seniors now. We've grown—all of us. And Lucas Fuller might be different, but I'm different too.

This is my time to take risks, to experience life and to fall in love for real.

I want Lucas Fuller to be a part of my story, but I know for that to happen, I need to know the truth about our past.

Acknowledgments

It started at Home Game. I thought, "Yeah, all those requests were onto something. Peyton does have a story."

And then came Wyatt.

And now, I am not sure how I will ever let these two go.

This next generation series is such a wonderful creative gift, one I never expected. But this story has me in its grip, and I cannot wait to share book 3 with you all. Because I think it might just literally be EVERYTHING!

Game Face was inspired by real athletic warriors, primarily Corey Hahn and Isabella Picard. I've followed them both for years, and as I was developing Peyton's journey, I really started pull from those lessons and experiences they've shared. I won't go into their individual stories here, they are lengthy, but I encourage you to check them both out. Isabella in particular. She's in Peyton's fabric for sure.

I have to thank my team for standing behind me for this series. Autumn, there are no words good enough, but I'll stick with thank you, I love you, and you are the one I lean on. Endlessly grateful to you.

Brenda, my editor, you make all the good stuff sing. You are quite literally an angel, and a wizard. Both. For sure.

As always, Mom, you are my strength. And my boys, you are my heart.

In the end, it is because of you, my readers, that I get to do any of this. I read every email you send, try to hunt down every post on social media, love every share when you love one of my books, and am in bliss when I get to meet you in person. Thank you for taking a chance on my stories. I'll keep them coming as long as you want them.

If you enjoyed Game Face, please consider leaving a review. Those little stars and reviews make all the difference in whether a book is seen or not seen. And if you don't yet, be sure you follow my newsletter (link in my about me section). I send out goodies, previews, and always announce what's coming there first.

And this next book for Peyton and Wyatt? It's gonna be a doozy!

XO,

Ginger

About the Author

Ginger Scott is a *USA Today, Wall Street Journal* and Amazon-bestselling author from Peoria, Arizona. She has also been nominated for the Goodreads Choice and RWA Rita Awards. She is the author of several young and new adult romances, including bestsellers Waiting on the Sidelines, The Hard Count, A Boy Like You, This Is Falling and Wild Reckless.

A sucker for a good romance, Ginger's other passion is sports, and she often blends the two in her stories. When she's not writing, the odds are high that she's somewhere near a baseball diamond, either watching her son swing for the fences or cheering on her favorite baseball team, the Arizona Diamondbacks. Ginger lives in Arizona and is married to her college sweetheart whom she met at ASU (fork 'em, Devils).

FIND GINGER ONLINE: www.gingerscottbooks.com

facebook.com/GingerScottAuthor

instagram.com/authorgingerscott

tiktok.com/@authorgingerscott

Also By Ginger Scott

Final Score Series

The Tomboy & The Captain

The Wallflower & The Running Back

The Best Friend & The Short Stop

The Boys of Welles

Loner

Rebel

Habit

The Fuel Series

Shift

Wreck

Burn

The Varsity Series

Varsity Heartbreaker

Varsity Tiebreaker

Varsity Rule breaker

Varsity Captain

The Waiting Series

Waiting on the Sidelines

Going Long

The Hail Mary

The Waiting Series - Next Generation

Home Game

Game Face

Final Down - Book 3 Coming 2025

Like Us Duet

A Boy Like You

A Girl Like Me

The Falling Series

This Is Falling

You And Everything After

The Girl I Was Before

In Your Dreams

The Harper Boys

Wild Reckless

Wicked Restless

Standalone Reads

The Moon and Back

Southpaw

Candy Colored Sky

Cowboy Villain Damsel Duel

Drummer Girl

BRED

The Hard Count

Memphis

Hold My Breath

Blindness

How We Deal With Gravity

www.ingramcontent.com/pod-product-compliance
Lightning Source LLC
Chambersburg PA
CBHW011130190726

48289CB00012B/2986